BLAPHAUS MAXIMUS AND THE NEW GALAXY DAY

By Jason Peverett

Way, way into the future in one small galaxy of 23 planets...

CHAPTER 1

His friend and boss laid on his back in the middle of the busy space-port, his tie pushed to the side and his hat laying a few feet away. Wearing the outlandish colorful suit that looked like it was tie-dyed, he knelt next to the body wondering why no one was coming to help, even though help was called about twenty minutes before. He had no idea if his friend was dead or alive, but he knew they missed their flight. Their robot stood looking down at them feeling hopeless, as his job was to take care of both men... but with one sprawled out on the shiny floor and the other one kneeling, not saying a word there was nothing for him to do. Blaphaus, a tall green potato-like looking species with no legs and big feet and really long arms, wearing a purple jacket stood watching this whole event. He earlier watched the two humans run through the spaceport and the one that was laying on the floor slide on the shiny service and go up in the air and come down backwards hitting his head. Stupid humans, Blap thought. Always running. He was kind of jealous of the running part as he has no legs and had to shuffle everywhere. He hated being the species he was "forced" to be. What he hated more was having to wait for the two children that he had to pick up.

He watched as the alpha medics finally arrived on the scene and started to examine the human that was on his back. Blap half hoped the human was dead... just so there was one less in the galaxy. Nope, the human startled to mumble, and explain what had happened. His friend or business associate or brother or boyfriend, Blap couldn't figure out the relationship between the two. Humans were so hard to figure out. His friend was so happy that there was a sound coming from the other human that he started right cry. Blap watched the medics lift the man onto the hover stretcher and the other one take out his info-pad and start asking the other questions. Blap tried to listen when he heard the announcement that the shuttle he was waiting for had arrived at Gate B. He huffed and shuffled away from the scene before he found out who the two men were.

Blaphaus Maximus was from the planet Tooberosum, so he told any-body that asked, and Toobs, as they are often called, ever leave the planet. But not Blaphaus, he decided to get a job as a transport driver and leave the planet... which what he wanted everyone to know. He made good money but wondered what the hell he was doing. Now what he was doing was waiting for two children to take them back home. He had no idea who they were and why they were traveling alone but they were his next pickup, so he went to the spaceport. He watched the crowd of different species walk out the hallway and into the arrival area. He went over to where other pick-up drivers were waiting, waved his long fingers over a screen and in the air two names appeared that said Romana and Nate. He watched everybody closely when two kids approached him, a male and a female, both human and both happy. They saw their names "floating" in the air and skipped towards Blap

"Are you our driver?" asked the boy, his brown hair brushed forward over his eyes.

Blap sighed and said in a deep growling like voice, "Do you see your names floating above my head?"

The girl with the long brown hair frowned and looked up and read the names. She just nodded.

"We have to get our bags, sir." the boy said.

Sir? No one ever called Blap "sir" in a long time. He kind of liked it, but didn't know how to show it. He just shuffled after the children to baggage pickup.

The children didn't have to wait long for their bags on the conveyor belt and Blap was glad he didn't have to grab their bags.

"Okay, sir, we're ready to go." the boy remarked.

"Follow me to my vehicle." Blap told them.

They followed him through the spaceport, he turned his body to see that the human male who fell was now gone, as well as the man who was with him. Blap grumbled and sighed.

His vehicle was parked amongst the other vehicles, but easy to find. It was white and shiny with a large front door for his six foot tall body. There was no seat in the front section as Toobs did not sit. He opened the back door and the two children climbed in, carrying their bags. Blap got in the front, started the vehicle up and it moved off from his parking spot.

"Don't you want to know why we are by ourselves?" the boy asked.

"Nope." Blap replied.

"We were visiting dad at his job. He works for..."

Blap interrupted Romana who spoke up for the first time. "I don't care."

"Are you always like this?" Nate asked.

"Like what?"

"Rude. If we tell mother she would give you a bad rev..."

Blap checked the map on the vehicle's info-pad to see where he was going.

"I don't care. We have another five minutes to go so why don't you sit back and enjoy the ride and stop speaking?"

"You're a Toob, right? Toobs don't leave their home planet. Do you regret that?" Nate asked.

"Normally no, but right now... yes."

The man with the multi-colored outfit sat in the ambulance-vehicle across from the medic and his robot. The medic was scanning the other gentleman with a med-scanner, chocking the readings every few seconds.

"Well, doc, what do you think?"

"Actually, sir, he's just an alpha medical technician, an AMT as you humans call them. The doctor is at the hospital and..."

"Quiet, Ten. So, how is he? He's my boss, and I'm worried about him."

The medic looked up and replied, "Mr. Peezle, sir. As far as I could tell he broke his right humerus and it looks like he has a concussion. It's weird he's still barely conscious though."

Mr. Peezle, the one in the colorful outfit looked sad, and very worried. This was not good news.

"Do you think he'll be okay? Is he gonna... you know... not... I don't know how to say it."

"Die? Not live?" the medic asked. "It's hard to tell. I don't think he'll die."

Just then the med-scanner beeped a very long beep. The medic looked down at it and frowned.

"What's that sound mean?" Mr. Peezle asked.

Ten, the robot replied, "I think he's dead, sir."

Blaphaus' vehicle pulled up outside the pretty big house in the fancy suburbs. Humans and their big houses, Blap thought. Why do they need such big houses? He got out the vehicle and opened the door for the two kids. They could easily open the door themselves but he was required to do so. They climbed out, carrying their own bags.

"Home, you two. Have a nice life."

"You too." Romana, the girl replied. "Can we give you a hug? You need a hug."

"No. You won't be able to put your little human arms around me and it'll be awkward."

Nate went up the path to the front door and knocked on it. A small little servant robot popped out the little door at the bottom of the main door, rolling on four wheels.

"Children, did you have a nice trip visiting your father?" the robot asked.

"Yes, we did. O-U."

"That's good. Your mother is not here yet. So I can't let you in the house. My programming will not let me look after you two alone."

"What shall we do?" Romana asked.

Nate turned to the vehicle and saw that Blap was standing in it, just ready to leave.

"How about you take us to mother, sir?"

"Huh? Wot? That's not part of the trip."

O-U said, "But it's a very good plan."

"No it's not, and you have to book a ride, and you did not." Blap said matter of factly.

O-U opened his arm to reveal a number of buttons. He pushed two and looked up.

"I just booked a ride for the two children."

"Well, I didn't get the..."

Blap's info-pad in the vehicle beeped and a red circle appeared on the screen circling the exact position and coordinates he was at now. He muttered something under his breath.

"Did you swear, sir?" Nate asked, "Mother doesn't like swear words."

"Well, your mother is not here, is she?" Blap argued.

"You will be with her in a few minutes." O-U replied. If the robot had a mouth they'd be able to see a smile.

"Bye, O-U." Romana smiled, "Do you want to hug?"

"Sure, little Romana, I love hugs."

And hug they did as Blap groaned. Too much saccharin he thought.

The ambulance-vehicle pulled up to the hospital which was a tall tower like building. The back doors opened and Ten stepped out followed by Mr. Peezle and the medic. The driver stepped out from the front as the hover stretcher with Peezle's boss moved out. A team of doctors and nurses walked out the hospital, with a bunch of medic-robots. One doctor looked down at the man on the stretcher.

"He's dead." the doctor claimed.

Mr. Peezle sniffed, "Is their anything you can do?"

"That would take a miracle. I'm afraid he's dead."

"But he broke his shoulder and got a concussion. How could he be dead?"

Just then the man in his stretcher opened his eyes and spoke one sentence.

"There was a Tooberosum at the spaceport." And his eyes closed again.

The Toob drove up to the little building that the music was coming out of.

"What's that noise?" asked Blap.

"Music." Romana said, hopping out the vehicle.

Nate stepped out as well and turned to Blap.

"Thank you, sir. You can go now. It was nice to meet you."

"Well... thank you. Have a nice life."

Just then Romana walked out the building with a tall red headed woman in a tight pink outfit that showed a lot more of the female body that Blaphaus has ever seen in a long time. If his green skin could turn red it would've.

"Mr. Toob, your skin is turning red!" exclaimed Romana.

"Wot? Impossible." muttered Blap.

Romana just giggled. There was no way his skin good change color… no way… not on the outside anyway.

"This is our mother, sir." Nate smiled.

"That's good for you." Blap said, "I figured."

Their mother looked Blap up and down very closely. Blap wanted to take off but was half afraid of running her over.

"What race are you?"

"A Tooberosum."

"I think I heard if them, but they're rare, right?"

"Not rare, I'm one of millions." he scoffed.

"Not rare on this planet, definitely rare on *this* planet. Were my children scared of you?" she asked.

"Mother, we are never scared of any species." Nate said.

"I know, Nate, but look how big he is. And green, and lumpy."

"Look, I get it, lady." Blap muttered, "I'm a wonderful looking species, a rare alien on your planet. Your children were a joy. I'd love to stay and chat but I have other people to pick up."

He looked down at his info-pad hoping he'd see another red circle, but there wasn't any.

"Your computer is not telling you where to go, sir." Nate said.

"No. Not yet."

"You sound kind of worried... do you have a name? Do Tooberosum's have names?" the woman asked.

"Of course I have a bloody name. It's Blaphaus Maximus."

The two children giggled at his name. Blap's yellow eyes glared at them.

"That's a fancy name." their mother grinned, "But I like it. So, as you have nowhere to go would you like to come into my dance studio and meet my class of children? They'd love to meet you. I'm sure none of them have ever seen one of your species before."

Just then a red circle appeared on his computer screen.

"Oh, look at that, I have a new pick up. Have a good life."

She stepped back as he drove his vehicle off, maybe quicker than he should've.

Me. Peezle paced back and forth in the hospitals waiting room. Ten stood a few feet away, not moving at all, just listening

"His family needs to know, then the Cabinet, then the press... or maybe the employees, family and press. Or press first... no, then his family and the Cabinet would find out through the press and that won't be good."

"Sir, I think that the Cabinet should find out first." Ten said. "But it's not my programming to decide."

"No, it's not." scoffed Peezle. "Where's our freaking ride?" He looked out through the glass doors. "We have a lot to do. We have to get off this planet and go back home. 10-E-C, did you book a ride?"

Ten shook his head, "I'm not program..."

"Forget it! I'll do it myself!" Peezle stormed off towards the receptionist desk that the receptionist robot was behind.

The figure on the street corner was tall, chubby, furry and orange with black spots all over him. Oh no, thought Blap as he drove towards him. A Cyrakuse, the happiest damn species around. This certain Cyrakuse was grinning from one side of his round feline looking face to the other. It looked so happy to see the white vehicle drive up and even more so when he saw a Toob was driving it.

"Hey! You're a Toob!" cried out the Cyrakuse. "I've never seen one before!"

The vehicle stopped and the Cyrakuse skipped over. Blap glared at him, hating the fact that this Cyrakuse was so happy... and loud.

"Hello, you must be..." he glanced down at his info-pad to read the name. "Tostone."

"Yes, my green friend. I'm so excited to meet you."

"We are not friends, and if you want me to take you somewhere you might want to climb in the back of the vehicle." Blap said stepping out and opening the back door.

"Of course, of course. So, how would you like a new job?" Tostone asked as he got in the back seat.

Blap closed the door and got into his position in the front.

"A job? A job doing what? I have a job."

"As my bodyguard."

Blap frowned, thinking after this trip he was going to go home and rest. He had enough for a day... but his day was not going to be over.

At first glance you'd think Doctor Macca was a human, with his gray hair and giant bushy mustache but once you got close you'd see he had gray skin was more leathery and he had webbed hands and a fin tail sticking out of his white doctors coat. Dr. Macca was one of the top doctors at Jubilee Hospital, but his matter of fact attitude earned him the nickname "Macca of Fact." He stood facing Peezle and Ten in the hallway outside the room Peezle's ex-boss was in.

"It was an heart attack." Macca told them, "It's just a coincidence he had it as he fell and hit his head. Or maybe the fall gave him the heart attack. Needless to say he's dead. I hope he wasn't an important man."

Important? Thought Mr. Peezle. The man was the most important man in the galaxy of twenty-three planets. The problem was he was very shy and no one knew really who he was but a handful of people. Humans were plain and boring, and didn't stick out in a crowd. They also didn't have a planet to call their own. They were the one species that was scattered throughout the galaxy.

Mr. Peezle sighed and wiped away a tear. "Can I go and give my last respects to my boss?"

Dr. Macca shrugged, "You do you, sir. The morgue will be here to pick him up soon. They'd want to know if it'll be disposal or a funeral." Macca shuffled off leaving the two behind.

Ten said, "I'm not programmed to pay respects. I also don't have currency."

"That's fine, Ten, I won't be long." Peezle replied, opening the door and going into the room. "Ten, check to see if our ride is here."

Blap parked his car outside a tall apartment building, in the parking lot full of other vehicles.

"This is it?" he asked.

"This is it! Thank you." grinned the Cyrakuse.

Blap shuffled out the vehicle and opened the back door seat door for Tostone who stepped out.

"Nice job! You'll definitely get a five star review from me."

"That's nice. Have a nice life." Blap remarked as he closed the door and got back into his vehicle.

"Think about the bodyguard offer. You're big, and mean looking and a Toob. You'll be the best bodyguard ever. I can pay a lot."

"You want me to be a bodyguard because I'm a Toob?" Blap asked.

"Yeah, that's good, right?"

"No. No it's not."

"Well, I can triple whatever you're making driving people around."

Blap replied by driving off leaving Tostone to wave. Blap was happy he could go home and rest now, no more riders for the day. Just then another red circle appeared on the info-pad screen. He looked at it and saw it was at a local hospital a few blocks away. One more trip he thought won't be too bad.

Mr. Peezle walked up to Ten in the hospitals lobby.

"Did you pay your respects?" Ten asked. "I hope it wasn't too expensive."

Peezle looked around at the few different species, mostly humans though in the lobby who were sitting and waiting for some news from the doctors.

"Is our ride here yet?"

Ten replied, "Not yet."

"How long does it take? We missed our flight to go back home, now we have to get a hotel room for the night. I don't even know this planet or this city on this planet that well."

Ten said, "Sir, I hope it's not over-stepping my line but doesn't Zalez live on this planet?"

Peezle sat and thought for a minute. "Yes, well, he works on a space station, he's hardly ever on this planet."

"But his family does live on this planet, and they love you. Should I make a call to them?"

Peezle replied, "It wouldn't hurt. Of all the planets this has to happen on... why Ceilingida?"

Outside the hospital Blap parked his vehicle and a few seconds later shuffled into the hospital lobby, going over to the receptionist desk where the receptionist robot was. He was aware that everyone in the lobby was looking at him. He wasn't aware that two of them more than the others.

"I'm here to pick up Mr. Noj Peezle and his robot 10-E-C." Blap told them receptionist.

Peezle walked over smiling, "What a coincidence! You're the Toob from the spaceport."

Blap turned his body towards Peezle and the robot, realizing who they were.

"You're the bloke who was with the poor bastard that fell. Did he make it?"

Peezle looked sad, "No, unfortunately he passed. It wasn't the fall that killed him though. He had a heart attack."

Blap wanted to say he was glad, but he also wanted a good rating so instead he said, "Well, shall we go?"

They walked towards the vehicle and Blap opened the back door for them. Ten had a hard time getting into the vehicle and realized he couldn't fit as he wasn't able to sit.

"Guess you'll have to ride in the front with the Toob." told Peezle.

"There's no bloody room in the front for both of us. Have you seen my size?" Blap remarked.

Ten said, "He has a point, sir. It's okay. I'll walk to the house. I'll be there sometime in the morning."

"Just walk to the spaceport, Ten, we'll be leaving in the morning."

Ten replied, "Yes, I'll be waiting at the spaceport at whatever Gate you'll be going on. I'll make sure the flight is booked."

Blap asked impatiently, "Can we go now? I had a long day. Not as long as you I'm sure, but long enough."

Peezle hopped in the backseat. "Sure, my Toob friend. I'm understand."

Blap slammed the door shut and muttered, "I'm not your friend."

As Blap drove he couldn't get his mind off the other human who had died. He had a heart attack? Did his heart make him fly into the air and come down on the back of his head? Why was he left at the hospital? What will happen to him now? Blaphaus wasn't the kind to ask questions, he didn't really care enough, but he really wanted to know some answers. It bothered him that he wanted to ask. He had no idea what Peezle was doing in the back seat behind him. Peezle wasn't doing much, but looking out the window. After picking up the two children who wouldn't shut up, then the Cyrakuse who definitely wouldn't shut up, Blap realized he didn't like the silence. So he thought he might as well say something.

"So... Mr. Peezle, you have no luggage? Or is it back at the spaceport?"

Peezle was kind of startled that Blap spoke and asked him a question. Obviously he knew Blap could speak but didn't expect him to until they got to their destination.

"Um... it was just a day trip and Ten was baggage enough." Peezle chuckled.

Blap smirked, "So, you two are not from this planet?"

"No, we had a meeting and the meeting went over and we had to rush to the spaceport otherwise we'd miss our flight back home"

"Which you did anyway. I saw your other human friend slip and go up in the air and come down hard. I had a feeling that was it for him." Blap was really bad at small talk. "Why would you come to this planet just for a meeting? You can always holo-call."

"That's what Mr. Traf said, but I thought it'll be best he had the meeting in person."

"You know he'd be still alive if you didn't suggest that."

Peezle huffed, "Look, you're not very good at this talking business. I know you're supposed to be chatting to your passengers for extra stars in your review but you don't have any manners."

Blap was almost taken back by Peezle's reaction. He looked at the map on the info-pad screen, then he looked out the window and realized he was somewhere where he was earlier in the day. His day was going around in circles.

"So, your friends name is Traf?" he asked.

"Yes, Algar Traf. I'm sure you heard of him."

"Nope. Never have."

"You don't know the name?" a surprised Peezle asked.

"Nope. Is he important?"

"Important? He's only the most important man in the galaxy."

"He didn't look that important to me when he went up in the air."

Peezle sat back in his seat and sighed. He looked out the window to see they were now in the suburbs. He just hoped Ten called ahead to Zalez or his family.

The white vehicle drove up to the huge house for the second time in a few hours. The front door opened and the woman who was the kids' mother walked out, wearing a flowing black dress. A part of Blap was disappointed that she changed her outfit. She waved as Blap got out his vehicle and opened the back door for Mr. Peezle.

"Children! You'll never guess who is back?" she called out.

Terrific, thought Blap. She's going to make another circus out all this. Peezle walked up to the front door.

"I really appreciate you letting me stay..."

"THE TOOB!" the children cried out in unison running out the front door.

Peezle looked confused, looking at the kids and back at Blap.

"You've seen him before?" he asked.

"Yeah, he picked us up from the spaceport." Nate remarked.

"Who are you?" Romana asked Peezle.

"My name is Noj Peezle, I'm a friend of your father."

"He works with Galaxy President Traf." smiled Nate.

"You know who G.P. Traf is?" asked Peezle.

"Nate's a geek, he knows all those important people."

"Not personally of course but I have heard of him." Nate explained.

Peezle turned to thank Blap who had already driven away while the conversation was happening.

Thirty minutes later he pulled up to his little house in the small town he lived in. He got out his vehicle and went up to his front door, waving his hand over the lock. The door opened and Blap walked in. As soon as the door closed behind him he had his jacket off. He hated wearing the jacket, but he wouldn't be allowed to walk around "undressed." He went to the kitchen and opened the fridge taken out a beverage. He was calling it early for a change. She beings were so tiring. He thought about looking up on his info-pad to learn more about who this Traf was just for the hell of it but thought about watching something kids shouldn't watch instead.

The shiny red vehicle pulled up outside the house early the next morning. Nate and Romana looked out the window and looked disappointed to see it wasn't Blap's car.

"Maybe he has a different car today." Romana said hopefully.

A human man stepped out the vehicle and approached the house. The buzzer ran and O-U went and opened the front door.

"I'm here to pick up a Noj Peezle." the driver said.

O-U said, "He's in the kitchen. I'll get him." The robot went into the kitchen where Peezle was talking to the kids mother. "Hello, sir, your driver is here."

"Is it the Toob?" asked Peezle.

"Negative. It's a human."

Peezle smiled, "That's good. Well, ma'am, thanks for having me stay the night."

"No problem. Zalez talks highly of you all the time, and the G.P."

Peezle smiled, "Zalez is a good guy, even though he's a bit hairy for my liking, but you're lucky to have him."

The next morning, Blap walked out of his house and looked up at the big sun that was shining over the planet. He thought he hated sweating, but at least his sweat was inside of him. He thought he might try and be a good Toob and go pick up the man in the multicolored outfit. He then thought he didn't want to go to the house and see those children again, but their mother might be there and she might be wearing that right pink outfit, with the cleavage.

The red car dropped Peezle at the spaceport and left quickly. Peezle thought the driver was more pleasant than Blap but without the novelty of being a Toob. He made his way to Gate A where he was pleasantly surprised to see Ten waiting for him.

"Ten! You made it."

Ten nodded, "It took all night but here I am. I have two tickets purchased to go back home as well."

"Brilliant, Ten. We have a long day ahead of us."

Ten said, "Actually, sir, *you* have a long day. Technically I don't have to do anything."

Peezle smirked, Ten had a point.

Blaphaus' vehicle pulled up to the big house just as a red circle appeared on the computer screen. He wasn't happy he already had a pick-up to do but he wanted to see Peezle first. He got out the car and shuffled up to the front door. The robot rolled out robot door and looked up at the 6 foot tall Toob.

"You again." O-U remarked.

Blap said, "I'm here to pick up Mr. Peezle."

"He's gone all ready. You're late... did you get a job to pick him up?"

Blap said, "Forget it."

He turned and headed back to his vehicle. That's what he gets for being nice, he thought.

Nate and Romana were two years apart, Romana being ten-years-old and Nate being just eight. But because Nate was so smart he and his sister shared the same class at their school. They sat at their desks as their classmates shuffled in and went to their own desks. Nate turned to his best friend Nog who sat behind him. Nog wasn't the most popular kid in the school, let alone the class but Nate was his best friend and looked out for him.

"Nog, guess what I saw yesterday?" Nate asked.

Nog shrugged his chubby shoulders, "No telling, Nate."

"A Toob."

"A tube? What's the big deal about a tube?"

"Not tube... but TOOB. A Tooberosum. From the planet Tooberosum I think..."

"Oh. How? They never leave their planet. I remember my granddad talking about them once. Is that where you went over the weekend?"

"No, Nog, he was here on this planet. He picked us up at the spaceport."

"No way, Nate! You always have the best life. I heard that Toobs don't speak. Is that true?"

"Oh, he spoke all right." Nate smiled.

A few desks away Romana sat listening to this conversation. She didn't have any friends really in the class to share about her weekend, so when their teacher walked in to start the class Romana got up and went over to the teachers desk.

"Hello, Ms. Beezlee. Guess what I met yesterday?"

Ms. Beezlee was a young and cheerful teacher, who loved her class. But there were some open ended questions she was asked over the years she had no idea how to answer.

"Romana, that could be anybody. Who?"

"A Tooberosum named Blaphaus Maximus. He was so nice."

"Romana, Tooberosum's don't have names."

"This one did. He was our driver, picking us up from the spaceport."

"And they definitely don't drive, Romana. Now go sit down so we could start class."

Romana looked down sadly and went back to her desk, going past Nate.

"Don't worry, Romana, they'll see. Maybe he can be our driver again one day." Nate told her.

"You're late!" the fat old human male yelled as Blap's vehicle pulled up next to him.

"Actually we have a window of ten minutes before and after the time and I'm only six minutes late." Blap replied.

"You're still late. And you're an ugly creature! What the hell are you?!"

"Gone." Blap replied, driving off leaving the man on the curb waving his fist in the air.

"I'll have your job! You'll get zero star ratings!"

Blap's arm stuck out the window and his long middle finger flipped the man off.

"Bloody humans."

Because who he was, or associated with, or just because Ten knew what he was doing, Peezle got to sit in first class. Ten meanwhile wasn't able to sit so like in every flight he was in the robot section which was in the back of the shuttle.

"So," a very black and sleek looking robot said to Ten, "Did you have an interesting trip?"

"Well, my owner died and I met a Tooberosum." Ten replied.

The black robots red eyes blinked a few times. "A Tooberosum? What was *that* like?"

"A lot to take in really. Even for a robot."

Back at the school later in the afternoon it was recess time and Nate was holding court as the kids stood around him listening to him talk and answer questions about Blap.

"What color was his skin?"

"Green."

"Did he speak?"

"Yes."

"Did he have an accent?"

"All species have an accent. Unless they're mute of course."

"What did he smell like?"

"Is it true they are over sixty feet tall like giants?"

"How do you get to be so lucky, Nate and Romana?"

Romana sat by herself at a picnic like table watching and listening to all this. She was kind of surprised everyone was so fascinated by Mister Blaphaus. Yes, it was rare for one to be seen off their planet, or to have a job like his, or even anyone to be an acquaintance but a whole class of children? Even her own mother was taken back. She thought to herself she's going to learn about the Tooberosum species. Or ask Nate because he knew everything.

Meanwhile, Blap dropped off his next rider who patted him on the back of the head as he opened the door for her to get out.

"Thank you, Mr. Toob. That was a pleasant ride."

"It's Mr. Maximus, and you're welcome. Have a nice life."

He closed the door and got back into his vehicle. There was no red circles on the screen, so he had time to relax. He then realized he wasn't far from the dance school where he first met the two young humans' mother. Maybe she's wearing that tight revealing pink outfit again. He thought he should just drop by and see how everything was going. No, that wasn't the Toob way... or at least Blap's way.

They were just annoying humans, and humans were everywhere. Oh, what harm could it do? He thought and he drove off.

Peezle sat in his seat with a small info-pad on his lap where he could take notes. He tapped his finger on his chin, thinking. He never felt so alone. Sure, he had the Cabinet to help him when he got back but what was their reaction going to be like? Plus he had a funeral to take care of, plus G.P. Traf's family had to be told. That was the first thing he was going to have to do. He never had to do anything like that before. He turned to the man that sat next to him. The man wore a nice gray suit, and looked very "professional." He looked like he knew a lot and was at least thirty years older than Peezle was.

"Hello, hi." Peezle said awkwardly, "Can I ask you something?"

The man turned to Peezle and nodded, "Yes, you may."

"Have you ever had to tell someone's family that someone had passed away before?"

"That's an odd question, sir. Do you have to do that?"

"I think so. Or I might get someone to do it but I think it'll probably be me."

"Who passed if you don't mind me asking?" the man asked.

Peezle wanted to say who but he had a feeling this gentleman would know who the G.P. was and that would be bad.

"My boss. He had a heart attack yesterday."

"That's too bad. Would it be a promotion for you now?" the man asked.

Peezle didn't know what to say. He just sighed and said, "How do I tell the family?"

"Well, I would start off with a joke. Like this for example... what is the difference between marriage and death?"

"Ummm..."

"Death is free." he let out a loud belly laugh. "Get it? That's good, right?"

"Not really. No."

Just then a voice spoke over the intercom, "Please sit back and out on your seatbelts, ladies and gentlemen. We'll be descending shortly."

Thank the Creator, Peezle thought.

Blap got out his vehicle at the dance school called Belhopsa School of Dance. He wondered if that was the children's last name... Belhopsa. That annoying music was coming out of the building again which made him wince. He kept clenching his long fingers into fists, thinking he shouldn't be doing this. This was not part of the job. He looked through the window at the side of the building and saw a few human adult women standing around. None of them he recognized though. Suddenly one of them screamed, watching him peer in. He saw one of the woman, who was chubbier than he thought most female women were, especially at a place like this, march up to the door. She stepped outside and came around the -corner, waving her finger at Blap's face.

"What do you think you're doing, you big green monster?"

"Green monster?" Blap was taken back by the insult. "That's kind of racist and rude don't you think?"

"You scared Lilly, looking though the window like that. What do you want?"

"I don't want anything, fatty. I was look..." he wondered if he should say the real reason he was there. "Yesterday I picked up two children from the spaceport and dropped them off here. I was looking for their mother."

"Two children? Their mother? You dropped them off how?"

"I flew above and dropped them." he said sarcastically.

"Toob's fly? How?" the woman looked confused.

"No, we *don't* fly. I dropped them off with my car. I'm an Ultra driver. Anyway, I guess she isn't here, so I'll leave you to stand around to this annoying music."

He started to leave and she touched his arm. "Wait, you must mean Nate and Romana's mom, Mal. She teaches the children's class in the afternoon."

"Oh. Thank you."

"Should I tell her you stopped by?"

"Yes. No. Yes. No." Blap stuttered. "That's up to you. Have a nice life."

He walked back towards his vehicle. The lady put her hands on her hips thinking that Toobs were weirder than she ever was told.

Blap drove off, swearing under his breath. He felt stupid, and embarrassed which is a thing he didn't normally feel, and that woman called him a monster. He then wondered where Mal was. She wasn't at home, or the dance school. Where else could a human woman go? Shopping? The place they go to to get their hair colored and changed?

Back in the classroom the children were doing their work on their info-pads. Nog tapped Nate on the shoulder and he turned his head.

Nog whispered, "What company did the Toob drive for?"

"What do you mean?" Nate whispered back.

"Was it Ultra? Or Hoyst?" Nog whispered.

"It was Ultra."

"We should call Ultra for a ride and maybe the Toob will come to the school. That's a good idea, right?"

"Nog, that's a *terrible* idea. Why would we do that?"

"So I can meet him and see him in being.. or see him in Toob. No, that sounds too weird."

"Shssss, boys." Ms. Beezlee said, "Do your school work."

Nate apologized and went back to work thinking Nog did have a point. He would like to see Mr. Blaphaus again. Nog discreetly took out his info-pad and looked up Ultra to order a ride. Romana meanwhile decided not to do the lesson but research Tooberosums.

    At the end of the school day the children left the school building and headed to the school bus transports, or to their parents who were waiting in their vehicles, except Nog who stepped out of line and went the opposite way.
"Where are you going?" Nate asked.
"I ordered a ride." Nog smiled. "I'm hoping your Toob will pick me up."
Nate sighed, "Do you know how many drivers they must have working for them, Nog? The chances of it being Mr. Blaphaus is rare."
Just then a light blue vehicle drove up and a gray leathery Leetric stepped out.
"Are you Nog Lerboy?" the Leetric asked.
Nog looked disappointed and nodded, "Yeah."
"Well, I'm Trebb, and I'm your ride. Hop right in, young man"
Nog turned to Nate who grinned, "Told you."

    Blap meanwhile was back at the spaceport outside the gift shop waiting for three other people he was supposed to pick up. He watched as the crowd walked down the hallway towards him. He waved his long fingers over a computer and three names appeared in the air... Sargan, Ieme and Erick. They saw Blap and appeared him. Blap frowned as the two women looked exactly the same, dark haired, and chubby. One of them carried two babies and the male was a Leetric, just like Nog's driver.
"Hi, you must be our driver." Erick said.
"Unfortunately, yes." muttered Blap.
"Oh great," the woman who was holding the babies said. "You're cute."
"Let's go." Blap turned his back to them and walked off. Body guarding was looking better and better. He wondered where he could find that Cyrakuse.

    Launderington C.G. is the big main city on the planet Launderington, which was in the center of the twenty-three planets in the galaxy. People did live on Launderington but mostly it was a work planet, home of the G.P. and his Cabinet. Of course right now there was no G.P., and only a few beings knew that. Not every planet was part of the Cabinet and in the galaxy government. Outside the spaceport on Launderington the chauffeur Rubyspears stood besides the long black limousine vehicle waiting for the G.P. and his Assistant Peezle, and their robot 10-E-C. He wore a chauffeur's outfit and cap which was pulled down low. Rubyspears might as well be a Chordattian, which is one of the hairiest species in the galaxy. A Chordattian was part of the Cabinet, and was the closet species to the human species. Rubyspears was a human, but had as much hair on his face with his facial hair that he often got mistaken for a Chordattian which bothered him. He looked up to see Mr. Peezle and 10-E-C walk out the glass doors amongst the crowd but oddly enough there was no G.P. That's odd, Rubyspears thought. He bit his fingernails wondering if he should say anything.

"Rubyspears, in time as always." Peezle said.

"Of course." Rubyspears said in his gruff voice. "Do you want me to 'adjust' the robot for you, sir?"

Ten hated that word, and hated to be "adjusted." One of Rubyspears' jobs was robot maintenance. Ten couldn't sit in the limousine so Rubyspears would have to remove the legs.

"Sure, Rubyspears. But can you do it quick?"

Rubyspears nodded, and squatted down in front Ten. Peezle could't help but chuckle like a child.

The three in the backseat of Blap's vehicle would not shut up. Even Erick the Leetric kept chatting, which was rare for his species.

"So, do you make enough money driving, Toobie?"

"Honey, that's a personal question." the one named Ieme said.

"Look, he's a Toobie. He could make a lot of dosh."

"How do Toob's procreate?" Sargan asked. "Are you hatched out of an egg?"

"Sar, that's a very personal question. But it's a good one. You see, we never came across one before."

"I take it I'm supposed to answer these questions or get into a conversation with you." Blap commented.

"It is part of your job, to chat to your passengers." Erick said. "You'll get good reviews for chatting, right? Five moons or something."

"Stars. And I get paid pretty good."

"I sell things from other planets, like goods and stuff. What are Toobs into? I get stuff from your planet is..."

"Wait." interrupted Blap.

He saw the Cyrakuse walk up the steps in front of a building. Blap had about as far as he could take picking these annoying people up. He parked on the side of the road.

"Is this our stop?" Ieme asked.

"I don't think so. The seller is supposed to be..."

"This is your stop now. Please get out." Blap got out his vehicle and opened the back door, motioning for them to get out.

"But this is not our stop." Erick said, "You can't just drop us off where you feel like it."

"I just did. Now I don't care if you give me zero stars and a bad review, I am dropping you off here."

Sargan said, "Will I be able to see you again?"

"I hope not." Blap told her. "Now if you can get out."

Erick, Ieme and Sargan all climbed out, Sargan still holding her babies.

Erick said, "I really don't think this is smart for you to kick us out like this."

Blap replied, "It is for me."

He slammed the door closed and headed across the street to the building with the steps. He looked up at them and sighed. One thing about most humans, and other species' themselves was stairs and steps. His body wasn't "built" to climb steps as he had no legs. He cursed under his breath and turned around to go back across the street. The three passengers still stood next to his car.

"Get back in the vehicle." he said waving his arm.

"Yeah! I knew you'd come back to me!" Sargan said hugging her babies. "Girls, he could be your new father."

Blap just groaned.

"Dead?!" exclaimed Rubyspears as he drove the limo-vehicle. The legless Ten and Peezle sat in the backseat.

"Yes. Heart attack unfortunately." replied Peezle. "You know you can't say a word, Rubyspears, and tell anyone."

One thing that no one really knew was Rubyspears loved to gossip. It's no wonder everybody across the galaxy knew who Traf was. He loved to boast and gab and the attention of being the chauffeur for the Galaxy President, but now that G.P. Traf was dead he could not say that.

"So, who will be G.P. now, Mr. Peezle?"

"That hasn't been decided yet."

The Galaxy President was not nominated, he was chosen, all for different reasons. Traf was G.P. for many, many years, and still no one really knew who he was, and they couldn't tell you who was the G.P. before him, or before him or before him. One thing though every G.P. in the past was human. No one ever questioned that either.

"Where are you going anyway?" Rubyspears asked. "We are not heading to the House."

"We are going to *a* house, just not *the* House." Peezle replied. "We are going to Traf's family's house. I have to tell them that Algar had passed."

Rubyspears frowned, he never heard Traf get called by his first name before... by anyone.

The shadowy figure stood on the corner outside the little house. He watched as the white vehicle drove up and stop. Blap got out and opened the door once again for the three. They all got out with no hassle this time.

"Here you go." Blap told them, closing the door.

"Thank you, Toobie. If you ever need another job, I could pay you a lot for smugg..."

Ieme elbowed him in the side.

"Delivering goods."

Blap replied, "I'm good. Have a nice life."

Sargan kissed him on the side of his face where his cheek should've been.

"I hope to see you again."

"There's a slim chance." told Blap. "But the way my life has been going... I wouldn't doubt it."

Erick went over to the shadowy figure and they started to whisper. He motioned to the two women and the babies. The shadowy figure nodded and led them to the front door of the house. Blap got back into his vehicle half wondering what that was about. There was no circle on the info-pad screen so he thought he could just wait and go to the building the Cyrakuse went into and wait. How long could he possibly be in there?

At the Belhopsa Dance School, Mal walked in the front door, wearing the tight pink outfit that she wearing when Blap first saw her.

"Hello, Fadonna." she said to the chubby dance instructor who confronted Blap. "How is your day going?"

Fadonna replied, "Mal, you never guess who was here earlier."

Mal frowned, "Is he famous?"

"No. Not really."

"Then who?"

"A Toob. He was looking through the window and was asking about you."

"Really?!" Mal was surprised, "Did he say why? Did he give you his name?"

"I can't remember and he never said why... just he picked up your children. Isn't it weird that he's Toob? They are rare."

Mal nodded, "I totally agree, but for some reason this one isn't."

The house where Traf's family lived was up on a hill in the country with a gate around it. The limo-vehicle drove through it and parked right in front the house. Rubyspears got out the vehicle and opened the back door for Peezle, who stepped out.

"Ten, I'd love you to come in and help me tell them."

"Sir, I have no legs, are you willing to carry me?"

"No, you're too heavy. Rubyspears, carry Ten for me."

"That means I get to meet the G.P.'s family as well?"

"Yes, but let me do the talking."

Rubyspears nodded and reached in to get Ten as Peezle walked up to the front door and pushed the door buzzer. The door opened to reveal a tall shiny purple robot who had a slightly looking female body. She looked down at Peezle and Rubyspears who was holding Ten's upper torso in his arms.

"Greetings, I am One-Four-Three, could I help you?" she said in her sexy feminine like voice.

Rubyspears stared at her, slightly getting aroused.

Peezle cleared his throat and said, "Hello, I'm Noj Peezle and this is Rubyspears and 10-E-C, I am the Assistant to G.P. Traf. Is *Mrs.* Traf in?"

One blinked her glowing pink eyes. "G.P. Traf is not here and is not with you. Is he okay? Why doesn't your robot have legs?"

"I had to take them off so he could ride..."

Mr. Peezle cut Rubyspears off, "I *really* need to talk to Mrs. Traf if she's here."

"She is. Wait there. I will get her."

One-Four-Three turned around and walked deep into the house.

"You know, sir, that robot detects something is wrong and might tell Mrs. Traf." Ten remarked.

"I hope you're wrong, Ten, I really do."

Just then Mrs. Traf walked up to them at the door. She was also tall with long brown hair. One stood behind her, watching the three very closely. Rubyspears had to look away as he was getting *really* aroused now, not because of Mrs. Traf but because he was thinking deeper thoughts about One.

"You're Mr. Peezle, Algar's Assistant." smiled Mrs. Traf. "We met a few time's at certain banquets and events."

Peezle nodded, "Can we come in, ma'am? I need to talk to you."

"Yes, you may. And I'll have my children put new legs on your poor legless robot here. Come in." She led them into the house and into the living room.

"Ma'am, I do not need legs, but thank you." Ten told her.

"Nonsense, how are you going to walk anywhere without legs? This poor Chordattian cannot carry you around forever, isn't that right?"

"I'm not a Chordattian, I'm human, and I have to admit this robot is getting heavy." grumbled Rubyspears.

Mrs. Traf clapped her hands three times and two children, a boy and a girl went running into the living room. They were in their teens, quite a few years older than Nate and Romana.

"Children, can you take this legless robot here and have some legs out on him?"

"Yeah, mother." the boy said.

Ten was passed to the boy who carried him out the room. The girl followed him.

"That's Narob and Hoeka, they are good kids."

"Getting so big, I remember when they were born." told Peezle.

"Haha. Of course. Take a seat, gentlemen, would you like One-Four-Three to get you any beverages or snacks?"

The two men sat on the couch and Rubyspears was the first one to speak.

"Yes, please. I'll have whatever you have. Thank you."

Peezle replied, "No, we are good, thank you."

Mrs. Traf nodded and sat down across from them. "So what brings you by today, Mr. Peezle? Where is Algar?"

This was the moment Peezle was dreading. He swallowed and rubbed his hands on his knees.

"Um... well... um..."

"Just say it, Noj. He's dead or in prison, right? No, he wouldn't be in prison. Is he dead?"

"Why would you think he was dead?" Peezle asked.

"I'm not stupid, Mr. Peezle. You wouldn't be here alone... I mean without him otherwise, or be here at all actually. How did he die? I know he wasn't assassinated... no one knew who he was really, so they wouldn't bother. He was too shy and quiet and didn't really do a whole lot. He was a fantastic husband though and great in bed, and a really good father to his children but not the best Galaxy President. So I'll ask you, how did he die? Was it a stupid accident?"

Peezle did not know what to say or think. This wasn't how he expected this conversation to go. But here it was.

"We were running through the spaceport and he slipped and fell..."

"It WAS a stupid accident!" she exclaimed.

"Actually, he has a heart attack that killed him."

"A heart attack? But he was pretty fit, for someone his age."

Peezle shrugged, "Guess it was a fluke thing."

"Wow. I can't believe it. Where's his body now?"

"At Jubilee Hospital on Ceilingida. We were there to meet with the Governor of that planet. Heading back was when he fell. I'll arrange for his body to be brought here to Launderington and arrange for the funeral."

"Thank you. Who else knows about this?"

"Just myself, and..." he didn't want to say who else. "I have to tell the Cabinet and then the press but I wanted you to know first. Do you want to say something to the press?"

"Yes, when you make the announcement I'll be there and I'll say something nice." she looked up at One who was still standing there. "Can you fetch the children, please? They won't hear my hand clapping."

One nodded and left the living room.

"Mrs. Traf, I'm glad you're taking things so good. We'll always be there for you."

"I know. A heart attack? So weird, right?"

"Yeah, very surprising."

"Look at me!" Ten's voice complained as he walked in. He had very short legs now, which were purple. "I feel like a Smidge."

Smidge's were the shortest species in the galaxy.

"Oh, One's old legs!" laughed Mrs. Traf, "Good job, kids. One used to be a shorty before she was made into the beautiful tall robot she is now."

"You look good, Ten." smiled Peezle.

The kids stood in the doorway of the living room.

"Children, Mr. Peezle has something to say about father." she turned to him. "You can tell them."

"Me? Um, okay. Your father unfortunately had a heart attack and passed away. I'm so sorry."

"He was a loser anyway." muttered Narob.

His sister Hoeka cried out, "NOOOO!"

Back on Ceiliningida, Blap was wondering why he was standing outside the building for so long, waiting for the Cyrakuse. Did he live there? Was he ever going to come out? Blap's mind wandered to Mal, wondering where she was. Then he realized it was the afternoon and she might be back at the dance school. He sighed and walked back to his vehicle. For now he was giving up on the Cyrakuse.

Again the annoying music played at the dance school and the children and Mal were inside dancing. Romana took part in the class but Nate sat, playing on his hand info-pad. He looked up the company Ultra and tried to see how many drivers they had on the planet but there was no info on that at all. He wished there was a way for the Toob to get in touch with them. Just then he looked up at the large window and got his wish. There was a Creator after all. Blaphaus again was peering through the window.

"Mr. Blaphaus!" he exclaimed jumping to his feet. Everyone else turned to the window and saw Blap standing outside.

"Why on the galaxy?" sighed Mal.

"That's it!" shouted Fadonna. "That's the Toob!"

"He's an 'he,' not an 'it.'" pointed out Romana.

Nate let Blap into the dance studio and the children surrounded him like he was their favorite thing on the planet. Blap raised his arms feeling very uncomfortable.

"Children, give Mr. Blaphaus some space." told Mal.

They all stepped back one step.

"Why are you here, Mr. Blaphaus?" asked Nate.

"I... I..." Blap realized he didn't have an answer. Well, he did but wasn't sure if he should say anything. "I was driving by and wanted to say hello to my favorite human children."

That was a lie, and it did not sound convincing but no one questioned it.

"Aren't you a sweetie?" Mal smiled, "Hey, we all should capture this moment with an image-scan."

Fadonna a picked up a holo-cam to take the image.

"Turn around and face the 'cam, everybody." Mal said.

Fadonna took the image of Blap and the children and Mal.

"You should come over for dinner." Mal told him. "Do Tooberosum's eat human food?"

"I eat anything." he replied.

"Do you have a wife or girlfriend... or boyfriend?" Mal asked.

"No."

"Well, you know where we live, I'm sure the kids would love you to come over for dinner. Right, children?"

"Of course!" Nate exclaimed, "Please come over."

Blap grunted, this was no where near what he expected. These humans were too nice.

"Okay. I'll be there. I have to go now." He turned and left.

"That thing is so weird." Fadonna commented.

"He's *not* a thing." Romana said seriously.

"Why was he here?" Nate asked his mother.

Mal just shrugged, "I have no idea but everyone should know Tooberosum's are really nice. At least that one is."

Rubyspears drove the limo-vehicle as Ten, now with his short purple legs and Peezle sat in the back seat.

"Where are we going now, Mr. Peezle?"

"Take me home, Rubyspears. Tomorrow I'll get the Cabinet together and we will figure out what to do next."

"The funeral." Ten said, "And press announcement and put my old legs back on."

A few hours later, Mal was putting the food out on the dining room table... food for four as O-U watched her and moved towards her.

"Miss, why four places if you don't mind me asking? Is Zalez coming back tonight?"

"No, O-U, I invited the Tooberosum over for dinner."

"The big green Tooberosum driver?"

"Yes, that's him."

"Don't shut me down after this question but why would you invite him over for dinner? I think he could be dangerous."

"Dangerous? Don't be silly, O. He showed up at the dance school to say hello. He's just lonely I think."

"Miss, he also showed up at this house looking for you. I have a bad feeling about him."

"Oh, you're being really silly now. What does your programming know about Toob's anyway?"

"Not a whole lot. And that is what worries me."

"Everything will be fine. Don't you worry."

Just then the buzzer went off.

"Children, come down for dinner! Mr. Blaphaus is here!"

O-U went out through the little robot door and looked up.

"Oh my. Hello, sir. Welcome back."

Back on Launderington that evening, Peezle sat up in bed, a million thoughts going through his head. His husband slept in bed next to him, not knowing anything that transpired in the last few days.

Mal was surprised to see her husband standing in the living room.

"This is a big surprise, Zalez."

Zalez was a Chordattian, his big thick long beard and hairy face and hands revealed that. He stood there still in his blue work overalls. Zalez spotted that the dining room table was set up for four people.

"Surprise? Are you sure?" he asked. "There's four places set up at the table. Unless the robot can now eat..."

"Father!" the children cried out running down the stairs. "You're here!"

They both gave him a big hug.

"Father, we have a visitor coming for dinner." told Nate.

"You'll like him, father." Romana nodded.

"Like? Like who?" Zalez asked, looking surprised.

The door buzzer rang and O-U rolled over to the door and through the robot door once again. He looked up to see Blaphaus standing there.

"You're in time, Tooberosum."

The front door opened to reveal the Toob standing there.

"Mr. Blaphaus! Meet father!" Romana smiled.

A little bit later they were sitting at the table... except for Blap who had to stand.

"You didn't touch your food, Mr. Blaphaus." Zalez pointed out.

"You're a Chordattian. These are your children? How?" Blap asked.

"The children are adopted, Toob." Zalez replied, "What is a Toob doing off Tooberosum and why become a driver?"

"Have you been to Tooberosum?" Blap asked.

Zalez shook his head, "No, they are not part of the sixteen planets that are part of the Cabinet."

"There's twenty-three planets in the galaxy." Romana remarked.

"But only *sixteen* are under the G.P. and Cabinet. The others are not." explained Nate. He loved showing off.

"Darling, why don't you tell Mr. Maximus who you are, or work for?" Mal said to him, smiling.

"I don't think he'd know what it is or would even care." Zalez told her. "Toobs only care about themselves... and a free meal apparently."

"Actually looking at the logo on your outfit I'd say you were part of Dook Energy, the company responsible for all power on the sixteen planets."

"Well done." smirked Zalez. "You're pretty smart of a Toob. But fifteen planets. One planet in the Cabinet has their own company."

"Zalez, your friend and Assistant of the G.P. spent the night here. Did he get in touch with you?" Mal asked.

"No, his robot Ten did. That's why I'm here now. G.P. Traf wasn't with him?"

She shook her head.

"You didn't ask why?"

"I know why." told Blap.

"You do? Why is that?" Zalez glared across the table.

Blap gave a half smile. "Because your Galaxy President is dead. That's why."

All four humans gasped.

Peezle's husband turned his head and leaned up in bed. He opened his eyes to see the holo-call of Zalez standing at the end of the bed, arms crossed, looking annoyed.

"Noj, wake up!" the holo-call shouted.

Peezle woke up startled and cried out, "Zalez! It's late. Did the power go out on any of the planets?"

"Why didn't you tell me G.P. Traf is dead?!"

"Wha... how do you know?" Peezle rubbed his eyes.

"A Toob told me." glared Zalez's holo-call said. "Of all species. This is not good, not good at all."

Mal and the children watched Blap walk to his vehicle.

"We'll see you again?" Mal asked.

"I doubt it." he muttered, "I'm keeping away from your family from now on... as long as I can help it."

Or so he thought...

CHAPTER 2

The "home" of the Cabinet on Launderington was in the middle of the city. It was a beautiful domed building with white and grey marble walls. Huge steps were in front of it and it faced a long reflection pond and a large white ball made out if sugar... that was the rumor anyway, called the Launderington Monument.

Inside the House there was a meeting where there was a long table. On one side of the table sat eight figures, the other side sat six others. One was missing. They were all Governors for the twenty-two planets... Launderington didn't have a Governor... it had the Galaxy President... normally. There was a chair at the end of the table where normally the Galaxy President sat. But not now. Now for the first time ever their was no Galaxy President. The doors at the end of the room opened and Peezle walked in wearing wearing his colorful suit.

"Gentlemen, ladies..." he said nodding to them.

Three of the fifteen there were women, two humans and one that wasn't.

"Where is Tostone?" asked Peezle.

"Forget Tostone. Where is Traf?" the Chordattian Governor Zeb asked, scratching his brown beard.

"Maybe they are together... the Cyrakuse and the G.P." a Struthioian named Lluhdor asked.

Struthioian's were a feathered species with long skinny necks and a long skinny beak, and not known for being the smartest and bravest species.

"Zucaritas, you're from the same planet as Tostone, where do you think he is?" asked one of the females.

"Yeah, but I am the Governor of our own planet, not another like he is."

Zucaritas was feline looking as well, with orange fur and stripes, and looked a lot meaner than Tostone could ever look like.

"I'm not going to say anything until the full Cabinet is here." Peezle said.

Zeb said, "Technically you shouldn't be addressing the Cabinet at all, human, you are just Traf's assistant, not a Cabinet member."

Peezle gave the Chordattian a dirty look. He had no idea what to do. Zeb, did have a point though. Peezle was in over his head. He looked at the Cabinet closely, thinking which one he was closest to and who he could talk to one on one. He then saw the Cyrakuse's empty seat. Of course the one who wasn't there. Did he have a heart attack as well?

Testone was actually running out of his house literally, down the walk way to the waiting car... Blap's vehicle. Blap half smiled when he saw his pick-up was the Cyrakuse. He opened the door for Tostone.

"Hello... ummm... what's your name again, Toob?" smiled Tostone getting in the vehicle.

Blap closed the door and got in himself.

"Blaphaus Maximus. Good to see you again, Mr. Tostone." he drove the car, glancing at the address on the info-pad which just said "spaceport."

"You're going off planet?" Blap asked.

"Yes, to work. I got a holo-call late last night and woke up late. The Cabinet is waiting on me. I'm never late."

"Well, I'm glad I got you for the ride, Mr. Tostone. You are a member of the Cabinet?"

"Blaphaus, call me Charcat. That's my first name. Yes, I'm the Ceilingida Governor. Exciting, right?"

"Not really. Sorry about the G.P. kicking the bucket. You're going to be the next G.P.?"

"The what? Traf died?!" exclaimed Tostone. "How do you know that?"

"Well, honestly, I saw him slip, fly up in the air and come down hard. The thing is though apparently he had a heart attack. The job didn't seem that stressful, so who knows what caused it."

"You saw him fall?! Did you know who he was?"

"Not really, I don't follow politics, and didn't give a flying boink. His friend was concerned..."

"You don't understand, Blaphaus, he was just here visiting me. He and his Assistant Mr. Peezle..."

"That's the human in the gaudy outfit. Yeah, he told me what happened to the G.P."

"At the time Traf fell? Why would he speak to you?" Tostone was so confused.

"Because I picked him up from the hospital."

"And he told you Traf died?"

"Yup."

"Why would he tell you?!"

"Because I asked. People tell me all kinds of bloody stuff, all day long. No one knows how to shut up. That's why I stood outside a building for a few hours, waiting for you to come out. I'm interested in the bodyguard gig, but now I know you're a Governor you'd have to pay me a lot. Do the other Governor's have bodyguards?"

The vehicle pulled up to the spaceport as Tostone rubbed his furry head.

"Maybe. I don't know. I feel sick. There's a lot to take in. Why didn't Peezle tell me about the G.P.?"

Blap's body wasn't built to shrug so he just waved his arm.

"Maybe you weren't important enough."

****

Back on Launderington, Peezle stood at the end of the table as the fourteen members were glaring at him. A long necked spotted Jiraffa named Gillian, the third female, blinked her huge black eyes at Peezle and waved her hand.

"Mr. Peezle, I don't think it's a good idea to wait for Tostone. If something happened to the Galactic President you have to let us..."

"Now." ordered Zeb.

Peezle sighed, "Okay. I guess we'll fill Governor Tostone in whenever he shows up. Speaking of Governor Tostone, the G.P. was called to Ceilingida to meet with Governor Tostone. I was not part of that meeting, it was private. That will be up to you lot to ask him about it. Anyway, the meeting ran over time and we rushed back to the spaceport. He slipped and fell on his back, breaking his humerus and got a concussion..."

"Where is he now?" Governor Lluhdor asked.

Peezle looked sad, "He had a heart attack and he passed away unfortunately." He fell back into the G.P. chair.

"Dead?" Southington, a blonde female human asked, "And you're telling us now?" She was the Governor of Mencken, a very religious planet.

Zeb asked, "Are you the only one that was there?"

"We took 10-E-C with us of course."

"He passed away at the spaceport?" Gillian asked.

"No, the hospital I believe."

"And Tostone didn't know?"

"No, I did not tell him."

"So, just the hospital and you and the robot knew he passed?" Southington asked.

"Well... a Tooberosum knows. He saw the G.P. fall and knows he died."

The short Smidge at the right end of the table scratched his head.

"Let me get this straight on behalf of this whole friggin' Cabinet... you're not a member of the Cabinet but are here for our daily meeting with the G.P. who you say had a heart attack and is dead. Governor Tostone, the Governor who met with Traf secretly is not here now. Doesn't anybody but me find this all suspicious? And the witness of Traf falling is a friggin' Toob? Does Traf's wife and children even know or, Peezle, did you keep your secret from them as well?"

"Ummm... well, I did tell Mrs. Traf and she told her children. She wants to be there for the press conference and I said..."

"You had no right to tell her." Zucaritas snapped. "All you were was Traf's Assistant... as soon as Traf was dead, before he turned blue you should've contacted us and, at least Tostone. It's up to the Cabinet to inform his family and the press. Did you arrange a press conference yet?"

Peezle shook his head, "No. I thought I'd tell you first."

"I will let the news know." Southington pointed out.

The Smidge named Noam said, "Who is in favor for having Tostone arrested and held for questioning of Traf's death raise your hand?"

Everyone but Peezle raised their hands.

"Good. Peezle, what hospital was Traf in?" Noam asked.

"Jubilee Hospital on Ceilingida."

"Who was his doctor that told you he died?"

"I think his name was Macca… he was a Ruswal I believe."

The Leetric Governor named Thaw nodded. "He's a popular doctor. I can go to speak to him."

Zeb nodded, "Okay, and after all this we need to figure out who could be the next G.P."

Noam stood upon his chair and told everyone, "Great. Peezle, you are now banned from this building. Your boss is dead, there's no reason for you to be here now."

Peezle nodded and stood up. "Thank you, everyone. I'm sorry I didn't tell you all sooner."

He turned to sadly leave the room.

At recess, back at the school Nate was holding court again, telling Nog and his other classmates how Mr. Blaphaus showed up at his mother's dance school.

"Wow!" Nog said, "Why would the Toob go to your mom's dance studio?"

"I don't know. He never really said. But we have a holo-image of it. He didn't stay for long."

"Nate, you got to tell them about dinner as well." Romana said, "While you're at it."

Nog's mouth opened wide, "Don't tell me he showed up to your house for dinner too."

Nate smiled and nodded. "But he didn't eat. Which was weird…"

Blap's eyes rolled to the back of his head when he saw who he had to pick up. The three idiots and the two babies. Why out of all the drivers, with two companies in the galaxy on the few planets did it have to be that gang of idiots? They weren't too far away from where he was driving so he thought it might be a good thing, especially if they were going back to the spaceport and leaving the planet.

In the hallway of the school Nog whispered to the little girl that stood next to him.

"Don't tell the Belhopsa kids but every kid in the class is going to order a Ultra ride. One of us will be sure to have the Toob as a driver."

"Are you sure that's okay?" she asked.

"It'll be fine." Nog smiled, "Pass it on and tell the next kid to pass it on but don't tell Nate and Romana."

The little girl nodded.

"Toobie!" Erick smiled as Blap shuffled out his vehicle. "Can't believe it's you again!"

"Vice versa." Blap muttered.

The two identical women stood behind him, one holding the babies.

"Hello!" the one with the babies smiled. "I've been having thoughts about you."

"Terrific. Get in the vehicle, please."

They did so in the backseat and Blap slammed the door. He got in the front and said to them. "Please tell me you are going back to the spaceport."

Erick nodded, "Yeah, but we'll be back. We might move to this planet."

Blap just groaned. This was it, take these back to the spaceport then he was done for the day.

"Do you know who the G.P.?" he asked. He was curious what these three would say.

"Yeah, some guy named Traf or something. He doesn't do anything." Erick remarked.

Sargan said, "Do you have any kids, Toob?"

"Lady, I'm not going to be your significant other and the father of your children."

Erick asked, "Why did you ask about Traf? Did you have him in this vehicle?"

"No. And I'm not saying."

Blap did not feel like spilling the beans about Traf dying. Not to these three anyway.

"Do all Toobs look like you?" Sargan asked, "I had my looks changed by surgery to look like Ieme."

"It's great, right?" Ieme asked.

Blap rolled his eyes, these humans were really getting on his nerves. He decided just then he only liked a handful of humans, or any species. But it was still better than living on his own planet.

That afternoon the kids filed out of school and everyone from Nate's and Romana's class went the opposite way from the yellow school transports.

"Hey! Where is everyone going?" asked a worried Nate.

"Is there something happening?" Romana asked.

Nate followed them to see where they were going.

"Nog! What's going on?!" he cried out.

"Nate, you and Romana can't be the only ones to see and meet and interact with the Toob. So everybody in the class ordered an Ultra ride to go home, hoping to get the Toob as the driver."

"What?! That's the most ridiculous thing I ever heard! Your parents are going to be mad... it costs money to ride in a Ultra vehicle. It's not free you know."

"If we get in trouble it'll be so worth it." Nog smiled.

"Nate, not one vehicle is white, or looks like Mr. Blaphaus' one." Romana pointed out.

Nate looked and smirked, "You know what... nineteen vehicles, nineteen drivers and not one of them is Mr. Blaphaus' vehicle. All those drivers and not one is a Tooberosum. Nog, your experiment failed."

"What?! No! Oh, man, my fathers gonna be mad." Nog started crying real tears.

The other kids started calling him names, and blaming him. Nate actually felt bad for his friend, and started to wrack his brain on how Nog can meet Mr. Blaphaus.

Back on Launderington, Peezle walked out the House followed by two security guards, with a box under his arm. He packed up his stuff and left. He was out of work and had no idea what to do next.

"Sir, where are you going?"

Peezle turned to see Ten walking out as well, still with the short purple legs.

"Ten, I was kind of let go. No one wants me as an Assistant."

"Well, considering the Galactic President has died I guess I'm out of 'work' now as well."

"You can come with me if you want, I have to tell my husband that I'm no longer employed."

"Wait!" the Leetric Governor ran out, waving his arms. "I want you as my Assistant! Don't tell anyone though. Can you come with me to meet with Doctor Macca?"

Peezle said, "Um, sure. Are you sure it'll be okay?"

"Yes. And we need to find out where Tostone is. Chances are as soon as he gets to this planet he'll be arrested, if I know my other Cabinet members well enough."

Tostone walked out the spaceport on Launderington to find Rubyspears waiting by his limo-vehicle.

"Governor Tostone." he nodded, opening the passenger for Tostone. "You look perplexed. You heard the G.P. is dead, right?"

"What? You know as well? How?"

"Mr. Peezle told me."

"Oh. That human has a big mouth."

"How do *you* know the G.P. is dead?"

Tostone frowned, "A Toob told me."

"Talking about a big mouth." chuckled Rubyspears. "You know a Toob?"

And just then they were surrounded by four black vehicles and a hovering craft hovered over their heads. A man stepped out one of the vehicles, holding some sort of hand weapon.

"Governor Tostone, you're under arrest for suspicion of murder."

"Murder?! I'm a Cyrakuse! Murder of whom?"

"Galactic President Traf." the Galactic Bureau of Investigation agent replied.

Rubyspears thought to himself he can't believe his life the last few day's... very exciting. Tostone thought to himself what did Peezle say?

CHAPTER 3

The next day at the school on Ceilingada, Mal and Zalez sat in chairs in front of the school's principal.

"I'm glad you two are able to come and meet with me on such a short notice." the human principal said.

"What did Nate do?" Zalez asked. "How much trouble is he in?"

"He's not really in trouble, Mr. Belhopsa."

"Romana is?" Mal asked.

"No, not her either. But there *is* a situation. It seems Nate and Romana both mentioned a Toob... ahem... a Tooberosum being in their lives. Like picking them up at a spaceport and going to your dance school... even going to your house for dinner. They said he was a driver for Ultra, which we know that's not true. I don't know how a Toobersum could drive with no legs. Anyway, I had over fifteen parents call me yesterday to complain that their children ordered a ride... from Ultra, just to see if they can meet the Tooberosum. Well, guess what? Not one driver was a Tooberosum. Nate is the smartest student this school has but he for some reason has a very wild imagination. And he's getting his sister involved. You know how shy she is."

"I knew the Toob would cause problems." grumbled Zalez.

"So, you know about it?" the principal asked.

"Principal Garcey, it's true. But I don't know why they are talking about it at school so much. We'll pay back everybody back for the rides..."

"You think it's true, Mrs. Belhopsa?" Garcey asked.

"It is. Look." she took her info-pad out her purse and an image showed up above it. It was the holo-image of Blaphaus and the dance school students, with Nate and Romana and her in it as well.

Garcey didn't know what to say when a woman walked into the office.

"Sorry for interrupting, Principal Garcey, but G.P. Traf has passed away and Governor Tostone has been arrested as a suspect for the murder. That's the latest news."

"Thanks. I like getting the latest updates... I'm a big fan of the Governor. Sorry for the interruption."

"What?" Zalez asked her, "How do you know this?"

They ready knew, but didn't want anyone to know that, especially not the principal.

"It's all over the news. It's on GNN right now."

Blap walked into Ultra's headquarters, picking up his weekly paycheck. A red and black robot with the Ultra logo on its chest rolled up to him.

"Mr. Maximus, Mr. Calasteel would like to see you in his office."

"I just stopped by to get my weekly check. I'm not staying."

"He said do not let you leave until he saw you."

Blap sighed, "Terrific. This better be good."

He went to Calasteel's office door which said on the glass 'Vistrat Calasteel.' Blap knocked on the door and a voice said from inside.

"Come in!"

Blap opened the door and walked in to see his boss sitting behind his desk in his black suit and his matching greased black hair.

"I hope this is quick, I have work to do. I might be picking up the Governor again."

"Really? Governor Tostone you mean?" Calasteel asked.

Vistrat Calasteel looked human, with pitch black eyes but was actually a Chordattian who shaved. He figured he'd get more respect looking that way and be able to have more females fall for him, which normally worked. He even wore black leather gloves to hide the fur on his hands.

"Yes, that one. I gave him a ride twice."

"I know. You might want to see this, Maximus."

Vistrat waved his hand over his desk info-pad and above the desk appeared an image of Tostone as a female voice was speaking.

"...When asked how he knew about the G.P. passing away he said this..."

Tostone's voice spoke, "I was told by my Tooberosum Ultra driver."

"Governor Tostone is being held for questioning by the Galac..."

Calasteel turned off the hologram projection and looked up.

"Explain."

"There's nothing to explain, Chordattian."

"Except did how do you know the G.P. died?"

"I was told."

"By who?"

"You're an owner for an on-call transportation company, not a private investigator, or the bloody GBI. I'm not going to tell you my source. Have a good day, Calasteel." he turned to go.

"One more thing, Maximus, you're fired."

"Good, Chordattian. I am going to get a job as a bod..."

He stopped when he realized the one who offered him the bodyguard job was now under investigation. He walked out the door and through the area where the other drivers were and shouted for everyone to hear.

"Calasteel is really a Chordattian monkey ass!"

Peezle, Ten and Governor Thaw made their way through the spaceport. Peezle stopped walking and looked down at the floor.

"This is where the G.P. fell." he pointed out.

Thaw nodded, "The floor *is* slippery. I can see how he would fall running through the spaceport here. I don't know how he would have a heart attack though."

Peezle nodded, "He always seemed so fit and never was sick. If he was, he sure hid it."

"I apologize for interrupting, sir, but look at the holo-screen." told Ten waving his hand up.

Above were some holo-screens that was telling the weather, flight info, and GNN. They saw Tostone's large holo-image head and the words under it said that a Tooberosum told him he knew Traf had passed away.

"How is that possible?" Thaw asked. "Why did he open his mouth?"

Peezle shrugged, walking off. "I have no idea. Maybe Toobs like to gossip."

"Why and how did you come across this Toob?"

Peezle said, "He was our driver... he drove for Ultra. It was a coincidence he was here and saw the G.P. fall and then met us at the hospital to drive us back here."

"This Toob could be a problem." Thaw remarked. "We need to track him down."

Ten said, "We know where he works."

Peezle nodded, "Want to go to Ultra's headquarters first?"

Thaw said, "No, the hospital. We have to arrange for G.P.'s body to be sent to Launderington. Then we'll go find the Tooberosum."

Ten said, "Well, I ordered an Ultra vehicle so with luck he'll be the driver."

When they went outside they saw the vehicle waiting for them but it wasn't Blaphaus' vehicle. A human stood besides it, and smiled when he saw one of the passengers looked important in his grey suit that matched his skin.

Principal Garcey, Mal and Zalez sat in the principals office as Nate and Romana stood there in the doorway.

"Children, you two are so smart and such good kids but I have to ask you please no more talk about the Toob, or anything about a Toob. Do you understand?" the principal told them.

Nate said, "But he's a family friend! Right, father?"

Zalez shook his head, "Son, we know nothing about the Toob..."

"He has a name... Blaphaus." Nate pointed out.

"Whatever his name is he's *not* a family friend and I don't like how he's stalking you. If I would've known that he was going to be your driver when you came back home from visiting me on the space station I would've arranged something else. I have to go back to work later but I want to make sure the Toob stays away from you two, and your mother." he turned to Mal, "So no inviting him over for dinner."

Mal nodded, "I understand. Children, do you?"

Romana said, "Yes, but if Mr. Blaphaus comes by what do we do?"

"Contact us." Zalez told her. "Do I make myself clear?"

Both of the children nodded.

"Now go back to Ms. Beezlee's class. I'll see you later, children." Principal Garcey told them.

The children hugged their parents and left the office.

"So, I don't think it's a good idea to tell the children about the report that Governor Tostone was told about the G.P.'s death by this Toob." Zalez said.

Garcey nodded, "Make sure they stay away from the news."

"I don't think Blaphaus has anything to do with it." Mal said, "The G.P. had a heart attack. And just because he knew and told Tostone... we don't know if that's true."

Zalez crossed his arms. "Well, before I leave this planet I want to have a talk with this Toob."

On the way to the classroom Nate spoke to Romana. "The Governor of this planet, Tostone was arrested for investigation of G.P. Traf's death. And I'm afraid that Mr. Blaphaus might be in trouble as well."

"Why, Nate?" Romana asked.

"Because Governor Tostone claims Mr. Blaphaus told him about it. He saw the G.P. fall at the spaceport when he was there to pick us up. After school we need to find Mr. Blaphaus. But don't tell mother... especially father."

"How are we going to find him, Nate?"

"I have not figured it out yet. But I will, Romana. Trust me."

On Launderington, Governor Tostone sat at a table at the Galactic Bureau of Investigations headquarters. Across from him sat Governors Zeb and Zucaritas.

"So, what happened? What was your secret meeting with Traf about?" Zucaritas asked.

The normally cheerful Tostone replied, "It wasn't a secret meeting. Traf was wondering if he stepped down who would take over from him. He asked if I'd be interested. I said I don't know."

"Why was he going to step down?" Zeb asked.

"I don't know." Tostone shrugged.

Zucaritas said, "Why did the meeting go on too long which made him rush to catch his flight back here?"

"We just spoke a lot. He talked about family, and how we could get the other seven planets to join the Cabinet. I told him we wouldn't be able to get all of them."

Zeb frowned, "Why not? Anybody else who was G.P. could probably. He just had no backbone and nobody knew who he was."

Tostone said, "Zucaritas, do you think you'd be able to convince the other planets to come together with us? They have no one in charge... no Governors. They are simply on their own."

"How would you, Tostone, get all the planets together?"

Tostone smiled for the first time in days. "I told him if he could go to Tooberosum and he can find a Tooberosum and get them on board. Then luckily a Tooberosum fell on my lap. That's why I told him. I offered for him to be my bodyguard. But I think we might need to find this Tooberosum... Blaphaus Maximus... he works for Ultra. If you can find him, bring him to me. I need to talk to him. What do you say?"

Zeb said, "Let me get this straight, Tostone, you want us to find this Toob driver and bring him to you?"

Tostone nodded. "Yes. That's what I told Traf, travel to Tooberosum and see who he can find there that would be perfect to convince them to join the Cabinet. But there's one rogue Tooberosum who left his planet and became a driver on my planet where I am the Governor. How fantastic is that?"

"Again you want us to find this Toob and bring him to you?" Zeb asked.

"Yes. That's what I'm saying." Tostone said.

Zeb and Zucaritas both laughed out loud in Tostone's face.

At Jubilee Hospital back on Ceilingida, Traf's face was as blue as it gets. Doctor Macca turned to Peezle and Thaw who stood there, staring at Traf's blue face. Peezle thought he was going to throw up.

"It was definitely a heart attack." the doctor told them. "As I said before. Guess the stress of being a 'do nothing' Galactic President got to him."

"He was a good G.P., doctor." Peezle said, "Maybe not the best... what do you say, Governor Thaw?"

"He was a nice man." Thaw replied.

Dr. Macca said, "Well, nobody I know really knew who he was. No one seems to care that he's dead. Life is still going on. I hope the next G.P. is more 'visible.' if you know what I mean."

"Anyway, doctor, he wasn't poisoned or shot or anything?" Thaw asked.

Macca shook his slimy grey head. "No. He did hit his head hard, and broke his humerus but what finished him was a heart attack. How? Who knows? It's that what killed him. So, is it going to be a public funeral or should we just put the body in the furnace?"

"That's up to his family." told Peezle. "But no furnace. He will have some sort of funeral."

"Or the Cabinet's decision." Thaw replied. "By the way, doctor, have you ever had a Tooberosum here as a patient?"

"A Toob? Ha! You're funny, my planet mate. Nope. I never even met a Toob. Ugly creatures they are I heard though."

"Didn't the Toob pick you up from this hospital, Mr. Peezle?" Thaw asked.

"Yeah, but he was in and out. Doctor, you had a Toob in the lobby of this hospital. There's one on this planet at least"

"Yeah, the one that Governor Tostone claimed they told him the G.P. passed. Yeah, everyone is talking about him."

"Really?" asked Thaw.

"Yeah, crazy, right?"

"Not as crazy as you think." muttered Peezle.

Blaphaus drove his vehicle, wondering what his next step in life would be. He didn't hundred percent know why Tostone mentioned his species in the news but at least his name wasn't out there. That's the last thing he wanted or needed. That put him out there but most just were surprised he was a Toobersosum. Rumor was that Toobs kept to themselves and were a quiet bunch, their planet was very different. It was one of the rare planets out of the twenty-three that just had one species living on it, which led to so many rumors about the race and even the species themselves.

For Blaphaus it was really easy to get a job on another planet, on Ceilingida. Vistrat did not even blink his eyes when Blaphaus applied. He got the job right away. Not having a body that's able to sit was hard, and having no legs, just feet. But he had to drive, he was too slow to shuffle anywhere and he thought if he had to drive he might as well made some dosh. Blaphaus had an attitude, that was just the way he was but he often got good reviews, and five stars. Maybe because he was unique, being a Tooberosum. Or maybe it was people felt bad about him. He didn't care why... he was just thankful. He decided he was still going to approach Tostone somehow and ask him about the bodyguard job. But why would he want a bodyguard? Then again why was he being investigated? He wasn't there when Traf fell, and as far as Blaphaus knew Tostone didn't look like the murdering type. Blaphaus wished he didn't see Traf fall but it was one of those things. He then thought of the children, and their mother, and then their father. He wondered what did their mother see in that hairy ass? He was rude... but that was the norm for the Chordattian race. They were one of the oldest species and legend says that they were once the rulers of the galaxy. There were so many rumors about so many of the planets.

He saw the sign for the highway and thought maybe he would just drive out the city... and see where he could end up. Then he passed the headquarters for the company Hoyst, and smiled a big smile. He wondered what the owner of *this* company was like. He couldn't be any worse than his last company owner.

The red and black robot at Ultra rolled into Vistrat's office.

"Sir, you fired Blaphaus Maximus, the Tooberosum?" the robot asked.

Vistrat sat behind his desk, feet up on his it, taking a nap. He opened his eyes and nodded.

"Yeah, he was a liability to the company. He somehow knew the G.P. was dead, and was the one that told this planets Governor. How did he know about Traf?"

"Sir, yesterday over ten children ordered cars from Ultra..."

"We get over a hundred calls a day, Ultra-robot."

"Yes, sir, but these children were from the same school and the same class."

"So?"

"So thirteen of the drivers... which is pretty much all of them that were there told they wanted Maximus to be the driver... sir. He's like a celebrity. I think he's good for the company. And since the news report on what Governor Tostone said we have quadrupled in calls for rides."

"Really? Why?" He slid his feet off his desk and sat up.

"They want the Tooberosum to be the driver."

The robot turned and wheeled out just as Peezle, the short Ten and Governor Thaw walk in.

"Hello." the robot said to them, "Governor Thaw, what brings you to Ceilingida and Ultra?"

"We are looking for a Tooberosum." Peezle told the robot.

"Really." the robot remarked. "Follow me."

He led them over to Vistrat's office and rolled back in.

"Sir, we have visitors."

"Are you here for a job?" Vistrat asked standing up.

"Mr. Calasteel, I'm Governor Thaw. This is my Assistant Peezle. We are here looking for a Tooberosum."

"You are? Well, Governor, your timing sucks. I fired one this morning."

"Why would you fire him?" Peezle asked.

"Did you see the news? He told Governor Tostone, this planet's Governor that the G.P. had passed away. And then Governor Tostone goes on the news and mentions this company and the Toob."

"He had nothing to do with Traf's death..." Thaw said.

Peezle said, "And the Tooberosum witnessed the G.P. falling."

"How do you know that?" Vistrat asked.

"Do you have his address?" Thaw asked, ignoring the question.

"No. He probably lives in a swamp or something. I hope whoever the next G.P. is more out there and not in the shadows like Traf was. He did nothing for the galaxy. Good luck, gentlemen, finding the Toob."

Blaphaus stood waiting in the Hoyst lobby waiting to meet the company owner or whoever would be the one hire him. A skinny black spotted orange furred Cyrakuse came out an office and was startled to see a Tooberosum standing there.

"Hello. Can I help you?"

"Have you seen the news today?" Blaphaus asked.

"No, am I on it? Or Hoyst?" the Cyrakuse asked.

"No. I don't think so. So, I'm looking for a job. I have a vehicle. What do you say?"

"I have to do a background check."

"Do you see what I am? What bloody background? I'm a Tooberosum. As far as the twenty-three planets go we have no background."

The Cyrakuse shook Blap's hand.

"Welcome to the team. I'm Mr. Cheeetoe. I'm the manager of Hoyst."

"Blaphaus Maximus."

Calasteel looked up at his doorway to see a Chordattian standing there wearing a blue overalls with the Dook Energy logo on his left chest. The Ultra robot stood next to him.

"Sir, you have a new visitor, and you'll never guess who he is looking for."

The robot wheeled off and Zalez stepped forward.

"Are you a Chordattian?" Zalez asked, studying Calasteel.

"Ummm... you are I see."

"Yes. Are you? You smell like one."

"Close the door."

Zalez did so and asked, "So, you left Chordatt to be in disguise?"

"It's a long story. Humans get more respect. You know that."

"Tooberosum's do as well apparently. I heard one works for you. He picked up my children from the spaceport and because of him a bunch of your drivers were 'called' to their school hoping they'd see him. I met Blaphaus, even had dinner with him. There's something about him, he seems to be interested in my wife. I need to talk to him. So, can you get in touch with him?"

"Have you watched the news? He also knew about G.P. Traf's death. He told Governor Tostone." Vistrat pointed out. "So, with someone like that I fired him."

"You fired him? I would have put his big green face up on the outside of this building. He's becoming the most popular being on this blasted planet right now."

Mal looked up at the Belhopsa Dance School building to see a huge holo-image of Blaphaus' head. Her jaw dropped and she wondered who would do that. And why. She walked into the building to see Fadonna dancing with the other women to the music Blaphaus would think was annoying.

"Fad, do you know there's a huge holo-image of Blaphaus on the roof of the building?"

Fadonna's chubby face smiled, "Yes. Do you love it? I got it from the holo-image I took when he was here. I thought about putting you and the children up there as well. But was going to ask you about that. Do you like it?"

"Like it? I'm confused why it's there."

"The Toob seems to be loved by the children. So I thought it'll attract more students and get the attention of the public."

"Fad, Zalez is not going to like this. He doesn't want Blaphaus anywhere near us."

"He isn't. Just his likeness. And no offense, Mal, but you own the dance school, not him."

"Still, Fad, take it down please."

Outside a black vehicle drove past the dance school, and the two passengers in the back seat spotted the giant Blaphaus head.

"Hey, that's Blaphaus." the human driver smiled. "He is a Ultra driver like I am. I wonder why his head is on that building. Not his real head but you know what I mean. It's his head but an holo-image... he's a Toob. I only met him once and he was pretty standoffish, but I'm a human and I don't think he's a fan..."

"Turn around and go back to that building." one of his passengers said.

In the back seat of his vehicle were Governors Zeb and Zucaritas.

"Yessir." nodded the driver.

Blap threw his old info-pad from Ultra in the trash can on the curb and put in the new Hoyst computer. He peeled off the "Ultra" sticker on his windshield and replaced it with the Hoyst sticker. Same old, same old he thought, but at least until he saw Tostone again he should be good. Now to start his "new" job.

The two Governors got out the vehicle and walked into the dance school.

"Hello, gentlemen, can I help you?" Mal asked.

"Are you Belhopsa?" Zeb asked.

"Yes, sir, Mal Belhopsa. You're a Chordattian like my husband."

"Zalez Belhopsa... head of Dook Energy. Yes, I know him. I'm Governor Zeb and this is Governor Zucaritas. Do you know the Tooberosum that's image is on the roof of this building?"

"Yes, sir, he's a friend."

"What's his name?" asked Zucaritas.

"Blaphaus Maximus. Is he in trouble?"

"No, but do you know where we can find him?" asked Zeb.

"No, sir, but he works for Ultra which is a transport company."

"We know what it is. Thank you, Ms. Belhopsa. If you see your friend again please tell him we are looking for him. We are not going to leave this planet until we find him." Zeb told her.

"I will, sir, I will."

She watched them walk outside and turned to Fadonna and grabbed her by the shoulders.

"Please get that image off the building."

"Definitely, Mal, but can you believe two Governors came here to your studio? This is exciting, right?"

"No, no, it's not good, Fad."

Outside in the car Zucaritas said to the driver, "Take us to your Ultra headquarters, driver."

"Certainly, Governor, it'll be my pleasure." the driver grinned.

The vehicle drove off as Blap's "head" disappeared from the roof.

Peezle, Thaw and Ten were back at the hospital... on the roof next to the hospital shuttle. President Traf's body was already in the shiny black burial capsule, ready to go and was placed into the shuttle by the medics.

Thaw said you Peezle, "I'm going to head back to Launderington, and will arrange the funeral You need to stay here and find the Tooberosum. When you find him contact me right away and I'll come right back."

Peezle nodded, "Give his family my regards. Thank you, Governor Thaw, I really appreciate this."

"It's my pleasure, Peezle."

Ten said, "I guess I'm staying here with you, sir."

Peezle nodded, "Yes, Ten. Order a vehicle for us please."

Thaw sat in the shuttle, the doors closed and Peezle, and the medics as well as Ten stepped back quite a few feet as the shuttle lifted to take Thaw and the G.P. back to Launderington. A tear fell down from Peezle's cheek.

"Sir, are you crying?" Ten asked.

"No... what are you talking about?" sniffed Peezle. "You're seeing things."

And he walked off. Where would Blaphaus be?

Blaphaus was driving with the annoying human in his back seat.

"Are you the Toob that Governor Tostone mentioned on GNN? You knew the G.P. died?"

Blap replied, "I'm not going to comment on that."

"How about this, Toob? Are you the Toob whose holo-image was on the roof of a dance school?"

"Wot?" Blap asked. "Wot dance school?"

"The one by my house... Bel something or rather. I always hear the best music coming out of it. So, is that you?"

Blap frowned. He had no idea what was going on. As soon as he was going to drop this human off he knew where his next stop was.

The robot went back to Calasteel's office thinking he never saw his boss this many times in a day... ever.

"Mr. Calasteel, you have two more visitors. I think I could guess why they are here."

He moved aside and the two Governors walked into the office. Vistrat jumped to his feet and walked around the desk to shake their hands.

"Welcome to Ultra. It's a pleasure to meet you, Governor Zeb."

Zeb glared at Vistrat and asked, "Are you a Chordattian?"

"Yes, sir, no disrespect to our race..."

"That is disrespect." Zeb pointed out. "You shaved your fur... you don't have a beard."

Zucaritas said, "We are here looking for a Tooberosum who works for you."

"Oh, Blaphaus..." muttered Vistrat. He could not believe that in one day he had three Governors and two random types looking for the Toob. "Unfortunately he doesn't work for me anymore. He... quit. I tried to keep him here but he refused. I have no idea where he is." he lied.

"Hmmm." Zeb rubbed his brown beard. "When did he quit?"

"Just today. I wish I could help you more."

"Where do you think we'll be able to find him?" Zucaritas asked.

Vistrat shrugged, "Back on Tooberosum maybe? I don't know."

"I doubt that." Zucaritas remarked. "I bet he's still on this planet. We will find him. Someone like that should stick out in a crowd."

Blaphaus parked his vehicle outside the dance school and got out. He looked up at the building but all he saw was the words "The Belhopsa School Of Dance" but no holo-image of him or anybody else. He grunted and thought he was going to go into the school but chose not to. Maybe the human lied. But why would he do that? He went to get back into his vehicle as another vehicle drove up to the building. In the back seat Nate and Romana sat, excited to see Blaphaus standing there. But also confused. The driver of the vehicle, their father looked very annoyed.

"Children, stay in the vehicle."

"Sure, father." Romana said.

Nate just nodded as their dad got out the vehicle.

"Uh oh." Romana said, "Nate, what's going to happen?"

"Romana, I don't know. But I need to talk to Mr. Blaphaus as well."

Blap turned to see Zalez approaching him.

"Hey, Tooberosum, what are you doing here?"

"You're not going to believe me, Chordattian. I was just leaving anyway."

"Are you stalking my wife?"

"Stalking? No."

"Then what would you call it?"

Blap then saw the children were in the vehicle. "Your children are here. They look scared, Chordattian."

Zalez looked over his shoulder towards his kids. They didn't look scared but they were staring.

"Blaphaus, how did you know that the Governor passed away?"

"What are you, detective now? You should stick to engineering..."

"Look, most Chordattians have a short temper. I don't. I just want you to stay away from my family and explain how you knew about Traf's death."

"He's just Traf now? Not G.P.? He's only been dead for a few days. That's disrespectful..."

"How did you know? Governor Tostone mentioned you to the press..."

"He mentioned a Toob. Not me."

"You very well know he was taking about you."

"Prove it, Chordattian." snorted Blap.

"Look, I just want you to stay away from my family. And if you know anything about Traf... the G.P.'s death..."

"Heart attack. He's the lucky one. And his Assistant told me. The one who stayed at your home when you weren't there. I don't think you have anything to worry about... I don't think your wife is his type. I was his driver, and took him from the hospital to your house. I was there when Traf fell, I happened to be there at the hospital after he died. Nothing more. Yes, I opened my mouth and told the Cyrakuse he died, but you'd think he would know already, being on the Cabinet. Great communication there. No wonder seven plants don't want to be part of the bureaucratic government."

Zalez thought for a minute, rubbing his big black beard.

"Blaphaus, I get it. Just stay away from my family. You're under a radar right now."

"Look, I'm just living my life, driving people around. Have a nice life."

Zalez watched Blap get back in his vehicle and drive off. Zalez motioned for the children to get out of the vehicle.

"Children..." he hugged them when they got out. "I have to go back to the station soon, let me know if Blaphaus comes around you again... or mother."

They nodded and went into the dance school. Zalez thought to himself Blaphaus said he's driving people still so either Blap lied or Calasteel lied. And if Zalez was a betting Chordattian he would bet it was Calasteel that was lying.

Peezle and Ten stood outside the Belhopsa's big house. O-U wheeled out the robot door in the front door like he usually did.

"Greetings." he saw Ten was short with purple legs. "What happened to your legs?"

"It's a long story." Ten replied.

Peezle said, "We tried to get in touch with Zalez or Mrs. Belhopsa but had no luck. Do you know when they'll be here?"

"Do you know that telling the Tooberosum that G.P. Traf had passed away is causing all kinds of problems?" O-U asked.

"Yes, thanks for being obvious. Do you know when they will be here?"

"Mr. Belhopsa is heading back to the space station, but Mrs. Belhopsa and the children should be here soon."

"Can we wait for them inside?" Peezle asked.

"I don't think that's a good i..."

Ten looked down to O-U by three inches.

"We are going to wait inside for them. Mr. Peezle and I are spending the night."

Back at the dance school Mal taught the dance class as Nate sat on the floor doing his homework, and trying to figure out how to contact Mr. Blaphaus. He didn't want Blaphaus to get in trouble, and was stressed that he didn't know what to do. He looked up watching his mother dance, teaching the other children and his sister. Just then a holo-call from O-U appeared in front of him, about twelve inches high from his info-pad.

"Oh! Hey! Hi, O, what's up?" Nate asked.

"Is your mother busy?"

Nate looked up to see his mother taking a break from dancing.

"Okay, students, take a break and get some water." she said.

"Mother, it's O-U..." Nate carried his pad over to his mother with the holo-call above it.

"Yes, O, what's up?" Mal asked.

"Ma'am, that man Peezle is here and he won't leave. He's waiting to see you."

Mal frowned, "Why is that?"

"He says he needs to spend the night."

"Then let him in, O. We'll be home soon."

"But he has a robot with him."

"O, let him in." scolded Mal. "Mr. Peezle is a family friend."

She saw O look up at and say, "You're lucky she's nice."

A half hour later the figures in the black vehicle watched Mal and her two children get into her little blue vehicle and seconds later it drove off.

"Follow that car." the Cyrakuse in the back seat told the driver who nodded.

Zeb said to Zucaritas, "Do you think this is a good idea?"

"Zalez's wife somehow knows more than she says, and so does Zalez. We'll see where she goes, if she'll lead us to the Toob."

At the spaceport Zalez headed to Gate A which was all the way to the right end of the long building. All he could think about was his children and his wife and that Toob. Part of him thought the Toob was truthful but something still didn't seem right. He wondered if he should not leave the planet now and go home. A hand then touched his shoulder. He turned to see two GBI agents in their black tight uniforms and their shades.

"Can I help you fellas?" Zalez asked.

"Come with us, Mr. Belhopsa." one of them said.

Mal and her kids walked into the house to see Peezle sitting on her couch.

He stood up. "I really appreciate this. It's good to see you again, Mrs. Belhopsa."

"Mr. Peezle, what's going on?" she asked.

There was a knock on the door and O-U went through robot door and looked up to see the two Governors standing there.

"Hello, Governors. Can I help you?"

"Let us in, robot." Zucaritas ordered.

The front door opened and the Governor's walked in to see the two children, Mal and Peezle with Ten at his feet standing there.

"Peezle!" Zeb said raising his voice. "What are you doing here?"

"Governors." Peezle muttered. "Hello."

CHAPTER 4

On one side of their dining room table sat the two Governors, Zucaritas and Zeb. On the other side of the table sat Mal and Peezle. The children were sent to their rooms but Nate and Romana hid at the top of the stairs, out of sight and eavesdropping.

"Who are they?" whispered Romana.

"Two Governors... one from father's planet Chordatta and the other from Cyrakuse."

"Ooohhh."

At the table Zucaritas said to Peezle, "So, explain what you're doing on this planet."

Peezle said with his arms crossed lie a child, "I don't have to explain anything to you, Governor. Unless you're a part of the GBI I'm not explaining anything."

"That shouldn't be a problem, GBI agents are on the way here."

Zeb said, "Mrs. Belhopsa, how well do you know the Tooberosum?"

"Mr. Blaphaus? Not too well. He's an acquaintance." she replied.

"Are you sure?" he asked.

"Yes, I'm sure."

Zeb looked around at the floor and looked up at her. "Where's your robot?"

"O-U? He's in the living room probably."

"Call him."

"Okay, if you want. O-U! Can you come here please?"

The little black robot wheeled up to the table. Ten stood a few feet away from him. He knew what was happening. Robots are not programmed to lie, unless someone programs them to lie on purpose. She doubted O-U was programmed that way, so he knew Mrs. Belhopsa was in trouble.

"Robot, how well does Mrs. Belhopsa know the Tooberosum?"

"Well, he was..."

His head then went flying off and sparks shot out of his torso. Everyone looked stunned, Nate gasped and Romana started to cry. Robots are like pets, they are loved and part of the family. It was obvious what happen, Ten had swung his arm so quickly he hit O-U on the back of his head knocking it right off.

"Ten!" shouted Peezle jumping to his feet. "What did you do?!"

Mal knelt down and picked up the two parts of the family robot. Tears built up in her eyes. O-U was done for.

She spun to face Peezle and cried out, "Your robot killed our robot!"
Zeb said, "I think we all know what he was going to say."
Peezle picked up Ten by his shoulders and looked into his black visor that were his eyes on his round plain looking face.
"Ten, what did you do?"
"Saved everyone from the obvious, sir."
"You're not supposed to kill, Ten. Robots don't kill."
"Robots are machines. We are not alive, so can't be killed."
Zucaritas stood up, "Ma'am, what are you hiding?"
"Nothing! Yes, Blaphaus ate dinner here one night! Well, he didn't eat but still was here. Yes, he showed up at my dance school! Yes, he picked up the children from the spaceport! But we know nothing about him!"
"You don't know where he lives?" Zeb asked.
"No. No idea."
She put the two pieces of O-U on the dining room table. The door buzzer buzzed just then, but there was nobody to answer it. That was what O-U did, but not any more. The door opened anyway to reveal Zalez standing between the two GBI agents. Zalez saw who was in the room.
"What's going on here?" he asked.
Romana whispered to Nate, "Father is back?"
She was still sobbing. Nate frowned and put his fingers to his lips to shush her.

Back on Launderington, Governor Southington sat at her desk in the House as the Smidge stood on the other side of it. A GBI agent led Tostone into the office.
"You can leave him." Southington remarked, "Thank you, agent."
He nodded and left.
"Thank you, Jupha." Tostone told her, calling her by her first name.
"Sit down, Charcat."
He sat across from her and smiled at Noam who smiled back.
"So, I'm on your side. The other Governors might not be. That's why I had you do that press statement. You have to be honest with me though. Before the Tooberosum told you about Traf's death you had no idea?"
He shook his head. "No idea. I told Zucaritas and Zeb the same."
"Why was he meeting you on Ceilingida?"
"He wanted to talk to me about who would be his successor."
"His successor? Did he know he was sick? Did he have a feeling he was going to die?"
"I don't know. He was thinking of stepping down though. I told him a few ideas on what he could do."
"Like what?" asked Noam.
"Like... I told the other two Governors already all this but they laughed at me."

"I don't laugh." the Smidge said.

"No, no you don't. I think that I have an idea about the next Galactic President should be."

"Who?" Southington asked.

Blaphaus looked up at the sky over Ceilingida to see a few GBI crafts hovering above the city. He frowned as he drove, wondering what or who they possibly be looking for. The human in the back seat also noticed the hovering shuttles.

"Mr. Toob, those are GBI shuttles..."

"I know." muttered Blap. "I see the bloody logo on the side of the shuttles and well as the letters 'G.P.I.'"

"Usually crafts hover like that if they are looking for someone."

"I know." Blaphaus remarked. "You're an observant human, aren't you?"

"Sometimes."

Zalez sat in the chair at the end of the table, elbows on the table and head in his hands.

"Why is O-U headless?" He looked up at the Governors. "What's going on? Did you two do this?"

"We are looking for the Tooberosum, Zalez. We figure you might know where he is." Zucaritas told him.

Zeb asked him, "Where did you see him last, Zalez?"

Zalez wanted to tell them it was a few hours ago but actually wanted to protect Blaphaus. "I don't know."

"For a Toob he's sure hard to find." muttered Zucaritas.

"Why is father lying?" Romana whispered to her brother at the top of the stairs where they still stood.

"He's protecting Mr. Blaphaus." Nate replied.

"Why and from what?"

"I do not know. But everyone seems to want to find Mr. Blaphaus."

Peezle said, "I wish everybody would just relax. I made a big mistake in telling Blaphaus about the G.P. passing away. I wasn't thinking. I should have told the Cabinet as soon as I found out. This is all totally my fault."

Mal put her hands on her husbands shoulders. "Mr. Blaphaus did not do anything wrong. I don't know what's all the fuss about."

"We know he didn't do anything wrong, but we want to talk to him." Zeb replied. "It might be good for everyone."

On Launderington, Southington frowned. Neither her or the Smidge laughed at Tostone but didn't agree either.

"The problem is finding him." Southington told him, "Zucaritas and Zeb went to Ceilingida looking for him."

"I know. But I think I'll be the one to find him. Let me go back to Ceilingida. I promise I can find him. After all, he was looking for me."

"Good. I'll make sure the press will be waiting for your return and the announcement you're free, and the investigation being over." Southington pointed out, "And I'll let the rest of the Cabinet know, and the two Governors on Ceilingida can meet you there. I'll also get in contact with a shuttle company to give you a private flight."

Tostone smiled a huge big smile. He would get Blaphaus to come out of "hiding."

Back at the big house on Ceilingida where the Belhopsa's lived Zucaritas told the couple, "We are going to leave an agent outside your house in case the Tooberosum shows up again. And another outside the dance school..."

"And another at your children's school." Zeb added. "We will find the Tooberosum."

Mal and Zakez nodded. The two agents and the two Governors walked to the front door. Zeb turned to them and looked at the broken robot on the table.

"I'm sorry about your robot. But we know what he was going to say. We saw the holo-image on your dance school, remember?"

They then walked out the house, closing the door behind them.

"What holo-image?" Zalez asked.

"I'll tell you later."

Peezle said, "No, ma'am, what holo-image?"

"Fadonna, one of my instructors thought it'll be a good idea to put a large holo-image of Blaphaus on top of the school. It's not there now but those Governors saw it. They stopped there asking about him. They must have followed me and the children back here."

Zalez said, "Ever since this Tooberosum came into our lives..."

He thought that was his idea, telling the Ultra sleaze ball he should do that.

Peezle said, "Tell me about it. Anyway, I should get going... and try to get back to Launderington to help with a funeral. If you want me to leave Ten here..."

"No, take him." Mal said sternly.

Peezle nodded, "I'll replace your robot somehow."

"Stay." Zalez said, "For the night. Tomorrow we will go to Ultra's headquarters and look for Blaphaus. That's more important right now than the funeral."

"I was there today and I was told that he was fired from that company." Peezle remarked.

"I was there as well, Noj. But I also saw the Tooberosum today and he said he's still driving."

"You saw Mr. Blaphaus today?" Mal asked surprised.

"Yes, at the dance school. I talked to him outside."

"But you told the Governors..."

"I know." he said, "We are being watched anyway so I didn't want to make it worse. We have to find him again before they do."

Nate looked at his sister and said, "Everything is going to be okay. Father will see to it."

Romana smiled and hugged her brother.

CHAPTER 5

The next day at the spaceport on Ceilingida the press waited in an area where Governor Tostone would be arriving. GNN robot-cams hovered over head to record the arrival. To the side of the press stood Zucaritas and Zeb, ready to greet their fellow Governor. They both thought it was a good plan for Tostone to come back and later do a press conference at his office building. The GNN anchor stood a few feet away from them. He was a Leetric named Buterdau Kooper, who was one of the rare GNN anchors who got to travel from planet to planet. GNN was based on a space station near the Dook Energy space station and the gambling space station Firvegas and the Church station.

"Here we are at the Ceilingada spaceport waiting for the arrival of Governor Charcat Tostone. Governor Tostone was held by the GBI for questioning about Galactic President Traf's death. It's been noted that G.P. *did* have heart attack. We are still waiting for news on when his funeral will be. So far there's been no announcement on who the next G.P. will be. On Firvegas there's betting odds that the next G.P. will be Governor Tostone."

The holo-sign above the exit Gate where they all waited flashed green and said "Arrived."

"We just got word that the Governor's shuttle has just landed."

The Cabinet arranged for a private flight for Tostone so he wouldn't be bothered. The press corps all perked up as well as the two Governors. The Gate doors opened and Tostone walked through it into a bunch of flashes and robot-cams flying above him, getting him at every angle. The two Governors approached him and shook his hands.

"Welcome back, Tostone." Zeb smiled.

"Good to be back. Let's get to my office building and arrange for this press conference."

Zucaritas said, "We have an Ultra vehicle waiting outside. And no, the Tooberosum is not the driver."

Tostone chuckled. "He'll make an appearance today. You can put lucre on it."

On Launderington, Governor Thaw sat on the couch in the Traf living room with One-Four-Three standing by the door and Mrs. Traf sitting across from him in the chair.

"Of course all the other Cabinet members are going to be at the funeral. Would you want your husband to be buried here or his home planet, whatever that planet would be?"

"I would like him to be buried on this planet... and I understand the Cabinet had to be at the funeral. And I want to say something, as there was no press conference for his passing. Just the statement Governor Tostone said. I would like to know why this Tooberosum knew about his death before you lot as well."

Thaw nodded, "So do we."

"I want Mr. Peezle at the funeral. He had the right sense of mind to come to this house and tell me Algar had passed away. That shouldn't have to be his job. That should be your job, or any of the Cabinet members."

Thaw nodded, "I understand and it would've been if Mr. Peezle would've informed us first."

"Algar was a husband and father way before he was G.P., Governor. I want Peezle to be one of the speakers."

"That can be arranged."

"Good. And I want this over and done with. So the sooner the better."

Thaw nodded, "Tomorrow is the plan."

"Good. Don't let me down, Governor. Algar never let me down."

Blaphaus saw a few more of the GBI crafts flying above the city as he drove his vehicle. He realized they were close to the building where Governor Tostone worked. Could he be back on Ceilingida? That went through his mind. He approached the building and noticed GNN robot-cams hovering in the air. Yep, the Governor was either back or dead. He looked at his info-pad to see a blue circle for his next pick up, which was the opposite direction. He would pay a visit to the Governor later.

Peezle stood outside the Belhopsa's house with Ten waiting on the sidewalk Inside the house was Mal and Zalez and the children were back at school. Zalez walked out the house and joined Peezle who was no longer wearing his overalls, but a nice looking black leather jacket with the Dook Energy logo on the back of it. He looked casual in his jeans and blue shirt. Peezle even thought Zalez looked attractive but didn't want to say anything. His mind went to his husband who was back home on Launderington.

"Noj, the Governor is back on Ceilingida." Zalez told him.

"Really? Tostone?"

"Yep. GNN said he was cleared from the investigation."

A vehicle then parked in front of the house.

"Not the Tooberosum." Ten remarked. "Our 'luck' has ran out."

The driver who was a Cyrakuse stepped out the vehicle. He was feline looking but very skinny and had shiny pitch black fur.

"Hello! My name Broomthe. You look like an odd group... a badly designed robot, a fancy dressed human and a good looking Chordattian."

Ten asked him, "Do you know a Tooberosum driver?"

"You mean Blappy? Yeah, I know him. He was fired though."

"So he *was* fired?" Peezle asked.

"But he said that he was still driving." Zalez remarked.

"There is another company that does what Ultra does." Ten replied, "Called Hoyst."

Peezle said, "You don't think... that he went to the other company?"

Zalez said, "We are going to find out. Broomthe, you're taking us to the Hoyst headquarters."

Principal Garcey's holo-call was in every classroom at the school as he stood in his office, in front of the desk info-pad.

"Children, I am pleased to tell you that Governor Tostone is thankfully back on Ceilingida..."

Nate looked over his shoulder towards Romana who sat further in the back of the class, in the next row.

"Also you'll notice a GBI agent is at the school. Everything is fine, you have nothing to worry about. And hopefully he'll be gone tomorrow. Have a good day, children." His holo-call disappeared.

Nog whispered to Nate at the desk in front of him. "It's because they are looking for the Toob, right?"

Nate did not reply.

Tostone sat behind his desk as the robot-cam hovered in front of him. The other two Governors stood to the side.

Tostone said, "Hello, my fellow people on Ceilingida, and in this great galaxy. I'm so glad to be back on this lovely planet. I missed you all. Tomorrow will be G.P. Traf's funeral so I will be off planet again. Hopefully this week we will have a new Galactic President as well, which will be absolutely wonderful. Have a wonderful day, everybody."

The robot-cam turned off the camera and lowered to the floor. Tostone turned to the other two.

"Okay, so, Governor Thaw is handling the funeral, and Governor Southington is handling the press. Now we just wait."

"And you think the Tooberosum will come to you still?" Zucaritas asked.

Tostone nodded, "I certainly do."

The black vehicle parked outside the Hoyst headquarters. Broomthe got out and opened the back passenger door for the three passengers.

"Here you go. I hope they don't think it's funny an Ultra driver is at Hoyst's headquarters."

"It's really not that funny." Zalez commented.

The three went into the building and the Cyrakuse owner approached them.
"Hello, my name is Cheeetoe. Welcome to Hoyst. Can I help you?"
"We're looking for the manager of this company."
"I'm the manager, sir."
"We were wondering if you have a Tooberosum driver working for you."
"Yes, as a matter of fact I do. He started just recently. His name is Blaphaus Maximus. Nice fella. Is he in trouble?"
"No, but we need to talk to him." Zalez said.
Peezle looked down at Ten, "I can't believe this."
Cheeetoe replied, "I can send a holo-call to his vehicle and have come here."
Zalez said, "Perfect. But don't tell him why."
"Whatever you wish." nodded Cheeetoe.

In his vehicle Blap was startled when a twelve inch holo-call appeared above his info-pad.
"Mr. Maximus, can you come to headquarters?"
Blap frowned, "Why?"
"Ummm..."
"If you're going to fire me I'd rather you do it here."
"You're not going to be fired... you're getting a... raise."
Blap said, "On my way."

Cheeetoe turned to the Chordattian and Peezle and smiled, "He's on his way."
"And now he's getting a raise." Zalez commented. "Good job."

"Fired?" Tostone asked in his office. "Why would Mr. Maximus be fired? He was an excellent driver."
"Because you told the press that you knew about Traf's death from the Toob. He was considered maybe a liability." explained Zucaritas. "You shouldn't have said anything."
"I know. This whole thing is a mess. Mr. Peezle should've told the Cabinet. Anyway, we have to figure out another way to contact Mr. Maximus."
Zeb said, "I'd get to thinking if I were you. The funeral is tomorrow."

Blap's vehicle parked in front of the Hoyst headquarters. Moments later he walked into the building's lobby to come to face. Behind him stood Ten, Peezle and Zalez.
"What is this?" Blaphaus asked.
"Blaphaus, we need to talk." Peezle told him. "The GBI is looking for you."
"For me? Wot for? I keep my nose clean... well if I had a nose I would. What do they want with me? Traf dying was on your watch."

"I don't know. But I know you're number one on the list. You're really popular, Blaphaus."

"That's great." Blap turned to Cheeetoe. "You better not be lying about the raise, Cyrakuse."

"You'll get a raise. I really don't know what this is about, Mr. Maximus. They just came here asking for you."

"How did you find out I work here?" Blap asked them.

Zalez said, "We just figured it out. Once we found out that you were fired from Ultra..."

"You were fired from Ultra?" Cheeetoe squeaked. "Vistrat would have my hide if he found I hired you. I'm afraid I have to let you go."

"See wot you did?" Blap asked the other two. "That's two jobs I've been fired from since the bloody G.P. passed. Chordattian, I haven't been around your family again. Peezle, I would say it's good to see you again but I'd be lying. And your robot looks odd." He turned to leave.

"Blaphaus, where are you going?" Peezle asked.

"Away. It's none of your business. Have fun at the funeral."

"Blaphaus, there are Governors on this planet looking for you." Zalez pointed out. "Come with me and I'll take you to the Dook Energy space station until this whole thing blows over."

"Wot? I'm not going to your stinking space station. Or leaving this planet. I'm done with both of you."

He left the building and Zalez shook his head.

"There's nothing we could do. He's on his own,"

Peezle nodded, Zalez was right. There was nothing more they could do. He wanted to get back to Launderington for the funeral if he could go. Zalez had his family to take care of. The Tooberosum has been part of their lives way too long, and it was time to let him be. But he wasn't going to let that happen. He rushed out the building and over to Blap before he got in the vehicle.

"Blaphaus, we came here to your work place as we are concerned about you. You don't understand what the Governors are thinking..."

Blap turned to face Peezle and said, "Listen, fancy ponce, this has nothing to do with me. You and your bloody Governors all messed up. No wonder why the other planets don't want to be part of your 'club.' Do you know that no one has ever approached half of them to join the Cabinet? Traf was useless and everybody before him was."

Zalez and Ten walked out the building to hear what Blap was saying.

"And as your for you, Chordattian, your wife had my head on top of her dance school for everyone to see, and she was the one who invited me to dinner when you weren't even supposed to be there. And you thought *I* was stalking *her*. Ha!

You all need to figure out your lives. I have my own. Now put the proper legs on that bloody robot and keep out of my life. All of you!"

He got in his vehicle and they watched him drive off.

On Launderington, all the Governors except for Tostone, Zucaritas and Zeb met in the Cabinet room at the House. The three that weren't actually were "there" but not in person, just with holo-calls.

"Mrs. Traf wants to talk at the funeral." Thaw was explaining to them, "And she also wants Peezle there, and I'm sure he'll want to talk. I think only a few of us should speak there, not all sixteen of us."

"What about the press?" the green skinned Gink asked. Ginks were green skinned with little sword shape looking noses, black hair, and big bulging eyes. The males had antennas but the females didn't and this one was male.

"What about GNN? Are they going to be there?" the Gink named Guoz asked.

"Mrs. Traf doesn't want the press there at all." told Thaw, "But agreed Buterdau Kooper and GNN could be outside the cemetery gate."

Southington said, "Then I'll cancel the rest of the press."

Thaw asked, "Governor Tostone, any luck on the Tooberosum?"

"Not yet. But we are working on it. Apparently he's not driving for Ultra anymore."

"He got fired." Zucaritas said. "Because he knew about Traf's death. But GBI agents are everywhere. He will be found."

"You three have less than twenty-four hours." the Smidge remarked. "Toob's are pretty big apparently, it's not like you're looking for a Smidge like me."

Blaphaus drove his vehicle, heading to the building where Tostone worked. He noticed the GBI crafts were still above. He figured that Tostone would make them go away. He wanted the bodyguard job now more than anything. He approached the building which was on the right. He grumbled when he saw those steps... steps he wouldn't be able to climb. What a lousy design, he thought. He parked in the parking lot, and moments later he approached the building. He had no idea how to let anyone know he was there, and wanted to talk to the Governor. Just then a GBI approached him from the side.

"You, Toob. Do not move."

"Does it look like I'm going anywhere? If Tostone is here let him know I'm here for the bodyguard job but he needs to take care of these steps problem."

The holo-call of the agent appeared on Tostone's desk, a foot high.

"Governor Tostone, sir, the Toob is outside looking for you."

"He is?!" grinned Tostone. "Perfect! Bring him in."

"He can't climb the steps, sir, his body has no legs."

"Oh. Of course, which explains why he stands when he drives. I'll be right out."

The agent nodded, "I'll let him know, sir."

The holo-call disappeared and Tostone turned to the other two.

"See? He came right to us."

"Let's go meet this infamous Toob." Zucaritas remarked.

"Actually, I should go by myself. You two will spook him. I offered him a job as my bodyguard and that's what he'll think he'd be doing. Let the Cabinet know he's here. Get a shuttle ready... the plan is falling into place."

Blap watched Tostone come out the building and practically run down the stairs which was a humorous sight considering his built. Tostone had his arms open wide like he was going to hug Blaphaus.

"Don't hug me." Blap warned.

"I won't, Mr. Blaphaus. It's good to see you again. I hope I didn't cause any problems for you."

"I just was fired from two jobs because of you. And apparently have the GBI looking for me and some of your Cabinet members as well as Traf's errand boy and the head of Dook Energy. It's all been a giant big adventure, Tostone."

"I'm sorry. Getting the news about the G.P. came as quite a shock to me."

"Wasn't to me. Humans don't live that long normally. Your race is lucky, To-stone. Don't Cyrakuse's have eight lives or something?"

"Nine really, but that doesn't mean we can't die."

"It's still a good thing, maybe you can be the next G.P."

Tostone laughed, "That's funny, Blaphaus. So, what brings you by here?"

"You offered me a job as your bodyguard... unless you were talking out of your arse is that offer still open?"

"Yes, of course!" grinned Tostone. "This is all good timing. I'm going to need you to come with me to Launderington tomorrow."

"Launderington? I'm not leaving this planet."

"It'll just be for a day. I have to go to the G.P.'s funeral, Blaphaus. It'll be worth your time, and pay. Would 500 lucre's be sufficient?"

"For five hundred? I'd go *now* for that much." smiled Blap.

Tostone shook Blap's hand excitedly. "Tomorrow at seven in the morning meet me here."

"You got yourself a deal, Governor."

This was way too perfect, thought Tostone.

The holo-call's of Zucaritas and Zeb appeared in the Cabinet room back on Launderington, inside the House.

"It turns out the Tooberosum has showed up at Tostone's building here. I don't know how the conversation is going but we are hoping it's going good. The good thing is the Toob came to us. Don't ask why, but he's here." Zeb smiled.

Southington nodded, "That's perfect."

Thaw nodded, "If the Tooberosum can be convinced to come here that will be something."

At the school the GBI agent got the holo-call from Zucaritas to head back. The Toob had been found, the same thing for the one at the Belhopsa's house and the dance school.

The next morning Blaphaus was at Tostone's headquarters right on time in the morning. This was the earliest he ever got up and out in a long time, since he was back on his planet. He watched as Tostone walked down the steps wearing a black suit. Blap wasn't a driver anymore so didn't bother getting out the vehicle to open the door for the Governor. Tostone opened the door himself and got into the back seat.
"Morning, Blaphaus. Are you ready for your first day on the job? I hope you don't get sick of me."
Blaphaus said, "For 500 lucre's I can put up and deal with anybody. Hope you booked a flight for both of us."
"I did, but you can't sit so how are you going to be?"
"That's up to you to figure out.
"You might have to be in the storage area with the baggage and robots I'm afraid. I hope that's okay. As least it's a very short flight."
"Guess I have no choice." he muttered.

Zeb and Zucaritas were already on Launderington at the House in the Cabinet room with the others. Outside GNN robot-cams hovered in front of Kooper who was talking.
"Today is the day of Galactic President Traf's funeral. Traf's wife and children are supposed to be there as well as all fifteen Cabinet members. At the end of the day we also should know who the next G.P. will be. On Firvegas odds are that the new G.P. will be Governor Charcat Tostone from Cyrakuse but the Governor of Ceilingida. GNN is 'banned' from the funeral but I will be reporting on what is happening from outside the gate. Buterdau Kooper, GNN."

At the spaceport on Ceilingida, Blaphaus and Governor Tostone walked in just as the report was finished.
Blap said, "This trip better not be too long, Tostone."
"It won't be. It'll be worth it. Trust me."
"You're a politician. I know about you lot." grumbled Blap.

A few hours later Blap stood among the baggage and the robots in the storage hold of the shuttle. He held on to a bar of some sort on the bulkhead so he wouldn't fall over.

"What kind robot are you?" asked a shiny silver robot.

"The kind that can rip your arms off if you keep talking."

On Launderington, Peezle walked into his flat and was greeted by his husband with a big hug and kiss.

"Noj, I missed you! You've been busier since the G.P. passed away than when he was alive."

"I know, Yerkal. I have been really busy, wrapping everything up. How are you? How's work?"

"Ah, you know, the same. So, are you staying on Launderington now are going somewhere? Are we moving?"

"I don't know. Maybe the new G.P. will have me as his or her Assistant."

Yerkal smiled, "That would be great unless that one will have you working more."

Hours later, Blaphaus and Tostone walked through the Launderington spaceport and walked outside to be met by Rubyspears, who was standing besides his black limousine vehicle.

"Governor Tostone, and... you're a Toob, right?"

"You're a Chordattian..."

"Actually, I'm not, I'm human. But I look like... never mind. Nice to meet you. You're famous, you know?"

"Wotever."

"He's my bodyguard." told Tostone.

"Really? That's interesting. I'll open the sunroof so the Toob can stand on the seat and stick his head out the roof. Toob, welcome to Launderington. I'm Rubyspears."

"Blaphaus."

Launderington was a lot different looking than Ceilingida. Every building looked like it was made from marble, all black, grey and white with some gold trimming thrown in here and there. Tostone sat next to Blap who stood in the black leather seat with his head out the roof.

"We are going to the House, home of the Cabinet so you can meet everyone. Then the funeral."

"Great. This should be a blast," he said sarcastically. "I'll bet they'll love me."

"I hope so." mused Tostone. "I really do."

CHAPTER 6

"Greetings, everyone. My name is Algar Traf and I am your new Galactic President. It's a huge honor to be chosen and I hope I can do the whole galaxy proud. Right now there's only sixteen of the plants out of the twenty-three that are part of the Cabinet... with a Governor representing each planet. I hope to by the end of my tenor as Galactic President, whenever that may be to have the remaining seven planets all be in unison, under one planetary union. Thank you, and have a good day."

The holo-image of Traf froze on the holo-screens that everyone watched. Traf was a good looking well spoken man. He wore a black pinstriped suit, a tie and a fedora. He always tried to look his best, and be as Galactic Presidential like as possible.

Buterdau appeared on GNN and spoke, "That was Galactic President Traf who a few days ago passed away from a sudden heart attack. Today on Launderington is his funeral and hopefully by the end of the day we'll know who the new G.P. will be. Some now think it's a possibility it will be Governor Erlas Zeb from Chordatt. Others still think it's going to be Governor Charcat Tostone from Ceilingida. We will soon know the answer. Buterdau Kooper, GNN."

"Steps. Why does it have to be steps?"

Blap, Tostone and Rubyspears stood at the bottom of the steps in front of the House.

"Who designed this bloody building?" Blap complained, waving his long skinny arm at it annoyed.

"Ummm... it was built years ago." Tostone remarked, "Before any of us were here."

"Well, Governor, you're screwed. I can't go into your precious building, so unless you have another idea..."

Rubyspears remarked, "I've never seen a species with no legs before. Robots, yes, but species. That makes life hard for you I'm sure."

"Well, on Tooberosum we don't have steps. Or stairs. So, Governor, what are you going to do about this?"

"We'll figure it out." Tostone said, "The Cabinet will have to come outside to meet you."

"Just have them meet me at the funeral."

Tostone was annoyed that he didn't think of this. He knew Blap couldn't do stairs. He signed and turned to Rubyspears.

"Go to Traf's family's house to pick them up and take them to the cemetery. I'll take care of things here."

Rubyspears nodded, "You got it, Governor."

At the cemetery, Buterdau Kooper stood outside the big iron gate as the robot-cam hovered in front of him.

"I am here at the cemetery, where many have been buried before. Today though, Galactic President Algar Traf will be lowered into the earth. The fifteen Governors should be arriving soon."

Across the galaxy, on most of the planets so many people watched the live footage on GNN. At Nate and Romana's school every classroom watched the holo-vision of Kooper with the cemetery in the background.

"The vehicles are starting to arrive." Kooper was saying as the first vehicle was seen in the distance.

Rubyspears parked the vehicle by the grass and he got out, opening the back passenger door for Mrs. Traf and her teenage children, Narob and Hoeka, all wearing black. Hoeka looked like she had been crying, and Narob looked like he had no feelings whatsoever.

"It's hard to see the Traf family's expressions from this distance but needless to say they are upset."

The second vehicle arrived and Southington and the other two human Governors got out of it, also wearing black. One was female, the other male.

"Governor Jupha Southington, Governor of Mencken has arrived, as well as Joer Ace, Governor of Lesavia and Governor Cris Dawber from Canola have arrived."

The third vehicle arrived and Zeb and Zucaritas got out of that one.

"Now we have Governor Erlas Zeb from Chordatt and Governor Toney Zucaritas from Cyrakuse."

Everyone who was showing up to the funeral was wearing black so far. The fourth vehicle arrived and the Gink Governor and the Smidge got out of it. Gink's normally wore green outfits to match their green skin, but this time his whole outfit was black with green trim.

"Next we have Governor Guoz from Gink and Governor Noam from Homunculus."

The fifth vehicle arrived, with the Jiraffa's head sticking out through the sunroof. She bowed her head and got out and the feathered Struthioian followed.

"Next we have Governor Gillian from Savannahian and Governor Lluhdor from Struthionia."

The sixth vehicle then arrived and Thaw got out, followed by a tan furred hunched over Pilosa. Pilosa's had big eyes and ears on the side of their heads and hardly ever spoke.

"Next we have Governor Thaw from Siahl and Governor Waydau from Hittittippi."

The seventh vehicle arrived and the white furred Bipolarab got out followed by a silver species who looked like it had a bone shell on his head and back, which was covered by a jacket.

"Here is Governor Kaktovic from Ankerage and Governor Heckmondwike Sugden from Xenartha and Governor Bert Eastora from the long tongue twister planet Burdenchurdettu."

Sugden was actually an Illiger species, but from Xenartha, which was the only planet in the galaxy that had a military. The bald human male with a small goatee followed him, not looking happy he had to be with the other two. This human was older than the others and carried a cane. The eighth vehicle then arrived with Blaphaus' head sticking out the sunroof.

"This is an odd sight." Kooper voices said over the live GNN feed. "Either I lost count or there's something new happening. I can't tell from here but it looks like..."

Tostone got out the vehicle followed by Blaphaus, who looked around at the others carefully. What a real mixed lot, he thought.

"It looks like Governor Charcat Tostone from Ceilingida and what I believe is a Tooberosum..."

"What the...?!" exclaimed Vistrat Calasteel who was watching GNN in his office with his robot.

"Is that...?"

"Looks like Blaphaus to me, sir."

"Why is he at the funeral? What's going on?"

The robot chose to say nothing.

In the classroom the children couldn't believe it, especially Nate and Romana. Nog tapped Nate on the shoulder.

"Is that your Toob, Nate?"

"Mr. Blaphaus. Yeah, that's him."

"Why is he there at the G.P.'s funeral?"

Nate turned to where Romana was and shrugged. She was smiling to see Mr. Blaphaus was on GNN.

At the dance school Fadonna turned to Mal, as they both sat watching GNN. "That's..." Fadonna said. "Your Toob friend. What is he doing there?"

Mal shrugged, "I don't know but I'm glad he is. He's with Governor Tostone as well."

Zalez stood in his office on the Dook Energy space station watching GNN stroking his black beard. He had no idea what to think. He frowned, thinking this maybe this was either a bad thing or a good thing. What was the Cabinet up to?

The last vehicle arrived and Peezle and Ten got out. Blap turned to see them and smirked. Everyone there was approached by a middle-aged man, wearing long red jacket as they stood around the hole in the ground that the black shiny coffin sat by.

"Hello, I'm Nitsiuj Rellim, head of the Faeligion Church, the one Church in the galaxy. Often Algar Traf and his family would come to the Church space station and pray with us. Not as often we would like, but he would come. So, it is my honor to be at his funeral." Rellim turned to the Traf family. "I understand that you'd like to speak, Lilly."

"Yes. Thank you, Pastor Rellim." She went and stood on the small stage at the podium which looked down at the group that stood around the hole.

"Thank you all for being here. Most of you thought you knew Algar but you didn't. He was a great father and husband, and loved his children. He also loved you and this galaxy. When he was chosen to be the Galactic President he was very surprised. We never knew if he wanted the job but he did the best that he could, with what little he knew. I don't know why the Creator of this galaxy took him, maybe Pastor Rellim has that answer..."

Rellim shook his head.

"Algar was a fit man, so having a sudden heart attack was a big surprise to all of us. I will say though, that Noj Peezle, Algar's Assistant did what none of you Governors could do, and that was to tell me of my husbands passing." She glanced at Peezle. "I thank you, Noj, for being a great friend to Algar, not just his Assistant. If there's anything you ever need... I hope the new G.P. will have you as their Assistant. Anyway, on behalf of my children Algar Traf will be missed, and this galaxy will continue. Thank you."

She stepped off the podium steps and went to hug her children. Blap watched everyone's reactions. Most of them kept stabber faced, not saying a word.

"Next to the podium is... Noj Peezle." Pastor Rellim told them.

Peezle walked up to the podium and up the three steps. He looked down at everyone, and smiled at Mrs. Traf.

"You are welcome, ma'am. Galactic President was more than my boss... he was a good friend of mine. The day he made G.P. was the day he asked me to be his Assistant. No other G.P.'s in the past had Assistants so I was taken back by this, but was very honored. Algar Traf didn't tell me everything that was going on, like why we went to Ceilingida a few days ago to meet with Governor Tostone privately. Only one person knows what that meeting was about and he's there." he pointed to Tostone, who stood next to Blaphaus, who wondered how long this thing would last.

"We were in such a hurry that day and I wonder if the G.P. didn't slip and fall then, would he had his heart attack. Since then I've been lost, told I'm no longer welcome at the House, and I am now unemployed. But I'm glad to be here today to pay my respects. Algar Traf, thank you for being in my life."

A tear rolled down his cheek as the Governors grumbled to themselves. Thaw winked up at Peezle, hoping he saw it and know that everything was going to be okay. Peezle stepped down and went back over to Ten.

"You're crying again." Ten told him.

Peezle shushed the short robot.

"I understand we have one more speaker, but first we will watch as the capsule goes into its hole." the Pastor told them.

Programmed to do this the capsule rose off the ground and slowly lowered itself into the hole, watched by everyone.

"Rest in piece, Galactic President." they all said in unison, except Blap.

He was thinking this was some odd tradition. This was a lot of pomp and circumstance but not as much as he would think for a funeral for someone so important.

"The next speaker will be Governor Tostone." Pastor Rellim announced.

Tostone made his way up to the podium, looking down at them all.

"It's been a crazy few days, for me and everyone here. More some than others. It's true Algar Traf and I had a private meeting, with the other Governors knowing. He was the one who asked for the meeting, not I, but I wasn't going to say no. Algar Traf was thinking about stepping down as G.P. and wanted my advice and I gave it to him honestly. If he would've survived that trip we would already have a new G.P., and he would be sitting home with his family without worrying about anything. But fate would have it, the Creator somehow made sure the plan and idea would still happen. Maybe not the way we'd want, but still the plan. Mr. Maximus, can you come up here, please and join me?"

"You need a bodyguard now?" Blap asked.

"Not exactly. Please join me."

"Whatever, Cyrakuse." He went behind the podium and saw the three steps. "That's not going to happen."

Tostone nodded, "Of course." He got off the podium and went to stand besides Blap.

"I can't see exactly what is going on over there but it looks like the Toobero-sum is joining the Governor at the podium. I wonder, was he the cause of the G.P.'s death?" Kooper said on GNN.

"What is Mr. Blaphaus doing up there?" Romana asked.
"Shsss." Ms. Beezlee told her.
"I have a weird feeling..." Nate mumbled.

"What is going on?" Calasteel asked. "I have a sick feeling in my stomach." The robot still didn't reply.

The Governors all looked at each other, some more confused than the others. Peezle even looked confused as did Traf's wife.
"Ladies and gentlemen..." Tostone grinned, "This is Blaphaus Maximus... your new... Galactic President!"

CHAPTER 7

"I'm not sure what just happened, but I think I just heard Governor Tostone just announce to the Cabinet that the Tooberosum is now Galactic President." Kooper's voice said as the image scans on GNN showed a shocked and surprised Cabinet and others.

Nate stared at the image, trying to figure out what's going on.
"I don't understand what's going on." Nog complained.
Their teacher said, "Neither do I, Nog."
"Nate, what's going on?" Romana asked.
"Well, I think that Mr. Blaphaus is the new G.P." he said.

Back at the funeral the Gink's eyes were wider than usual, bulging out of his head, his antennae's sticking straight up.
Waydau looked up and actually spoke, but slowly, "This is the dumbest, most ridiculous, asinine feces I have ever heard! And I thought choosing Traf was a bad move!"
The old man with the cane rubbed his bald head and said, "No one knows anything about Toobs or their planet… and now we have one as our G.P.?"
"You can't just chose who you want to be G.P." Dawber, the female human remarked.
"Actually I can." Tostone replied, "You know that."
"It has to be at least a few Cabinet members to decide." told Joer.
Southington said, "Well, I knew, Noam knew, Zucaritas knew, Zeb knew and obviously Tostone knew."
"Southington, how can you approve this?" Dawber asked.
"Hey, you lot, did any of tossers ask me?" Blap asked, "Cyrakuse, I agreed to be your bodyguard, not the bloody G.P. You bait and switched me. You bloody lied! Your race is supposed to be a happy lot, not liars."
A robot-cam flew over and hovered in front of Blap.
"Get this bloody robot thing out of my face." he complained, threatening to hit the robot, and flipping it off.
Peezle said, "Blaphaus, I'm sorry, I did not know this was happening."
"If you did would you have said so?"
"Stop this!" Lilly Traf cried out, "This was Algar's funeral! Couldn't you have waited?"
"No, I couldn't." Tostone said. "We'll talk about this at the House…"
"The building that I can't even get into because of the steps?" Blaphaus asked. "Great thinking."

Zucaritas said, "We'll figure that out."

Blap said, "Pick another sucker. If you thought Traf was useless, I'm going to be worse."

Zeb said to Peezle, "Go grab that GNN Leetric quick."

Peezle ran to the cemetery gate, waving his arms.

Thaw said, "I think we decided to talk about this."

"You knew about it, Thaw." Zucaritas told him.

"No I didn't."

"You lot are bloody crazy. You can't agree on anything, and you blamed Peezle for being disrespectful? You sprung this on me at a funeral! Funeral of your past G.P. mind you." Blap said, shuffling off.

Peezle and Kooper walked over, a robot-cam following them.

Tostone motioned to Blaphaus, "Hello, everybody in the galaxy who is watching. This is Blaphaus Maximus, your new Galactic President." he grinned.

"It's official then." Kooper said, "We have a new G.P. and it's a Tooberosum."

The drivers at Ultra cheered, and in his office Calasteel heard them.

"How can they pick him as G.P.?! I don't get it!"

"He was the talk of the week, sir."

Nate and everyone else in his classroom cheered. The other classes the children did not know what to think.

"Mr. Blaphaus is the new G.P.!" Nate said jumping to his feet. "We knew he was special!"

"Mal! You are friends with the G.P.! Can I put his image up on the building again?" Fadonna asked.

Mal nodded, "Sure. Until Zalez comes back of course."

Blaphaus shuffled away from everybody at the cemetery.

"Where are you going, Toob?!" Noam the Smidge exclaimed.

"Anywhere but here, tiny."

Tostone over hurried to him, "You can't leave. You're really the G.P."

"Please. Traf did what he wanted, which doesn't seem to be a lot."

"Yeah, and he'd want you to be G.P. Can we go back to the House and talk about it?"

"Wot? By the steps? You keep forgetting I can't go up the steps!"

"Somewhere."

Peezle walked over, "Right now you don't have a choice I'm afraid, my friend."

"Who are you, Peezle? You don't count. And you're not going to be my Assistant. This whole mess is your fault."

"I know. But I know the law. My husband is a Solicitor. You really don't have a choice."

Blap said, "Fine. I'll listen, but I'm not going to the House. We'll meet at somebody else's house."

"Whose house?" Tostone asked.

The life sized holo-call of Blap and Tostone were in front of Zalez in his office on the space station.

"G.P. Maximus, let me congratulate you." Zalez said.

"Knock it off, Chordattian. You and I both know you don't mean it."

"That's not true."

"Wotever. I'm the G.P. and have to meet with the Cabinet losers. I'm coming back to Ceilingida... and I want to have the meeting at your house."

"My house? I'm not even there."

"I know. So you might as well get into a Dook Energy shuttle and get going."

The hologram-call ended.

Rubyspears drove his vehicle with the Traf family in the back seat.

"I'm sorry about the G.P., ma'am."

"I know, but life goes on. Algar will always be remembered..."

"Sorry, ma'am, he will but I was talking about the Toob. I can't believe he was picked as the G.P. What are they thinking do you think?"

"Knowing the Cabinet who knows? I'm sure there's some kind of underhanded plan..."

"It's because they can use him." Narob spoke up. "They couldn't use father because he was lazy and didn't do anything. The Toob will."

"Do what?" Rubyspears asked.

"Bring the whole galaxy together."

Zalez's holo-call was at the dance school, a foot high per norm. On top of the dance school was the large holo-image of Blap's head once again.

"Darling, can you believe that Blaphaus is the new G.P.? I'm so confused."

"You're about to be more confused, Mal. He's heading back to Ceilingida. He wants to use *our* house for the Cabinet meeting." Zalez told her.

"What? Why? Our house?! The Cabinet are all coming here."

"Yes, but don't worry, I'm heading there as well. I'd keep the children away from the house."

"I will. Why our house though and not *the* House?"

"Who knows? But really, I'm not surprised. Nothing surprises me anymore."

Mal laughed, "True. See you soon."

The holo-call ended and Fadonna clapped her hands excitedly.

"You're so lucky! All the Governors at your house!"

Mal said, "Yeah, lucky, I need to go and clean."

Blaphaus and the entourage walked through the spaceport on Laundering-ton, getting stares from everybody. The GNN robot-cams flew above and besides them, watching every move. In such a short time everything was changing. Peezle and Ten followed the group.

"Why are we still with them, sir?" Ten asked. "We are not wanted."

"I don't know, Ten, but we are going to stay close with them as much as possible. This will be interesting."

"That's good, because I have something I need to do."

"So, G.P. Maximus is heading back to Ceilingida with the Cabinet. No word yet why a Tooberosum was chosen as G.P. but hopefully we'll find out more soon. Buterdau Kooper, GNN."

The Cabinet boarded the shuttle, with the new G.P. and Peezle and Ten.

"You don't have to go to the storage bay, Ten." whispered Peezle.

"I wasn't going to."

Blap told them all, "I will just stand in the aisle, I'm the G.P., so this time I'm standing here,"

"You can do what you want." Tostone said.

"Actually, sir, safety says that you have to sit during the flight or go to the storage bay..."

Blap cut the flight attendant off, "Lady, I'm not going anywhere. I am the Galactic President."

"But safety says..."

Zucaritas said, "We have a private flight, no one will know. Tell the pilot we are good to go."

"Very well. I will let him know." she said before she walked towards the pilots cabin.

"So, how much money does a G.P. make?" Blap asked.

"Nothing." the Smidge said.

"Oh, that will change, trust me. Tostone still owes me..."

Mal picked her children up at the school, and was driving her vehicle with them on the back seat.

"So, children, we are going back to the dance school and will be there longer today."

"Why is that?" Nate asked.

"There's going to be a meeting at our house."

"Meeting? With who?"

"Mr. Blaphaus and the Cabinet. But don't get too excited... we are staying away."

"They all coming to our house? Why?" asked Romana.

"And why can't we be there?" Nate whined.

"I don't know, Nate. But I think we'll just get in the way."

'No we won't..."

"That's a lot of people in the house." Romana said, "Is there room?"

The black and red robot at Ultra went into Calasteel's office as Calasteel was watching GNN still.

"Sir, I think you'd want to know that nine drivers were booked to go to the spaceport."

"So what? That's not new. The spaceport is a major place to go to."

"But this was booked by one single robot."

"And?"

"The robot is 10-E-C, and he ordered the vehicles for a large group..."

"What large group?

The G.P. and the Cabinet, sir."

"The Cabinet?!" Calasteel said. "They're using my drivers? I knew Maximus was a good Toob. I always liked him." he lied. "In your face, Cheeetoe! Ha!"

A little bit later Zalez stood outside his house waiting for the entourage. He watched as Mal's vehicle drove up instead, with the children in the back seat.

"What are you doing here?" he asked as they got out the vehicle. "I said to keep them away."

"Nate and Romana were begging to see Mr. Blaphaus and Nate wants to meet the Governors."

Zalez sighed, "Of course he does. *I* haven't even met all the Governors."

An hour or so later it was a sight to be seen, the line of Ultra vehicles, with Blap driving his own, Tostone in the back seat.

"Here I am as G.P. and I'm still driving you around, Cyrakuse. This is feces."

"But it's different, right?"

"Yes. It's worse! You know I'm not doing this for free... being a G.P. You lot better figure out a way to pay me."

"We'll work something out, Blaphaus."

"You better. I never worked for free. Ever."

They approached the suburbs, going by the houses. The few that were outside stopped what they were doing to watch the entourage. The row of cars stopped outside the Belhopsa house, where Zalez was waiting outside. The Cabinet started to file out the vehicles as well as Peezle and Ten who stood in the back of the Cabinet members.

"Welcome to my house." Zalez said. "And Ceilingida."

"We appreciate you having us." Zeb shook his planet mates hand. "On better terms this time."

"We are only here because these idiots' House has a bunch of steps in front of it." Blap told him. He noticed the children looking out the front window. "Your ankle biters are here?"

"Yes, when they found out that you were coming..."

"Can't anybody keep a secret?" Blap asked.

"We'll make sure they will leave." Zucaritas said.

"No, keep them here." Blap remarked.

Southington stepped forward, "Hello, I'm Governor Southington from Mencken. We really appreciate this and promise that we won't be long. G.P. Maximus will be interviewed later though by Buterdau Kooper. Will that be okay?"

"Interview? I don't do interviews." snapped Blap. "You people really need to start telling me what to expect. I'm not happy about any of this."

"Let's just go inside and we'll talk." Thaw remarked. "I'm sure you in shock."

"You don't know half of it, Leetric."

When they went inside Mal smiled at everybody, especially at the new G.P.

"Hello, Mr. Blaphaus, welcome back."

"You are to call him G.P. Maximus." Noam told her, glad he was at least taller than the children.

"She can call me whatever she likes." Blap told him.

"Mr. Blaphaus!" the children exclaimed. They wanted to give him a hug but they knew better.

"Hi there, you two. Are you being good?"

"Of course."

Romana spotted Ten, "He's the one who killed O-U!"

Blap looked at the short robot. "You killed their robot? I wondered where he was."

Peezle said, "He is sorry."

"Let's start the meeting, shall we?" Zeb asked.

"You should leave." Zucaritas told Peezle.

"No, he's staying." Blaphaus told him. "For now."

The children were sent to their rooms, and Mal joined them upstairs. Zalez was told he could stay downstairs. The Cabinet was spread out all over the living room, some sitting, some standing. Peezle sat at the dining room table with Zalez. They could see into the living room and hear what was going on.

"So, one of you better explain how I got picked and what the plan was." Blaphaus told them. "I don't like lying and you are all a bunch of liars. Can I fire any of you if I want?"

Southington said, "Yes, we'll go over the rules and what your 'power' is but yes, G.P. Maximus, you can fire any of us... but you have to choose the replacement."

"Hmmm." he turned to Tostone. "You're fired."

Everybody looked shocked.

"What?! You can't fire me! It was me that wanted you to be the G.P.!"

"That was strike one. You lied to me about the bodyguard job, and you mentioned me to the press. I try to stay on the down low, but you didn't make that easy. You're a nice Cyrakuse, but a pain in the arse. You're fired."

"You have to replace him." Thaw said.

"Okay. So, what are the credentials?"

"The replacement have to be from or a resident of this planet." Southington explained.

"Okay. That's easy. Zalez, get in here!"

Zalez walked in and said, "I can't be the Governor. I'm head of Dook Energy."

"I wasn't going to chose you, we have one Chordattian in the Cabinet already. I want someone smart, and would be honest and likes me. So, I want you to pick someone as I hardly know anybody."

Zalez nodded, "I'll find somebody."

"Good. I also need an assistant and it's not going to be Peezle. Zalez, get your boy down here."

"Ummm... why?" Zalez asked.

"G.P. Maximus, I don't think..." Zeb said.

"Get your boy, Zalez "

Zalez went to the stairs and called for his son. Nate went down the stairs, watched by his mother and sister.

"Nate, right?" Blap asked the boy.

"Yes, sir."

"Sir. I like that. Want to be my Assistant?"

"Me?! Yes!"

"Wait, he's eight-years-old and still in school." Zalez said.

"I'm not going to say pull him out of school. But he's still going to be my Assistant. The days he misses is up to you."

"Thank you, Mr. Blaphaus." Nate smiled, heading back to the stairs.

"Where are you going, kid?"

"Back to my room."

"No you're not, you're my Assistant. Walk Tostone to the front door. He's no longer a Cabinet member and I have no idea why he's still sitting here."

Nate looked at Tostone, who slowly stood up.

"You're making a big mistake." Tostone said sadly.

"No, you did, Tostone. Have a nice life."

Tostone looked sad as he walked behind Nate to the front door.

"You really need to have a replacement right away." Thaw told Blap.

"Pick a replacement yet?" Blap asked Zalez.

"No, not yet."

"Think, Chordattian, think. Okay, any of you want to lie to me again you want to think twice." Blap said. "So, why am I the 'chosen one'?"

Zeb said, "Tostone and Traf had a meeting as you know. You are the best choice for G.P. We hope you can get the other seven planets to join the Cabinet."

"One of those planets is Tooberosum. That lot won't be part of the Cabinet."

"You will convince them." Zucaritas said. "And the other six."

"We'll see. So, how come you lot didn't have a back up plan if something happened to Traf? You went through days without a G.P."

"We don't think..." the Gink said.

"That's true. You don't think. What and who are you?"

"I'm a Gink... Guoz is my name. I'm from Gink."

"Terrific." Blap replied. "You lot should have a back up plan... how many hearts do you all have?"

"We each have one heart." Southington said.

"I have one heart but four chambers." Thaw remarked.

"Well, I have two hearts... so there's a slim chance they would all go bad like Traf's, but if they did and I would drop dead who is gonna be my replacement? You're going wait a few days before you get your feces together and fumble about?"

"What are you suggesting?" the long necked feathered Governor asked

"What's your name?"

"I'm a Struthionian..."

"I know *what* you are. Who are you?"

"Well, G.P., my name is Lluhdor. What are you suggesting? You're the G.P., if you die we'll figure it out."

"I'm saying that if I do die then someone should take my place right away. So, I think there should be a Vice Galactic President... someone who can do something that I can't. So, Lluhdor, it's you. Congratulations." Blap turned to Zalez. "Think of a successor for Tostone yet?"

"How about... the principal from the children's school?"

"Whoever that is. We'll go visit him later." Blap said.

Dawber said, "I don't think it works that way. It's supposed to be something we all discuss."

"If I have to wait for all of you..."

Zucaritas said, "Now it's time to tell you what's going on, Maximus..."

“That’s G.P. Maximus to you, remember?”

“Yes. I remember. You were chosen, Tooberosum, not because of your person-ality and looks. You were chosen because for some reason you were the center of everything these last few days and is unique, as Toobs never leave their planet. You’re a pawn... a political pawn and there’s nothing you can do about it. So, you are going to every planet that’s not part of the Cabinet. Those planets have Planet Mayors and you will convince them to become Governors and part of the Cabinet. One of us will go with you to make sure you do this right. Any questions?”

Zucaritas wasn’t going to lie... they all saw how reckless Blaphaus could be in firing who lied to him.

“Tooberosum is one of those planets and we don’t have a Planet Mayor or any-thing like that. No government, no leader, nothing.”

“Then you will go there and pick someone.”

Blaphaus sighed, “That’s not as easy as you think, Zucaritas. But wotever.”

The door buzzer buzzed and Nate went go get the door.

“It’s the GNN Leetric!” he called out.

Blap and Buterdau went outside as the robot-cam hovered before them.

“This is Buterdau Kooper, I’m here on Ceilingida with the new Galactic Presi-dent. How are you doing, Galactic President Maximus?”

“Like a big fat green idiot. I would say more but I’m guessing children are watching this.”

“Perhaps. Did you ask or want to be G.P.? Did you have aspirations on being G.P.?”

“No! I was happy being a bloody driver until Calasteel fired me as he said I was a liability.”

“Calasteel?”

“The manager of Ultra on this planet.”

“You lived for a while on this planet. What made you come here?”

“For the sunshine. And because it was easy to get to.”

“What was it like back home on Tooberosum?”

“So great I couldn’t wait to leave. So I did.”

“How *did* you leave?”

“That’s a long story, Leectric. It wasn’t easy.”

“So, how do you think life will be now you’re G.P.?”

“More work than the previous G.P. did apparently.”

“Well, I wish you luck. You’re going to need it.”

“Tell me about it.”

Ten then walked outside the house and said, “Sorry to interrupt but I have to show you something urgent, G.P. Maximus.”

“Can’t you see I’m being interviewed, robot?”

“This is important.”

“Yeah. Wotever.”

"It's good, I'll be talking to you again soon. This is Buterdau Kooper, GNN."

Blap followed Ten who walked to the side of the house.

"Are you going to try and murder me?" Blap asked.

"No, I'm not." he opened up the top part of his head and pulled out small silver fob.

"What's that?"

"Later when you're home alone push the side of it. That's all I'm allowed to say."

"Forget that, I'm playing it now."

"No..." Ten said as Blap snatched it from Ten's claw like robot hand. He pushed the side button and a holo-recording of G.P. Traf appeared, about a foot tall. This was the first time that Blaphaus got to see what Traf really looked like.

"You're alive?!"

"Hello, if you can see this recording I take it you are my predecessor. I hope the Cabinet chose wisely and didn't pick you because you are good looking and a good family man like I was. I am planning on giving up on being G.P. In a few years time I think this galaxy will be invaded... There's other galaxies out there and nothing's stopping them from coming to our galaxy. We need the other seven planets to be reunited with the sixteen. Even Tooberosum... which I can't find any-thing about anywhere. But I know Toobs are out there. So, whoever you are, I wish you luck. Thank the Creator you'll be able to do a better job than I could ever. Take care."

The holo-recording ended and Traf disappeared. Blap grunted and he put the disc in the inside pocket of his purple jacket.

"G.P. Maximus, that's a lot of information."

"No its not. It told me nothing. Don't say anything about this though. Not yet."

"I'm not allowed to."

Blap frowned. Invasion? No one is going to invade the galaxy. Not this galaxy anyway. He made his way around to the front of the house and went inside.

"How did the interview go?" Southington asked.

"Terrific. Are we done here?"

"Yes, for now." Zucaritas remarked. "Tomorrow we are going to Cyrakuse."

"Cyrakuse? Your planet is part of the Cabinet. Are they crying because I fired Tostone?"

"No, but the King wants to meet you."

"King? What bloody King?"

CHAPTER 8

"Mr. Blaphaus, you're going to like Principle Garcey. He's really nice." Nate was saying in the back seat of Blap's vehicle. His father was sitting one side of him and the Struthioian named Lluhdor sat on the other side.

"What species is he?" Blaphaus asked.

"He's human. Does it matter?" Zalez asked.

"Everything matters now." Blap replied.

"I think we should have Tostone come back, G.P. Maximus."

"Nope. He's a lying Cyrakuse."

"But he did what he thought and what G.P. Traf thought was best, and that's having you..."

"That's feces right there, Struthionian. Traf didn't even know me..."

"He knew of Tooberosums."

"How many Tooberosums have you met?"

"None. Well, you're the first, G.P. Maximus."

"Zalez, you work on a space station which powers all sixteen planets, right?"

"No, only about thrirteen..."

"Okay, big difference. How many Tooberosums have you met? I'm sure you've been to every planet..."

"Ummm..."

Nate stared at his dad wondering what his answer would be. Every day since Nate and Romana met the Toobeeosum since he picked them up at the spaceport he and Romana have tried to research the race and the species, but finding out nothing. Yes, there was word spoken about the planet existing and the race but that's all. No text, holo-images, holo-scans, nothing. But here was one, driving him again, and as the new Galactic President. But something did not add up or make sense.

They approached the school where Principal Garcey stood out front of. He waved and smiled as he saw the Toob driven vehicle. It parked and the four figures got out of it.

"Hello, Nate, Mr. Bellhopsa, how are you?"

"I'm good, Principal Garcey." Nate smiled. "This is Mister... Galactic President Maximus. I'm his Assistant."

"You're a what?"

"Assistant." Blap replied.

"I heard a lot about you, G.P. Maximus. Nate and his sister talked about you a lot. Did you know that?"

"Sure. I'm lovable." he said sarcastically. "This is Governor Lluhdor. I hope you're not allergic to feathers."

77

Garcey chuckled, "Of course not."

"Is this a human only school?" asked Lluhdor.

"Ummm... yes. There's other schools... they have mixed species..."

"Mr. Belhopsa, you're a Chordattian, why would you have your children go to an all human school?" Lluhdor asked irritated.

"Because my wife didn't want the children to have distractions."

"What kind of distractions?"

"Being surrounded by..."

"That explains why they were so enthralled with me." Blap said. "Boy, you know you're going to be around all different species being my Assistant, right, kid?"

"Yes, G.P. Blaphaus. I wish I was around different species all the time."

Blap pointed to the principal. "As G.P. you are to open this school to everyone... no matter what species..."

"We don't have the space..."

"You will figure it out, I'm sure."

Zalez said, "So, do you still want to offer the Governor role to Principal Garvey?"

"Him? No. Garcey, you had a chance. Fix this bloody school."

Blap headed back to his vehicle.

"Sorry, Principal Garcey." Nate told him.

"Governor? Of Ceilingida? What happened to Governor Tostone?" Garcey asked.

"The new G.P. fired him." Lluhdor replied. "You're better off not being Governor. This might be the worse decision ever."

Mal watched the other Governors drive off in their Ultra rides as Romana and Ten stood either side of her.

"Mrs. Belhopsa, I apologize for destroying your robot."

"It's okay." Mal said. "He might be able to get fixed."

Romana said, "Mother, do you think it's odd that Mr. Blaphaus is G.P. now?"

Mal nodded, "Everything is odd right now, Romana."

Peezle walked up behind them and sighed, "I don't know what I'm supposed to do."

Ten replied, "I do. Find a Governor from this planet."

Peezle joked, "Well, *I* can pretend I'm from Ceilingida."

"Where are we going now?" Nate asked, as Blap drove. "The Governors are heading back to Launderington, is that right?"

Lluhdor nodded with his long skinny neck. "Except Zucaritas and I. We are going with you to Cyrakuse tomorrow."

"Terrific."

"I'm going to Tostone's home." Blap told them.

"Why?" Zalez asked. "You fired him."

"Because I need to talk to him. It's a thing us G.P.'s do, have private meetings with him."

They pulled up to Tostone's house where Blap dropped him off once before. They all got out the vehicle again and made their way up to the front door. Blap pushed the door buzzer and moments later the door opened to reveal a female Cyrakuse, with orange fur and small brown rings all over her.

"Galactic President Maximus! Charcat said you fired him! You can't fire a Governor, you big fat ugly Toob!"

"Hey! That's not nice." Nate told her.

"Whose the runt?" she asked.

"My son and the G.P.'s Assistant." told Zalez.

"Who are you?" Blap asked.

"I'm Celley Tostone..."

"Tostone's sister?" Lluhdor asked.

"Rude! No! He's wife!"

"Tostone is married?" Lluhdor asked surprised.

"Yes. Are you?" she asked him.

"Yes. His name is Ume."

"Terrific. Everyone is married... Is Tostone here?" asked Blap.

"Yes, but he doesn't want to speak to you."

Charcat appeared behind her, wearing a silky red robe. "It's okay, Celley. I'll talk. Come in."

Blap told his group, "Private meeting. Stay out here."

They went inside and Blaphaus stood before Tostone, who sat on the couch in his living room. Celley stood to the side, arms crossed.

"This is a private meeting." Blap told her.

"Celley, my dear, can you go to the kitchen or the bedroom?" Tostone asked nicely.

She nodded and gave Blap a dirty look before she left the room.

"First of... your planet has a King?" Blap asked.

"Yes, why do you ask?"

"I'm supposed to meet him tomorrow."

"Wow! I wish I can go with you."

"You will. Zucaritas is going as well, but I want you there."

"Why is that? I'm not a Governor anymore."

"You know a Governor cannot be fired. Just replaced. And as I don't have a replacement... yet..."

"Okay, then, I accept, I'll go with you."

"Why did you leave if you know the way things work?" Blap asked, "You didn't stick up for yourself or argue or use any kind of backbone."

"Because my job was done... I made you G.P."

"Did you know Traf sent me a message?"

"He sent you a message? How? When?"

Blap reached into his jacket and pulled put the fob, pushing the button on the side. The foot tall holo-recording of Traf appeared again above it in Blap's hand and again he said the same message as before.

"Hello, if you can see this recording I take it you are my predecessor. I hope the Cabinet chose wisely and didn't pick you because you are good looking and a good family man like I was. I am planning on giving up on being G.P. In a few years time I think this galaxy will be invaded... There's other galaxies out there and nothing's stopping them from coming to our galaxy. We need the other seven planets to be reunited with the sixteen. Even Tooberosum... which I can't find anything about anywhere. But I know Toobs are out there. So, whoever you are, I wish you luck. Thank the Creator you'll be able to do a better job than I could ever. Take care."

After it ended the holo-recording disappeared.

"So, has Traf said anything about an invasion, Tostone?"

"Wow. No. Never. I didn't know he recorded this. I wonder..."

"So do I. See you tomorrow, Tostone. Give your wife my regards."

He headed to the front door and Tostone stood up.

"Blaphaus."

Blap turned around. "Wot?"

"Thank you."

"Wotever. You're a better Cyrakuse than you know. You don't need to lie. You could've asked me to be G.P."

"And if I asked you would've said 'yes'?"

"No. Are you stupid? I would've said 'hell no.' There's a reason I'm on this planet, and we all have secrets. Remember that."

Blap turned and walked out the house leaving Tostone looking confused.

Early the next day, Blap, Nate, Zalez, and Thaw made their way through the spaceport. Zucaritas was already there, waiting for them. Blap pointed to a spot on the floor.

"See there? That's where Traf slipped and fell. Who would've thought?"

Zucaritas said, "The King has sent one of his private shuttles for us. It's down at Gate F."

Blap said, "That's very majestic of him."

"G.P. Blaphaus, where is Mr. Tostone?" Nate asked him. "You invited him, right?"

"You invited Tostone?" Zucaritas asked. "Why?"

"He's still Governor until we find a replacement, Cyrakuse. It's his planet as well as yours after all where we are going."

Just then Tostone and his wife Celley went running up to them, each carrying a suitcase. Tostone was running pretty quick for his size.

"We made it! Hello." he smiled.

"Why is she here? And why do you both have suitcases?" Blap asked annoyed.

"I'm moving off this planet back to Cyrakuse. That was the deal... as long as he's the Governor we can live here..." Celley told him.

"Well, he's still the Governor until a replacement is found." G.P. Blap said interrupting Celley. "Just hope there's space for you on the shuttle."

"There will be I'm sure." Thaw said.

Zucaritas said, "I say we get going. We don't want to keep the King waiting."

The shuttle was immaculate, with a very plush inside. Seats, a couch, full buffet and bar.

Nate's eyes opened wide. "Father, is this food for us?"

Zalez nodded, "I believed so."

Nate smiled, "Yay!"

He started eating from the pile of grapes. There was every kind of food they could imagine. Blap laid on the couch, taking up all the space on it.

"Maybe I should be King... not G.P. We need a shuttle like this, Zucaritas."

Zucaritas nodded, "We'll look into it."

"Don't look into it. Do it."

Celley took a seat and said to her husband who sat across from her, "You chose *him* to be G.P. out of all the choices in the galaxy?"

Tostone nodded, "It'll be worth it. Trust me."

"This is your pilot, please everyone take a seat. We'll be taking off in five minutes. The King hopes you enjoy your flight." the voice said over the intercom.

Back at the school, Nog, Romana and the rest of the class filed into their classroom.

"Where is Nate?" Nog asked Romana. "He never misses a day at school."

"He's going to Cyrakuse to meet the King." she said.

"Cyrakuse? Why? With your father?"

"Yes, and G.P. Blaphaus. He's Blaphaus' Assistant."

Nog's eyes opened very wide, "No way! Man, he gets luckier and luckier all the time!"

"Okay, settle down, children." Ms. Beezlee told them.

"Romana, what do you think Nate is doing now?" Nog asked.

"I have no idea." Romana said.

****

Nate was in fact filling his belly on chocolate, fruit, cheese and crackers. He spotted these long yellow fruit things, which are hard to find on Ceilingida but on his fathers planet there was plenty. He grabbed two and showed his father who was sitting besides him.

"Father! Look!"

"Oh, yeah. Grororas. Those are hard to come by."

"You want one, father?"

"Sure. Why not?"

Nate passed his dad one and looked at Blap laying on the couch and frowned. He saw Blap's eyes were closed, and one hand was on his chest area, the other arm laying limp, hand on the floor of the shuttle.

"Father, does it look like G.P. Blaphaus is not breathing?"

Zalez glanced over at him and nodded, "A little bit. But his body is so different than a normal body. Who knows what he's doing."

Nate shrugged and unpeeled his grorora.

An hour later the shuttle came down to land in front of the massive palace on Cyrakuse. A human woman in a flowing dress with flowers all over it approached the shuttle. The side of the shuttle opened and a ramp descended from it. Four Cyrakuse guards, holding large spears and wearing armor approached as well, standing besides her. She watched as the group from the shuttle descend from it.

"Father! I thought *our* house was big!" Nate said.

Zucaritas stepped forward and approached the woman.

"Greeting, Lady Gerda. We appreciate you having us here." he motioned to Blaphaus. "This is Galactic President Maximus."

She frowned at Blap, and said seriously, "So you're a Toob?"

"So I'm told. You are?"

"Lady Gerda. My husband is waiting inside to meet you."

"Your husband is the King?" he asked.

"Yes. Follow me." She led them to the palace.

"So the King is human?" Blap asked.

"He's a Cyrakuse." Tostone replied.

"Who married a human? Hmmm. Cyrakuse scratch fever."

They went inside and into the throne room where the King waited. He was tall, with a long mane, and wearing red and gold robes, he even had a gold crown on his head. He smiled as he saw them all enter.

Zalez whispered to Nate, "Bow on one knee."

They all did that except Blap, whose body wasn't built for bowing, and he had no legs to kneel.

"You're not bowing before me, Tooberosum?" the King asked in a deep royal like voice.

"Does it look like I can bow? Or kneel?" Blap asked.

"It looks like you can do whatever you want. You're the Galactic President."

"He can't even climb steps." Zucaritas laughed.

The King laughed with him and motioned them all to stand. "Stand, everybody. I hate that kneeling mess unless Lady Gerda is doing it. Especially in the morning if you know what I mean."

Zalez, Zucaritas and Tostone all laughed along the King. Celley gave her husband a dirty look.

"What's funny?" Nate asked his father.

"I'll tell you one day, son."

The King looked down at Nate and frowned.

"What's with the child? Shouldn't he be in school?"

"That's Nate... he's my Assistant." Blap told the King.

Zalez said, "And my son. Hence why I'm here."

"Hmmm... you're a Chordattian... what did you do, shave the child?"

"He's adopted." Zalez said.

"I know this Chordattian named Calasteel who shaved his fur so he didn't look like a Chordattian." the King remarked. "I hate that faker."

Blap frowned, "Vistrat Calasteel? You know him?"

"Yeah, I met him a few times on Firvegas. He's a horrible gambler. And a liar. I have no idea where he is now though."

"He manages Ultra in Ceilingida... he fired me." told Blap. "I hate him too."

"Oh. Small galaxy. Come on in to the banquet room, we'll sit and chat. Except you, Maximus, you won't be sitting I take it. Having no legs must be a drag." He led them all off. "It's good to see two Cyrakuse Governor's here."

"Actually I'm not going to be a Governor for much longer." Tostone said, "As soon as I get replaced we're moving back to Cyrakuse."

"So you're a Governor short?"

"Only with the Smidge." Blap joked.

"Well, Lady Gerda is from Ceilingida. She doesn't talk much but you have a Pilosa Governor who doesn't say much. I'm guessing. So, want her as Governor?"

"Don't ask me." Blap said.

"You're the G.P., it's your decision. Why aren't you Governor anymore, Tostone?"

"I was fired."

"Fired? Ha! That's one thing about being Royal... you can't get fired."

Zucaritas said, "I say Lady Gerda should be Governor for Ceilingida."

"Then if that Cyrakuse says yes then yes. Tostone, you've been replaced officially." Blap told him.

They walked into the banquet room which had a huge long table and full of food. All kinds of food... you name it, it was there. The King sat at the end of the table and Lady Gerda sat to his left. The King ordered one of his Cyrakuse servants to move one chair to his right.

"Move that chair, the Toob G.P. can't sit."

The servant moved the chair to the side so Blap could stand at the table. Nate sat next to Blap and his father sat besides him, then Thaw. Across sat Zucaritas who sat next to Lady Gerda, then Tostone and his wife.

"So, Tostone, do you need a job? Anything you got lined up?"

"I haven't lined up anything, no."

"Then I'll put you to work. You should be Zucaritas' Assistant." he laughed.

"I don't need an Assistant." Zucaritas said.

"You're a good Governor, Zucaritas. I was proud that two of our great species were on the Cabinet. Why did you get fired anyway?" he turned to Blaphaus. "Why would you fire Tostone here? He's such a nice guy. Look at that smile.'

"He lied. I don't do liars." Blap stated.

The King looked into Blap's yellow eyes. "And you never lied? I think you're lying right now."

Blap was actually taken back. "I am? How?"

"You know. But it's not the time to say, is it?"

"So, why are you a King?" Blap asked.

"We always had Kings or Queens on Cyrakuse. Then someone decided that this planet should have a Governor and be part of the Cabinet. Zucaritas does a great job not stepping on my toes. G.P. Traf visited here once and said he'd let us be, not to interfere with this planet. We are a happy lot but don't want anyone to butt in where they are not wanted."

"Zucaritas, you don't seem happy." Blap told Zucaritas across the table. "What's the deal with you?"

"I'm happy when I need to be." Zucaritas said. "I was happy until Traf died."

"Zucaritas would make a good G.P., but it's funny, Governors are never chosen to be G.P.'s... just outsiders. And nothing is more of an outsider than a Toob. I have never seen a Toob before I saw you. Why are you so different?" the King asked.

Blap said, "I'm special. Wot do I know?"

"You're special all right. I wonder why I never saw your kind before. Hmmmm. Did anybody here see a Toob before?"

They all shook their heads.

"Odd, don't you think?"

Blap was getting annoyed. "What's your point?"

"I just want to know my new G.P. The other was useless. Use. Less."

"What's your name?" Blap asked. "And don't say the King because that's feces."

"Nobody asks the King his name." Zucaritas said.

"Wot? No one ever asked?" Blap asked.

The King laughed. "I appreciate his bluntness. My name is Tanja Leywes Miarjere. Some call me Tanja. Fancy name, right, Blaphaus Maximus?"

"I guess. I could see why you go by the King."

"It's what I am. So, keep out my affairs, take my wife as Governor, and don't be a stranger and we're good. Got it?"

"Wotever." Blap muttered.

"And Tostone, you and your lovely wife can live in the palace for as long as you want. Now eat up!"

The King's shuttle flew through space, heading back to Ceilingida. Inside Blap laid back on the couch again. Tostone and his wife stayed behind as did Lady Gerda, until the next Cabinet meeting.

"Father, that was fantastic! That's the first time I ever left Ceilingida… except to go to your work. Thank you, G.P. Blaphaus."

"Wotever, kid. Glad you enjoyed yourself. Zucaritas, what was the bloody point of all that?"

"Open relationship, Blaphaus. Keep the King happy makes life easier for me."

"Just you?"

"No. Everyone in the end. And you got a new Governor out of it."

"Sure. The King is pathetic. So, wot now?"

"Well… tomorrow you're going to start going to the seven planets."

"Six. Not going back to Toobersosum."

"We'll see."

"So, which planet are we going to first?" Nate asked excitedly.

"Son, you're not missing two days of school no matter how smart you are."

"But father!"

"Zalez, he's my Assistant…"

"And my child. So, the weekend he can go with you."

"What planet should he go to first?" asked Thaw.

"We'll discuss it…"

"How about Canis?" Thaw asked

"I'm not going to that one." Zucaritas said.

"Then wotever Canis is that's the one we're going to." told Blap. "Now will you all shut up, I'm going to sleep."

Nate watched Blap lay down on the couch again and saw Blap close his yellow eyes. He watched him closely wondering why Blaphaus wasn't breathing.

CHAPTER 9

The next day, Mal was driving her children to school. Nate looked tired as he stayed up late from his big trip to Cyrakuse to see the King. When he got home Romana asked him a lot of questions, and so did his mother. Then Zalez and Mal ended up staying up through the night. In a week or so their lives and the whole galaxies life had changed.

They reached the school and the children got out the vehicle

"Have a good day, children." Mal told them smiling.

"You too, mother." they said at the same time.

They walked into the school where Nog already was waiting.

"You guys are late today!" he said when he saw them.

"Nate didn't want to get up." Romana said. "He had a long day."

"You're so lucky, Nate! How was the King? What was Cyrakuse like? When is the Toob coming to the school to visit?"

Nate did not look himself, he was very tired and he yawned and said, "The King was nice, we didn't see too much of the planet, just his palace."

"And the Toob... how is he?"

"G.P. Blaphaus? He's okay." Nate said.

They went into the classroom with the other children and went to their desks.

Ms. Beezlee sat behind her desk and said, "Welcome, children. So, Nate, how was your trip?"

He did not answer, his head was laying on his desk and he was snoring.

"Nate! Nate! Nog, tap him on the back to wake him up."

Nog did so but Nate kept on sleeping.

Blaphaus walked into the spaceport to be met by the Smidge and the human Governor who had the cane. The other travelers who walked by them were given them looks. A few beings took holo-scans of them with their holo-imagers.

"You two?" Blap asked. "Anybody else coming with us?"

"No, Maximus, just us two." the Smidge said. "No one is keen on going to Canis. I got nominated because I look like a human... just a shorter version. And Eastora here has been around a long time. The Canis' love human males. In fact, that's pretty much the only species they do like... apart from their own."

"Did they send a private shuttle for us as well?"

Eastora said, "No, they don't have shuttles. So we will be flying a regular shuttle. And you having no legs is making this hard."

"You lot chose me for this. Should've thought about that."

Eastora said, "I did not choose you. I would never choose a Toob."

"I wouldn't choose a Cyrakuse either. Not one that worships a fake King."

Governor Noam said, "I think we better head to the shuttle."

"So I can hang out with the robots and baggage. Terrific."

Governor Eastora waved his cane, "Actually the spaceline Galaxy Spaceways has an area for you in first class. You can stand and still be buckled in. You're welcome."

"Progress." Blap muttered. "I should still have my own shuttle."

"So, G.P. Maximus' trip to visit the King on Cyrakuse was a success. Now today he and two Governors... Noam and Eastora are going to be going to Canis to meet with Planet Mayor to try to have that planet join the Cabinet. Hopefully G.P. Maximus will be successful. More on this later. Buterdau Kooper, GNN."

The other Cabinet Governors sat in the House conference room watching the holo-images of Kooper and Blaphaus and the two Governors go through the Gate and head to the shuttle.

"If that Toob can convince the Planet Mayor I'll be impressed." Zucaritas told them.

"You don't think he will?" Southington asked.

"He's a Creator-damned wild card." Zucaritas said. "We hardly know him or his damn species."

Thaw nodded, "That's one thing that I have to admit bothers me. We know nothing, no one knows anything about Tooberosums."

Lady Gerda, the newest member of the Cabinet who sat in Tostone's old chair finally she spoke up. "I don't know why the Tooberosum was chosen to be the G.P. but I will tell you this, the King does not trust him. There's a scientist named Doctor Sahii who might know something about the Tooberosum species. He's friends with the King."

"What planet is this doctor on?" Zeb asked.

"That I don't know, but he's a Rodentia."

"There is no planet called Rodentia, that's a species that could be anywhere." Dawber said.

"Lady Gerda, can you contact the King and see if he can arrange a meeting with this Doctor?" Zucaritas asked.

Lady Gerda nodded, "Of course."

Principal Garcey sat behind his desk as a sleepy Nate sat across the other side of it.

"Nate, are you awake?" the principal asked.

"Yes, sir." Nate yawned.

Just then his mother walked into the office. "Nate. What's going on?" she asked.

"Mother, what are you doing here?"

"Principal Garcey contacted me. He said you fell asleep in class."

"The class barely started." Garcey remarked.

"I'm just a little tired. I'll be okay."

"I think you had too long of a day and space travel made you sick and tired." Mal said, "I have to talk to your father and have him talk to G.P. Blaphaus but I don't think being G.P. Blaphaus' Assistant is good for you."

"No! He picked me! I'm fine!" Nate cried.

"We'll see, Nate. But you have never fell asleep in class before today..."

Garcey said, "We'll see. Your mother and father will discuss it."

"Go back to class, Nate. And try to stay awake."

He nodded and stood, "I'll be fine. I promise."

The flight to Canis wasn't bad for the three at all. They were the only ones on the flight. Only a few planets were traveled to, and Canis, not being part of the Cabinet was one. Rarely did Canis' leave their planet, and when they did it most of the time it was to go to Firvegas to gamble. No one knew why Canis wasn't part of the Cabinet of planets and that's what the Smidge told Blap that he needed to ask.

"No one asked before?" Blap asked on the shuttle.

Eastora said, "Well, I will tell you that years and years ago the Cyrakuse and the Canis got along very well... and the Canis were almost part of the Cabinet, but they had a fall out and they went to war. That's when both planets had a military... now only on Xenartha has a military."

"What was the squabble about?" Blap asked.

"There's been lots of rumors, but like I said no one really knows. You ask a Cyrakuse and they'll tell you one thing... and a Canis will say something else."

"Do Toobs have a military?" Noam asked. "Probably not I'm guessing."

"We used to." Blap said, "That's all I'm saying. So, that's why Zucaritas didn't want to come on this trip?"

"If they saw him they'd be no chance they'll want to be part of the Cabinet."

"And if they do and find out about him... and the King of that bloody planet wife is now a Governor... I'm sure they'd love that."

"Don't mention that." the Smidge said. "Or Zucaritas yet. The Canis might seem mean but trust me, they are all bark and no bite."

"Should be a cake walk then." muttered Blap.

The yellow furred Canis stood besides his long black and tall limousine-vehicle wearing his full limousine driver outfit including hat, just like Rubyspears would wear. He was using a small bone as a toothpick when the G.P., and two Governors walked out through the glass doors of the small Canis spaceport. He quickly tossed the small bone aside and stood up at straight and saluted them.

"What's with the salute?" Blap asked.

"I'm sorry. I never met anyone as important as you before. My name is Jake, I'm here to take you to the Planet Mayor's house. He is very intrigued about you I think."

"As he should be." scoffed Blaphaus.

"Look, Maximus, you can stand in the vehicle." pointed out Noam. "These Canis are on the ball."

The city they drive through looked like every other common city. Blap noticed there were fire hydrants on every block.

"Get a lot of fires?"

"What do you mean?" Jake the chauffeur asked.

"You have so many bloody hydrants."

"They are not hydrants, they are pee stations."

"Pee stations?" asked Eastora.

"Yeah, where we... you know..."

They then saw on the sidewalk a long skinny, brown Canis with short legs and arms stop and pee on the hydrant looking thing. Water came out of it afterwards to wash it down.

"I want to try that." laughed Noam. "Whatcha think, Toob?"

"How am I going to be able to do that?" Blap asked.

"You don't pee?"

"That's enough." told Eastora.

Jake laughed, "It's all good. Very funny."

Up ahead was a white building with a red roof and Jake pointed out, "That's the Planet Mayor's house. I bet he's so glad to meet you."

"I wish I can say the same." Blaphaus replied.

The vehicle stopped and they all got out.

"No steps, Blaphaus. Betcha glad about that, am I right?" the Smidge asked.

"Yes, thrilled." he said sarcastically.

Jake then dropped his pants and relieved himself on a pee station.

"I'm so jealous." the Smidge said, "When we leave here I'm doing that."

A black and white faced Canis with big ears pointing straight up walked out the headquarters and over to the three.

"Hello, Mistah G.P. and Govahners, I'm Burr, the Planet Mayor sent me down to fetch you. Follow me."

He led them in and Blaphaus whispered to Eastora, "What's with that accent?"

Eastora shrugged, "Beats me."

"What two planet are you the Govahners of?" Burr asked.

"Burdenchurdettu and Homunculus." Eastora replied.

"Are you both humans?"

"I look like one but I'm not. I'm a Smidge." the Smidge said.

"Ahh, Smidges are wicked short, right?"

"I wouldn't say 'wicked.'" Noam muttered.

Burr opened up two large wooden doors at the end of the hallway and went inside the office. Two Canis' were there, one with an holo-cam, wearing a trench coat and hat. His legs were proportioned with his body, they were kind of short and his fur was white with brown spots.

"Say cheese!" he said, taking a holo-image of the three newcomers.

The Planet Mayor stood up from behind his desk, and came around. He was smoking a cigar and wore a silky black suit on his short squat body. He had a wrinkly face and a pushed in nose, unlike the other Canis who had longer snouts.

"Well, I thought *I* was an ugly git." he scoffed, looking up at the tall Blaphaus. He looked down at the Smidge who was not much shorter than he was, and the bald human with the cane.

"So, the two Cyrakuse Governors you have were too pussy to come to this great planet of mine?"

"He has an accent like yours, Toob." smirked Noam.

"There's only one Cyrakuse Governor, I fired the other." Blap remarked.

"You did? Ha! That takes balls. Which pussy did you give the sack too?"

"You know about the Cabinet?" asked Eastor.

"Yes, I'm well aware of you lot. So, G.P., which one did you let go?"

"Tostone." Blap said.

"Nice. What did he do? Steal?"

"He lied to me."

"All politicians lie, G.P., it's a fact. I even lie sometimes. The missus asks me if she looks good in her dress and I say she looks grand, when I'm thinking no, that's ruddy ridiculous looking. That's just me. So, have a seat, everyone. Oh, you have no legs, that's awkward."

"You don't know half of it." Blap replied.

"Well, I'm going to sit. I'm old, you know."

He sat behind his desk. Eastor and Noam went to sit in the comfortable chairs to the side of the room.

"So, is Canis the first planet you visited since you became Galactic Pres?"

"No, I went to Cyrakuse, your favorite planet." Blap said.

"Really? For wot?"

"The King wanted to have a word."

"Oh, the bloody King. He's a ponce. He thinks he's sooooo ruddy wonderful. You know this planet and that planet had a war once... many years ago."

"I heard. What did you two fight about?" Blap asked.

Blap was starting to hate the fact he was asking questions, like he cared.

"We Canis see the Cyrakuse as prey and they see us as a threat. We tried to live on the same planet before but that didn't go over too well. The Cyrakuse are a bunch of pussies."

Burr chuckled from where he stood by the door.

"So, tell me, wot is a Toob doing off Tooberosum? You lot mostly stay put or so I heard. You are a mysterious lot."

"There was nothing for me there. Literally."

"Are you better off now? Do you like being G.P.?"

"So far no. I liked my life as a driver better. But here I am..."

"Yes, here you are. You are very unique, Blaphaus, you're like a novelty. Novelty's could be fun... or dangerous."

"And you can't be dangerous? You have a lot of power as Planet Mayor, am I right? Answering to no one?"

"Ha! You're not only ugly you're funny too. Who knew Toobs had a sense of humor. Who knew they really existed. So, what is Tooberosum like?"

"Planet Mayor... wotever your name is..."

"Losergram. Planet Mayor Losergram."

"Losergram, I'm not here to be interviewed by you. I'm here because those two losers over there want me to convince you to join the Cabinet somehow. So, either we do this or I'm out, and that's going to piss off a lot of beings. At least sixteen..."

"Okay, I'll tell you wot, Maximus, I like you. I don't know why but I do. I will send you to someone who I think will make a great Governor, the best... *if* he wants. Then this planet will join the others and be part of the Cabinet."

A surprised Noam and Eastora glanced at each other... they didn't think it'll be this easy.

"But before I tell you who this Canis is you have to do something for me..."

"Depends wot it is. I don't do leg work."

"That's because you have no legs!" laughed the Planet Mayor.

"Okay, I'm out of here." Blap turned to the two Governors. "Find another sucker."

"You're going to be as useless as the last G.P." the Planet Mayor said, sitting back, puffing on his cigar. "I had a feeling..."

Blap turned to face him. "You have no idea..."

"Look, G.P. Maximus, let's hear the Planet Mayor out." Noam said, standing. "You know you can't just quit..."

"I can go into hiding..."

"You know we'll find you. Now stop being stubborn and listen to the Planet Mayor!"

"Fine! But make it quick. I'm very impatient."

"You don't seem to like hard work so I'll be surprised if you do this, Toob. I want the Cyrakuse Governor Zucaritas and the King to come here, call a truce and then

I'll tell you who the one you should approach to be Governor. Of course there's a chance he'll say no, but that's the risk and gamble you have to take."

"You're right, that's too much work. Traf never worked this hard. I'm the G.P., I shouldn't be having to do this. You Governors should do the work"

"It doesn't work that way." Eastora pointed out. "Planet Mayor Losergram, you got a deal."

"Good! Cigars for everyone then!"

He handed out five cigars to everybody, lighting them. They all puffed on their cigars, except Blap. His just put it into his mouth and let it burn. The Mayor puffed a few smoke circles to the ceiling.

"I don't know what's a better trick, my smoke rings or you not inhaling, Toob. Schultz, take a scan."

The Canis with the holo-cam took the holo-scan of Losergram posing with Blap, who looked irritated.

The twelve inch holo-call of Mal appeared on Zalez's desk in front of him.

"Sweetheart, this is a big surprise." he said, "Last time you did this you were naked and did a nice dance for me."

"That was for your birthday. This is different."

"Is everything okay?" he asked.

"Yeah, but it's Nate. Ever since his trip to Cyrakuse he hadn't been the same. He's been very tired, and he even fell asleep in class. I was called to the school to meet with Principal Garcey even. I don't think being Blaphaus' Assistant is a good idea."

"He just had a long day, he'll be okay."

"I don't know, Zalez. I think you need to talk to Blaphaus and tell him he needs another Assistant."

"I will try and meet with him and see. I'm sure it'll all work out."

"I hope so."

"Don't worry, Mal, everything will be fine. But I will talk to him."

"Thank you. You're by yourself in the office, right?"

"Yeah, why?"

Her holo-call started to dance and take off her dress. Zalez sat back in his seat and grinned.

Jake drove the G.P. and the two Governors again, heading back to the spaceport on Canis.

"So, was it a good visit to see the Planet Mayor?"

"No. It was a waste of time." Blap said, "And more work for me."

"It was a good meeting." Eastora said, "We're halfway there... for this planet anyway."

“Sure. Wotever.” Blap said, “So, wot do we do now?”

“We will go to Launderington and talk to Zucaritas, and contact the King.”

“We don’t know if the bloody Planet Mayor is given us the runaround. He might not have someone in mind.”

“Oh, I don’t mean to interrupt, Mr. G.P., but I’m pretty sure the Planet Mayor is not lying.”

“I hope you’re right.” Noam said. "Oh, man, I forgot to use the pee station."

Blap didn’t say another word, he was just thinking he hated this political stuff. But he was stuck with it... he just had to go with the flow. He just wondered how long the “flow” would last.

Chapter 10

On Launderington, the Cabinet minus Noam and Eastora, who were on the way back from Canis, met in the conference room of the House.

"What are we going to do about Maximus coming here?" Zeb asked. "He can't walk up the steps. I have no idea why a Toob was picked to be the G.P."

"You know why." told Zucaritas.

"We can meet elsewhere." Dawber remarked.

"Or replace the Toob." Lluhdor added.

"That's not going to happen." Southington said. "We are going to have to meet somewhere else... until the step problem is taken care of."

Just then a holo-call of Noam appeared in the middle of the conference table.

"We just landed on Launderington... figure out the step problem yet?"

"No, we haven't." Southington said. "How did the trip go?"

"Welll... I'll let the G.P. tell you."

A holo-call of Blap appeared next to the Smidge's.

"I'm not happy. So far I have done more in a few days than Traf has done in all his years as G.P. You owe me, you lot."

"So, it went well?" Zucaritas asked.

"It would've went better if your bloody species and the Canis didn't fight, Cyrakuse."

"That's ancient history! That was my grandfathers days..."

"Well, they still hold a grudge... according to Losergram anyway."

"So you couldn't convince him to bring his planet to be part of the Cabinet and name a Governor?" Southington asked.

"He has someone in mind... but as always there's a catch. I have to bring Zucaritas to Canis... and the King. They need to announce a truce then he'll tell who he suggests to be Governor. There's no guarantee that Canis will want to be Governor. There you go. Balls in your court."

"Creator-damn it!" Zucaritas swore. "The King will not like this! I'll meet you at the spaceport, and we'll go to Cyrakuse right away."

"Are you going to contact the King first?" Thaw asked.

"I could tell you the King will not approve of this." the King's wife spoke up.

"Then you will help convince him." Blap told her. "You're coming with us."

Zucaritas said, "We have to spring it on him in person. Lady Gerda, be prepared..."

"It's not *me* he's going to be mad at." she said. "This could open up a whole new conflict."

Blap said, "Then you better not let that happen."

Blap's holo-call next appeared on Zalez's desk on the Dook Energy space station.

"Zalez, I need your son to come with me back to Cyrakuse..."

"Blaphaus, I don't think that's a good idea. Mal said he has been tired at school, he even fell asleep in class. I think space travel was too much for him..."

"He's fine. The King liked him, everyone likes children... I have to convince the King to go to Canis and announce a truce..."

"Blaphaus, you realize that that will probably not happen."

"That's why I need the kid. I bet he can help."

Zalez sighed, "Fine. I'll head to Ceilingida and pick him up. His mother will not like this..."

"You're the man... she'll have to deal with it. As soon as I make this happen then I can approach the other five planets..."

"You mean six..."

"No. I mean five." Blap said, "Tooberosum is off the table. I will not go back to that planet."

Lady Gerda went into a small room at the House, where nobody was. She pulled out her small info-pad and a holo-call of the King appeared above it.

"Hello, my lady, how is life being Governor?" he asked.

"Uneventful. We are coming back to Cyrakuse. I'm not supposed to tell you but thought you should know."

"Coming back here? Why?"

"Well... the Toob G.P. went to Canis to try to convince them to join the Cabinet but apparently the Planet Mayor told him he needs to bring you and Zucaritas to Canis and call a truce."

"A truce? Our two planets haven't been in a war in years... before I was born even. Our grandfathers fought in that war. There already was a truce... this is a waste of time."

"Well, as far as the Canis is concerned this is what is happening."

"It's all political feces, my dear. Have them come here to Cyrakuse, it should be interesting."

"I'm coming as well." Lady Gerda said.

"Good. Maybe I'll pull this planet from the Cabinet. Ha. Can you imagine? Wonder what they'd think of that." he laughed.

"They'll lose their minds."

"Yeah, I wouldn't do that even if I could."

"Well, I'll be there soon." Lady Gerda told him.

"It'll be good to see you again, my dear." he said right before his holo-call disappeared.

"Mother! Nate's asleep again!" Romana cried out from the back seat as Mal was driving. Nate was indeed sleeping in the back seat next to his sister, his head on her shoulder. Mal sighed, hoping Zalez could tell Nate he's no longer the G.P.'s Assistant. They got to their house and Zalez walked out the front door as he had arrived there not to long before.

"Father!" Romana cried for joy, running over to him and giving him a hug before she ran into the house.

"Zalez, Nate is sleeping in the back seat."

"Oh, great." he mused. He went over to the vehicle, opening the door and nudging his sleeping son. "Nate, wake up. Wake up. We're going on a trip."

"A trip?" Mal asked, "What trip? I thought we discussed…"

"Mal, Blaphaus wants Nate to go with him back to Cyrakuse…"

"Who cares what he wants? Since when do you listen to him?"

"Since the fate of the galaxy is in his hands. And not to mention he's the G.P."

"You didn't like him before."

"That's when he was a driver and in our lives too much…"

"Now he's in our lives all the time." she said.

"Why are you two arguing?" Nate said, waking up.

"We are not arguing, we are debating. Want to go on another trip?" Zalez asked.

"Yeah! Where to?"

"Back to Cyrakuse again."

"Again? I want to go to another planet."

"I've had enough." Mal said angrily, storming off into the house.

"What's wrong with mother?"

"I'll tell you later, son. We have work to do in the meantime."

The King stood outside the palace himself this time as his shuttle came down to land. His armored guard stood either side of him, ready to protect him if they had to. He watched as the Tooberosum G.P., Zucaritas and Lady Gerda walked down the ramp.

"Welcome back, my wife!" the King bellowed, giving his wife a big hug. "Greetings again, Galactic President and Governor Zucaritas. What brings you back to this lovely planet?" he winked at his wife, not saying he knew why they were there.

"That's a good question." Blap remarked. "This is not my idea." He looked around, wondering where Zalez and Nate were.

"The G.P. has a favor to ask you." Zucaritas told the King.

"Well, come on into my palace again, and we'll chat."

He led them to the palace and said to his wife, "Stay the night, my wife. I miss you so much. You know how I get when I'm lonely…"

They went into the banquet room but this time there was no food laid out for them, the long table was completely empty. The King took his seat at the end of the table, and his wife sat to the left of him and Blaphaus stood to the right with Zucaritas next to him.

"So, tell me, my Tooberosum friend, what brings you back here? Shouldn't you be visiting planets that are not already part of the Cabinet?"

"I should be home sleeping." Blap said, "But one of your kind suckered me into this feces."

"I feel your pain. It's not fun to be used."

"Nope. So, you're being used next. We went to Canis and spoke to that Planet Mayor and he said he wants you and Zucaritas here to go to Canis, and call a truce between the two planets. Then he'll let me know who he'll recommend who he thinks would be Governor."

"Ahhh. Well, my friend, guess what? I will never leave this planet, let alone go to that nasty planet."

"Okay then." Blap turned to Zucaritas, "My work is done here."

Just then a black furred Cyrakuse walked into the banquet room.

"Sorry to interrupt, but a Dook Energy shuttle landed outside. What should I do?"

"Is this something to do with you? Are you going to turn off all the power here for blackmail?" the King asked Blaphaus.

"No. It's Zalez and my Assistant. They're late." told Blaphaus.

"The boy and his father. Yes, fetch them, Blake."

Blake nodded and rushed off.

"What about if we invite the Canis Planet Mayor here?" Zucaritas asked.

"Bring his filthy Canis body here? No way. That's funny though." the King chuckled.

Blake then led a tired looking Nate and his father into the room.

"Ah, hello, lad." the King smiled when he saw them.

"You're late." Blap remarked.

"G.P. Maximus, I had to go to Ceilingida to fetch my son."

"Wotever. You're still late. The King said he's *not* going to Canis, so that's that. The great dream of all the planets being part of a union is done. I'm going home." Blap went to the door where they stood. "We'll use your Dook shuttle."

"Stop." Zucaritas said. "Maximus, you can't just walk out and quit!"

"Why not? What would Traf do if he were here? I'll tell you, he wouldn't be here… I played this game long enough. I'm done."

"You quit too easy." the King said. "Algar Traf was a horrible G.P., but a good gambler. I hung out with him on Firvegas a few times."

"You said you never leave this planet."

"To go to another planet, but not the Firvegas gambling space station. That place is fun, isn't it, Lady Gerda?"

"Yes, it is." she said.

"I'll tell you what, Tooberosum, you should go there. It'll be good for the galaxy to see you at places like that. And the Church..."

"I don't gamble or pray. So no."

"Hmmm. What about if I say my wife can't be your Governor?"

"Then she's not a Governor. I don't really care. I care less about any of this."

Nate spoke up, "Mister Blaphaus, you *do* care. I know it."

"Ha! The boy sees through you." the King said. "I see through you."

"What do you mean by that?" Blap asked defensive.

"Boy, if you were G.P. what would you do?" the King asked.

Nate frowned, "About what? I'm confused."

"The Tooberosum says he wants me to go to Canis, this planets enemy planet and call a truce with the Planet Mayor. I say no, I'm not going there."

"Why not? We should all be friends." Nate said, "If I was G.P. I'd have everybody meet on one planet and get them all together."

"Rainbows and flowers." the King said, "Through the eyes of a human child."

Nate gave a half smile not knowing if that was a compliment.

"Wotever it is, it's not going to happen. You lot put yourself into this mess. I think you're scared of leaving this planet, Cyrakuse. But you send your wife off easily. I don't want her as a Governor." He turned to Nate. "Kid, you're not my Assistant anymore. You're Ceilingida's new Governor..."

"What?!" cried out Zalez. "No."

"You lost your mind." Zucaritas said. "He's a boy!"

"Yet he seems to have more common sense than anybody I know. Even me. My goal was to stay under the radar and like a dumbass I flew straight into it."

Nate smiled, "I'm really a Governor?"

"Yes." Blap said.

"No." his father said at the same time.

Zucaritas shook his head, "This is ridiculous. This is not a game, Blaphaus!"

"Sure it is. You said so yourself I'm a pawn. So, I will do wot I want. The whole Cabinet should just break up... there's no point of it. You are all wasting your time."

The King was grinning a big toothy grin. "I love this! Okay, here's what I will do. Invite the Canis Planet Mayor here but he's not coming into the palace. We'll meet in a park. Invite GNN if you want."

"And if he says no?" Blap asked.

"Then I'll have my people attack his planet."

"Wot?"

"Kidding! We'll take it from there." the King laughed.

"The G.P. will holo-call Losergram right away." Zucaritas remarked.

"No. You need to go there and bring him here. But use the Dook Energy shuttle. The Canis is not stepping in mine." the King said.

"I'm not going to Canis." Zucaritas remarked.

"Yes you are. Don't be a pussy." Blap told him.

Nate blushed at Blaphaus' remark.

Zalez's holo-call appeared in front of Mal in the Belhopsa living room. She could see he was sitting down somewhere.

"I want to tell you what's going on, Mal, I'm glad you're sitting."

She was sitting on the couch.

"What now, Zalez?"

"Ummm... I'll let Nate tell you."

Nate's holo-call appeared and he said, "Mother, I'm Ceilingida's new Governor! We are going to Canis to pick up the Planet Mayor. Are you proud of me?"

"Governor?! How is that possible? You're a child. Zalez, what's going on?"

"It's a long story. After this trip I will talk to Blaphaus. I promise."

"I hope so. I really do. I never thought I'd say this but I wish Blaphaus never came into our lives."

"I heard that." Blap said standing between the row of seats in the Dook Energy shuttle. "That hurt, Zalez."

"Well, I told her I'd talk to you about it. But later."

"Wotever."

Zucaritas sat quiet by himself.

"What's wrong with you, Mr. Zucaritas?" Nate asked.

"I'm going to my species' enemies planet. My parents and ancestors will be so disappointed."

"Suck it up. We all have to do something we don't want to do." Blap told him.

On Canis, Burr walked into the Planet Mayor's office where Losergram sat behind his desk.

"Planet Mayor, we just got word that a Dook Enaghy shuttle landed at the spaceport."

"Dook Energy? So? Maybe they're just doing a power check."

"Word is that the G.P. is on it. They called for a ride."

"Hmmm... well, send Jake. This should be interesting." he puffed on his cigar.

Jake stood outside the spaceport again, leaning on his vehicle. He watched as Blaphaus, Zalez, Nate and a very nervous Zucaritas walk out the glass doors. Jake could not believe it... a Cyrakuse was on Canis.

"Welcome... back... G.P. Maximus." Jake said.

"Yeah. Not my idea to be back. You didn't bring the Planet Mayor with you, right?"

"Ummm... no... was I supposed to?"

"It would've made life easier. But then again this is all a waste of bloody time." Blaphaus commented.

"Let's just go." Zucaritas said, "And get this over with."

"He's scared." Nate said, "But everything will be fine."

"It better be." muttered Blap.

Burr waited outside the Planet Mayor's house as Jake drove up again just like before. He got out and let the other four get out the vehicle.

"Welcome back. The P.M. is l'uking forward to... oh, that's a Cyrakuse. O'uh." Jake was startled.

"Just take us to the Planet Mayor." Zucaritas said.

The Mayor sat behind his desk as Burr led them into the office. The Canis in the trench coat was taking holo-images again just like before. He almost dropped his holo-cam when he saw Zucaritas.

"Welcome back, G.P. Maximus." the Planet Mayor walked around the desk and shook Blap's hand.

"And look... the Cyrakuse Governor came with you this time. Maybe you're not a pussy after all. But where is the King? And wot's with the Chordattian and the human boy? He's even shorter than the Smidge."

"I'm Governor Nate..."

"Governor?" the Planet Mayor chuckled. "Governor of wot? You're a child, am I right?"

"Yes. From Ceilingida."

"And you? A Chordattian Governor?"

"I'm Nate's father."

"Hmmm... you l'uk familiar." Burr said. "You came in a D'uk shuttle and you're wearing D'uk Enahgy ovahalls."

"I'm Zalez Belhopsa, head of Dook Energy."

"Ahhh. Of course." the Planet Mayor remarked, "You do a good job. You, Blaphaus, did half your job... where's the King?"

"Tell him, boy." Blap said, waving his arm.

"Ummm... the King said he's not coming here but wants you to go to Cyrakuse."

"So the King is the pussy..."

"Try not to use that word, Mr. Planet Mayor." Zalez told him.

"What does that word mean?" Nate asked.

"It's a slur for the Cyrakuse." snarled Zucaritas. "We Cyrakuse don't have a slur word for the Canis."

"Your kind used to." Losergram said. "Garbage guts, snoots... should I go on? I'm sure the child wants to hear more."

"That's enough." Blap said. "As G.P. I don't think I want this spudge of a planet to be part of the Cabinet anyway."

"Ha! Well, if the King can't be bothered to come here..."

"Isn't it something that *I'm* here?" growled Zucaritas. "The King said he'll meet you, but on his terms. GNN will be there for the meeting, don't you think it'll be a good thing for this planet and for you? When it's time for you to be re-elected..."

"Re-elected?" Blap asked. "The P.M. was elected? The Governor's and G.P. are doing it all wrong."

"That's what I say." Losergram said. "Do you think you'd win if you were running for G.P., Maximus?"

"No. Because I wouldn't run for the position. So, are you coming with us to Cyrakuse to meet with the King or not?"

"I'm not going to Cyrakuse. Tell the King I'll meet him on... Launderington. That's a good compromise I think." Losergram puffed on his cigar.

"Fine." Blap said.

"GNN will definitely be there?"

"Yes, we'll make it happen." Zucaritas said.

"Good. Burr, you're coming with me. If the King announces a truce then I'll tell you who I think will be acceptable as Canis' Governor."

The holo-call of Blaphaus and Zucaritas appeared before the King and his wife.

"He'll meet your, King, but not on Cyrakuse. He said he'll meet you on Launderington. Middle ground." Zucaritas explained.

"In front of that big round ball monument." Blap said.

"Hmmm. Was he vicious to you, Governor Zucaritas?" the King asked.

"No, he was blunt but not vicious. And no more blunt than the G.P. here. I think they have mutual respect for each other."

"I don't have respect for any of you politicians." Blap remarked.

"Ditto, Blaphaus, ditto." laughed the King. "Tell the Mayor I will meet him on Launderington."

"And GNN will be there as well."

"Of course. It's historic!" the King said, "Everyone in this galaxy will know."

On Canis, Zucaritas turned to Blap, "I think we are succeeding."

"Good for you." Blap scoffed, "Glad to be a useful political pawn."

"Here we are in front of the Launderington Monument ready for a monumental and historic meeting between the Canis Planet Mayor Losergram and the Cyrakuse King and Governor Zucaritas as well as G.P. Blaphaus Maximus. All the Governors will be present, as well as the latest Ceilingida Governor. Word is that it's the King's wife Lady Gerda. Buterdau Kooper, GNN."

"Don't flip out, Mal, but we are heading to Launderington for a meeting with the Planet Mayor and the King. All the Governors will be there, including Governor Nate." Zalez said to his wife's holo-call on the Dook Energy shuttle.

"Zalez, you need to tell Blaphaus..."

"He knows. When this meeting is over we'll discuss it. But GNN will be there, at the meeting. Nate's going to be 'out there' if you know what I mean."

"You know my feeling in this, Zalez. We don't want Nate all over the news... in the limelight."

"I know. I'll take care of it."

Mal said, "I already did."

Her holo-call went away.

"Father, I want to be Governor..." Nate whined.

"I know, son. We'll figure this out. Right now the truce comes first."

"But what did mother mean she already did figure it out?"

"I don't know." Zalez replied, wondering that himself.

On Ceilingida, in the living room of their house Peezle and his husband sat across from Mal.

"So, I appreciate you two coming to this planet. You know how important this is..."

"I know. We know." Peezle said, "I don't know what Blaphaus is thinking. He's so hasty."

"So, what would you want me or us to do?" Peezle's husband asked.

"Solicitor Yerkal, I want you to approach Blaphaus and tell him you want to be Governor... and that Nate is too young."

"Yes, I will. Being Governor for this planet will be perfect."

"But Yerkal is not a resident of Ceilingida... and they'll find out." Peezle remarked.

"That's not a problem." Yerkal said, "We'll buy a house here if we have to."

Peezle sighed, "Okay. You know the law."

"Yes. It'll work out."

Mal smiled, "Thank you, I really appreciate this."

On Launderington, robot-cams were flying around the grassy area where the Launderington Momument sat… a giant 500 foot white ball. A crowd started to form, and Kooper from GNN stood to the side. The Governors walked around the long reflecting pool that was between the House and monument. Galactic President Maximus was already there with Governor Nate, Governor Zucaritas, and the Planet Mayor and Burr.

"Quite a place you lot have here." the Planet Mayor remarked. "But how the hell do you go into your own House?"

"You mean that building over there? I don't. Idiots put steps in front of it."

The Governor's walked up to them and Zeb shook the Planet Mayor's hand. "We really appreciate this."

"I hope so, but where is the King?" Losergram asked.

"That's a bloody good question." Blap muttered. "He better show up."

Across the galaxy thousands and thousands watched GNN, and Mal was one of them. She did not like to see Nate standing there, but at least Zalez was with him.

At the school in the classroom the children were watching the holo-images of GNN. Nog's eyes almost popped out of his head.

"That's Nate! What's he doing there?!"

Romana shook her head, she was starting to feel left out.

"It seems that everyone is in place but the King has not arrived yet. No word yet on where he is or how long they're going to wait for him. Also notable his wife Lady Gerda is not with the Governors. Buterdau Kooper, GNN…"

"Look!" Nate pointed to the street besides the grassy area.

The King and his wife Lady Gerda approached everyone as the crowd standing around cheered, and the robot-cams followed them.

"Well, I'll be damned, he showed up." the Planet Mayor remarked.

Southington whispered to Blap, "Approach the King and shake his hand."

"I don't think so."

Everybody knelt and bowed before the King except the two Canis and Blaphaus. The Mayor and Burr didn't because they didn't agree with it and Blaphaus didn't because he couldn't.

"Ha! You are all too nice. I should be kneeling and bowing to you, my Tooberosum friend, you're making this possible."

"I'm not doing anything."

"You're doing more than Traf has done." the King turned to the Losergram. "Look at you, shorty, in your suit, looking all Planet Mayorish. You want a truce... but our two planets haven't fought in ages."

"I know, but you Cyrakuse are still enemies of the Canis."

"For no reason wotsoever." Blaphaus said, "Shake hands, become friends, kiss, make up, become drinking buddies, do wotever you want, but get this done. You two are wasting everyone's time, and I'm tired."

"This is the best G.P. you can ever have." the King said to the Governors. "So, Planet Mayor, you promise you have someone in mind to be Governor in the Cabinet to join Canis with the others?"

"Yes, I have someone in mind." nodded Losergram.

"Then tell them who it is and I'll announce an official truce, our two planets will no longer be enemies."

"Announce the truce first..."

"Ugh!" Blaphaus shouted, "I don't care about the Governor! Announce the bloody truce, Cyrakuse!"

"Okay, Maximus, I officially announce the truce. Balls in your court, Planet Mayor."

The crowd cheered and to the side Buterdau said, "You heard it here... for the first time in a very long time the Canis and the Cyrakuse are not enemies. G.P. Maximus pulled a miracle some say..."

"Who is the name of who you say will be Governor?" Zucaritas asked.

"I'll tell you in secret. Nudge nudge, wink wink. I will tell you back on Canis."

"Hey! Blaphaus! You're going to go to our planet next?!" someone shouted out from the crowd.

"A fan of yours?" the Planet Mayor asked.

A tall figure stepped forward, wearing a cape and hood. He pushed the hood back to reveal a reddish brown face with what looked like a helmet on his head, but it was actually the top of the head. He had two really long antennae's on his head and six arms.

"A Cakerlak?" Zucaritas asked.

"I'm speaking to you, Toob! Are you going to be going to Cakerlak?!"

Blaphaus said, "Not if they are all rude as you I'm not."

"We don't want your kind there!"

"Good, that will save me a trip."

"Father, what is that species?" Nate asked.

"A Cakerlak, son. They are not very nice and are scattered throughout the galaxy. They are believed to be the oldest species there is."

"And you want one on these in the Cabinet?" Blap asked the Governors.

"They are not all bad..." Southington said when this one pulled out a weapon and pointed it at Blap only to be tackled by two GBI agents and flung down to the ground.

"Take him away." ordered Zucaritas.

"What a dangerous life you lead, Maximus." the King said, "And you all were worried about the Canis and Cyrakuse who haven't fought in a hundred years. Good luck, G.P. Maximus. Come, dear, enough fun for a day. I'm tired."

He took his wife by the arm and led her off.

Mal did not like what she saw on the news... political life suddenly got dangerous. At least no one tried to assassinate Traf when he was alive.

"Let's go back to the House." told Thaw.

Zeb nodded, "Show's done here. Thank you for coming, Planet Mayor."

"You're welcome. It was more exciting than I thought."

"What now, father?" Nate asked.

Blaphaus said, "I'm going back to Ceilingida. You lot work out the next plan."

"We are going back home, Nate. I think we need to talk. And Blaphaus, I think you need to find another Governor again." told Zalez.

"So, the Canis and Cyrakuse finally have a truce, and a Cakerlak was arrested for the potential assassination of G.P. Maximus. What planet and what exciting day is the new G.P. going to have tomorrow? Buterdau Kooper, GNN."

CHAPTER 11

"Nate, sit down please."

His parents stood next to each other in the living room, as Romana eaves-dropped from the staircase. Nate sat on the couch, looking up at his parents, with a sad look on his face.

"I know you find it an honor that G.P. Blaphaus picked you as Governor, and as Assistant, but with you falling asleep in class and what happened yesterday on Launderington your mother and I think that you should not be Governor..."

"But I can do important work." Nate said.

"Yes, we know. But maybe when you're older..."

"But when I'm older Mr. Blaphaus might not be G.P.!"

"Oh, I'm sure he will." Mal said.

"Unless he does resign..." mused Zalez. "With him anything is possible..."

"Then what will happen?" Nate asked.

Zalez shrugged, "Who knows?"

"Does Mr. Blaphaus know I'm not allowed to be Governor?"

"He knows. But I will make sure I talk to him."

"He's going to have to replace me with someone... and that will be hard."

"Hopefully it won't be that hard." Mal remarked.

Zalez was about to ask Mal what she meant when when the door buzzer buzzed. Everyone waited for O-U to go see who it was there then realized he was still in two pieces in a closet. Nate got off the couch and went to the door. He opened it to see Blap standing there, just like the 'old days' Nate thought.

"Ready, boy?" he asked.

"Ready for what, Galactic President Blaphaus?"

"You don't have school today, so you're coming with me back to Canis. And I take it your father is coming as well."

Zalez walked over to the door, "Blaphaus, Nate is not going anywhere. You need to pick another Governor for this planet."

"Then I'll pick your daughter."

"No!" Nate cried. "She's older but I'm smarter. That's not fair."

"None of my children, Blaphaus." Zalez said strictly.

"Okay, Chordattian, then your wife..."

"Why does it have to be any of my family?"

"Because I know you lot. I trust you all. Yeah, you get on my nerves, and your wife is very attractive... for a human, but this kid is bloody smart and keeps me sane. I'm not replacing him."

Mal stormed over and waved her finger at Blap's face. "Yes you are! I have someone in mind that is heading to Launderington to meet you."

"Really now? That's great, but I'm here on *this* planet. I'm not going to Launder-ington."

"Then I'll have him meet you here." she said.

"That would be great. Wotever. But there's a shuttle ready at the spaceport to take me and your son here to Canis. Zucaritas and the Smidge are already head-ing there."

"Then you don't need Nate…" Zalez pointed out.

"Father, mother, let me go please." begged Nate.

"No, Nate. G.P. Blaphaus, good luck and have a good trip." Mal slammed the door in his face.

"Great. Forget you lot then." he muttered as he turned and stormed off towards his vehicle.

Wearing an immaculate sky blue suit, with his black hair slicked to a point the skinny human male walked up the steps of the House, walking through the main doors and went into the lobby. A robot approached him and scanned him from head to toe.

"Hello, can I help you?" the robot asked in a female voice.

"Hello, I'm here to see the G.P., Mr. Maximus."

"The Galactic President is not present on Launderington right now."

"Oh. Can you tell me where he would be."

"I'm forbidden to inform of the Galactic President's whereabouts for security reasons."

"Oh, I understand that. Let him know or the other Governor's know that Solici-tor Yerkal was here. I'm interested in being the Ceilingida Governor."

"Ceilingida has a Governor and that's Nate Belhopsa."

"Yeah, but the thing is he's a child… and the law says he's too young to be a Governor."

"I will let the Governor's who are present here know right away."

Yerkal smiled, "That would be great."

Zucaritas stood with Noam at the Ceilingida spaceport.

"We really need to figure out a better way to do this." Noam said.

"Once all the planets are part of the Cabinet we wouldn't have to." Zucaritas remarked.

"Yeah, that's if Blaphaus can convince his own species and the damn Caker-lak."

"They'll cave in once we get the other four."

Blaphaus approached them with the GNN robot-cam following him.

"Why are these bloody robot-cams watching my moves? If Traf had them fol-lowing him they would be able to record his fall. Imagine the ratings then. GNN missed out."

"You're a novelty, a Tooberosum, not a human." Noam said. "Eventually they'll go away."

"Yeah, when I do." Blap scoffed.

"Let's just get to Canis, and get this over with. The Planet Mayor has a name for us." Zucaritas said. "Someone who would be Governor."

"He better." Blap remarked.

On Launderington at the House, Governor Southington and Governor Thaw approached Yerkal in the lobby.

"Hello, I'm Governor Southington and this is Governor Thaw. We were told you're interested in being Governor for Ceilingida."

"Yup. That's true. I understand my planet has a new Governor, the third one in a week or so but the latest one is a child. He's too young. So, I'd like to offer my services." he smiled.

For the third time Blaphaus walked out through the glass doors of the spaceport on Canis. This time he was with Noam as well as Zucaritas. The Planet Mayor stood outside the black limousine vehicle, smoking his cigar. Jake was in the drivers seat already.

"Welcome back to Canis, Galactic President. Any run ins with a species trying to snuff you lately?"

"Nope. But it's early." Blap scoffed.

"No one will try to snuff you here. I promise you that."

"Yet." Blap said.

"So, who is this Canis you recommend?" Noam asked.

"You'll find out, pipsqueak."

"Rude." Noam remarked.

"So, where do we have to go?" Zucaritas asked.

"Not far. We are going to the country."

Outside the city on Canis was a beautiful countryside with hills, rivers and lakes and a lot of parks. They saw a few Canis here and there, who waved to the Mayor's vehicle. There was a nice sized looking house up on a hill that the Jake drove up the driveway of and stopped in front of it. The Planet Major, and two Governors got out the vehicle followed by Blaphaus. The Mayor walked up to the door and buzzed the door buzzer. The door opened and a brown and white Canis stood there, wearing a purple robe. The first thing Blap noticed was this Canis had one eye.

"Hello, Bodie. How are you, old chap?"

"Planet Mayor! Hello! Fancy seeing you here. Welcome to my... ack! That's a Cyrakuse!"

"Yep. Governor Zucaritas, old chap. You know that Canis and the Cyrakuse are no longer enemies, right?"

"Really? Wowzie. If I was a betting Canis... which I am, I would've lost dosh on that bet. So, who are these other two?" Bodie whispered to the Mayor. "That's the shortest human I ever saw and what an ugly bugger he is. What the bloody hell is it?"

"That's not a human, he's a Smidge. They are kind of on the short side, right? And that there is the Galactic President... Blaphaus Maximus."

"Galactic President, eh? You sure have a unique set of mates, Losergram. Well, come on in." he motioned for them to enter and closed the door behind him when they did.

"So, anybody want any Canis-weed?"

Noam almost said yes, but didn't.

"What do you think is in my cigar?" the Planet Mayor chuckled. "It keeps me happy. So, this Smidge is Governor Noam and the Cyrakuse is Governor Zucaritas. The G.P. has a question for you."

"No. I don't." Blaphaus replied.

"Yes, you do." Zucaritas said, "That's why you're here."

"I'm here because I'm 'forced' to be. This was your bloody idea."

"The G.P. wants you to be Governor for this planet." Noam told Bodie.

"Governor? Of Canis? We are not part of the Cabinet... are we, Losergram?"

"Well, I'm thinking now we are mates with the Cyrakuse we might as well be... if you agree."

"If not we'll move on." Blaphaus said.

"And find another prospect." added Noam.

"This is it. There is no other prospective. It's either Bodie or nothing." the Planet Mayor said.

"There's plenty of other Canis we can approach." Zucaritas told him.

"What would I have to do as Governor?" as Bodie.

"Beats me." Blaphaus said, "I can't figure out what *I'm* supposed to do let alone wot this lot does."

"We'll discuss it." Zucaritas said, "But you'll be going to meetings at the House on Ceilingida daily. You'll be in 'charge' of this planet, and the Planet Mayor would answer to you."

"Wot?" the Mayor gasped.

"Losergram would answer to me... I'd be in charge? Well, in that case call me Governor Bodie!" He shook Blap's hand.

Noam and Zucaritas both looked at each other and smiled. One planet down finally, six to go.

The holo-call of Blaphaus and Zucaritas appeared in the middle of the Cabinet conference table in the House's meeting room. The Cabinet sat around the table, with Yerkal in Tostone's old seat.

"So, success, we have a Canis Governor. We are heading back to Launderington real soon." Zucaritas explained.

The Cabinet cheered and clapped.

"That's good, Zucaritas. Well done, G.P. Maximus. We have someone here for you to meet."

"Great." Blaphaus said, "Then home to sleep."

"No, G.P. Maximus, you'll have to go to the next planet." Dawber told him.

"Nope. Not today. One planet a day is my new schedule."

"When you arrive here we'll talk about it. We have a suite for you at the luxury Icefence Hotel not far from here." told Dawber.

"I'm not paying for a hotel room." Blap told her.

"It's free, you don't have to pay for anything." she replied.

"Good."

"We'll be on the way." Zucaritas added.

The holo-call ended and they all sat there in disbelief... even Yerkal.

"So, we need to plan what planet he needs to visit next." Thaw said. "This was the easy one."

Southington replied, "Okay, let's lay them out... there's Old Eboracum, Mesas, Phytnes, Cakerlak, which a member of that species tried to assassinate Maximus already and of course... Tooberosum. "

The Gink said, "I think Tooberosum should be the last one... it'll be good for the press if he saves his planet for last."

"Good idea." Southington replied, "And I think the Planet Mayor of Cakerlak should come here, not send Blaphaus there."

Zeb said, "I think Old Eboracum... that planet has a huge mix of species, not one dominate one and that Planet Mayor is respected by the Chordattian's. I can go with Blaphaus there."

"Good, then that's what it'll be."

On Siahl, where it rained everyday, at a building a human male with dark hair slightly turning grey stared at five data-screens in a dark room, with the screens reflecting off his spectacles. He barely paid attention to them when something caught his eye. He sat straight, knocking his cup of drink on the floor. He had to tell someone what he saw, and had to tell them quick. He pushed a button on a console and spoke.

"Yourlinda, contact Governor Thaw please, I need him here as soon as possible."

CHAPTER 12

Old Eboracum was a pretty big, and popular planet for all the species to go to to live, shop, see entertainment or to work. It was also very self-sufficient, not relying on Dook Energy to power it, but it's own individual power company called Consolidated, which was owned by the Planet Mayor. Rumor was that hundreds of years ago Old Eboracum was the first planet to be inhabited by anybody, but some believed that was just a promo slogan as the Cakerlak was also believed to the the oldest planet… at least the Cakerlak race anyway. Old Eboracum had everything it needed, even Buterdau Kooper from GNN lived on the planet. Most of the planet was made up by one huge city, with just a third of it being country. The planet's Planet Mayor was a very tall, muscular human male named Kwoh Jaboney, who took over from his father twenty years before. Jaboney loved being Planet Mayor, he loved the power but secretly deep inside he wished he could be a Governor and even Galactic President. Every G.P. there ever was since he was Planet Major, which was Traf and now Maximus would never think of approaching him about joining the Cabinet, with his planet. Or so he thought. His day was about to change.

The Icefence Hotel was one of the most famous hotels in the galaxy, it was there that Traf and his wife had their wedding reception. The best part about the "U" shaped hotel was there were no steps. Blap looked out his hotel room window, naked, looking over the city and contemplating his life. He was starting to like the power he had. What he liked about Ceilingida to live on was that planet never really questioned who he was... or what he was. Now he was in the limelight, and he had to figure out how to get out of it. There was a knock on the room door and he went over to it. He opened it to see Southington standing there, who quickly looked away blushing.
"You... you're naked."
"Really? I walk around with just a purple jacket on and no one bats an eye."
He grabbed the jacket off the hanger in the closet. "So, you losers picked where I'm going today?"
He followed Southington down the hallway, after closing the door behind him.
"Yes, but first there's someone you need to meet. He's from your planet..."
Blap gulped, "Wot? Tooberosum?"
"No, silly. Ceilingida. He's really handsome as well."
"Well, that narrows it down who it's not."
They rode the lift down to the lobby and she led Blaphaus into the restaurant where Yerkal sat. He stood up as soon as he saw Southington and Blaphaus walk in. He shook Blap's hand.

"Hello, G.P. Maximus, it's a pleasure to meet you. I heard so much about you from Pee... people." He almost said Peezle's name.

"Wot people?

The word "people" was a an insult to non-humans. Everybody should be called either species or beings.

"You know, all people... species. Beings. You're are really popular."

"Except for that ugly looking six armed thing that tried to assassinate me." Blap said, "And the one family I liked. So, who are you and wot do you want? I'm very busy."

"I know. You have six more planets to go to, then the others after that. Twenty-three planets is a lot."

"Well, a few I'm not going to. So, you're just a fan or is there something else?"

Southington smiled, "G.P. Maximus, Mr. Yerkal wants to be the Ceilingida Governor."

"And I'm a Solicitor so I can help you."

"I don't trust Solicitor's otherwise I would've hired one a long time ago."

"Would you want to hear my pitch for Governor?" Yerkal asked.

"No. Because I don't care. You want the position, it's yours. As long as your parents won't object..." he said sarcastically.

"My parents are deceased, sir."

"All the better. And never stop calling me 'sir.' Now, Southington, where am I going? I'm taking skinny man here with me."

"There's a conference room here at the hotel. We are all meeting in there."

"Great." he said sarcastically.

They went into the conference room to see everyone sitting around the table already, including the Canis Governor Bodie. The only Governor that wasn't there was Thaw.

"So, it's official, Yerkal is the Governor of Ceilingida." Southington told them as they took a seat, except for Blap who stood at the end of the table.

"So, how are you doing, Blaphaus?" Zeb asked.

"How am I doing? Bloody tired, and feeling used. But that comes with the job I guess. No wonder you lot pick who will be Governor, no one sane would volunteer. Canis, you need a patch over that eye socket."

Bodie nodded, "I'll get one."

"Well, this is an historical moment, there's now sixteen Governors. Blaphaus, you're doing a good job." Zab smiled.

"Anybody could do this." Blaphaus said.

"Not really." Zucaritas replied, "Who would ever think a Canis and Cyrakuse would be sitting next to each other let alone as Governors."

"I'm happy for both of you. There's only fifteen of you here... where's the Leet-ric?"

"He had to go back to Siahl." Lluhdor explained. "He said he'll let us know what's going on."

"Is this normal?" Yerkal asked, "That Governors have to go back to their planet?"

"Always. Yes." nodded Southington.

"So, Blaphaus, you and I are going to Old Eboracum today. The Planet Mayor there does not know we're coming yet. I thought it was best if you holo-called him personally." told Zeb.

"Can't I just ask him who he recommends that way? Save time? And a flight?"

"No, it's best if it's formal." Zeb replied.

"Wotever. It's a waste of time if you ask me. Anyway, Yerkal is coming with us as well." Blaphaus told them.

On the rainy planet of Siahl, Governor Thaw walked into the gray bricked building to be approached by the human.

"Professor Phence, good to see you again. It's been awhile."

They both shook hands.

"Governor Thaw, it's good to see you. So, come to my office, I have to show you something very important."

"You don't sound good about it."

"Because it's not."

The female Cyrakuse walked into the office where the Planet Mayor sat behind his desk. Her fur was tan, and shiny. When she spoke everyone she had a very sexual sounding, sensual voice.

"Planet Mayor Jaboney, someone you might be interested in wants to holo-call you."

"I am interested in a lot of people, Bella. Is she female?"

Bella frowned, "Is who female?"

"The one who I'm interested in."

"You're interested in a lot of people."

"Bella! Who the hell wants to holo-call me?! GNN?"

"No, sir, the new G.P."

"What?! Really? Sure! Patch him through!"

She touched her hand info-pad she was holding and a twelve inch holo-call of Blap appeared on his wooden desk.

"G.P. Maximus? Am I right? What kinda species are you?" Jaboney asked.

Blap frowned, "You don't know?"

"Nope. On Old Eboracum we have every Creator-damned species there is but I've never seen anything like you."

"I'm a Tooberosum. From Tooberosum, a planet in this bloody galaxy."

"I don't care about the other planets, just this planet. But it's good to hear from you, G.P. Maximus. What can I do for you?"

"Nothing. Not for me. But I'm supposed to tell you that myself and two Governors are coming to Old Eboracum today."

"Come here? Today? Well, please do! It'll be great to analyze you in person."

"Wotever." the holo-call ended.

"Bella! Can you believe it? The G.P. is coming here! The last G.P. never came here... unless he did and no one noticed. What do we know about the Tooberosum?"

She shrugged, "You got me."

"Who would know? I know... that Rodentia Doctor... what's his name?"

"Doctor Sahii, I can try to reach him but he's underground a lot."

"Like most Rodentia's. Well, if you can't find him then I'll quiz this Tooberosum. How does he climb steps? He has no legs."

In his lab on Siahl, Professor Phence showed Thaw what he saw that prompted him to send for the Governor.

"I don't know what I'm looking at, Professor."

"Governor, this equation and info is stating this is not the *only* galaxy. There's other galaxies, with other planets. Maybe habitable planets... positively other habitable planets with different species."

"Are you sure? More than the twenty-three?"

"A lot more, Governor. Maybe hundreds!"

"What do you think this means for this galaxy?"

"Well, I know what it means... invasion, and I think it already started. A long time ago."

"Started? How? Who? What?"

"You can't tell anybody else yet until I do more research but... I think..."

The Old Eboracum spaceport was huge! And busy. So busy that when Blaphaus, Zeb and Yerkal walked through it, no one gave them any notice. And GNN robot-cam's didn't even follow them.

"I feel like Traf... no one is giving us a second look." told Blap. "Look at me, no one cares. I should've went to this planet instead of Ceilingida."

"People are in a hurry here, that's for sure." Yerkal said, "I wonder where they are heading to."

"Who knows? But there's every species here." Zeb commented. "I even saw a Canis."

"But not a Toob." Yerkal mentioned.

"Yeah, my kind doesn't like crowds. And I don't either."

They went outside where the weather was overcast.

"I do like this weather though." Blap said.

A black limo-vehicle was sitting there waiting for them. The driver walked around to see them.

He said seriously, "I thought you three landed half an hour ago. What took you so long? I've been waiting!"

"Ummm... it was a busy spaceport to get through." Yerkal said. "And you need to show some respect. This is the G.P. you're talking to."

"Yeah. I don't care. He's not *my* G.P. Get in the vehicle, the Planet Mayor is waiting.

"That's one rude human." Zeb remarked to Yerkal.

Red banners and a red carpet and balloons were hastily put out in front of the Planet Mayors headquarters. The Planet Mayor stood in front of it, with Bella by his side. GNN robot-cams hovered nearby, and a GNN reporter who was human stood there as well, holding a microphone.

"Here I am with the Planet Mayor in front of his headquarters waiting for the Galactic President to show up. With the G.P. convincing Canis to be part of the Cabinet we can only wonder what this meeting will be about. I'm Crisp Jaboney, GNN."

The vehicle drove up and parked in front of the building. The rude chauffeur got out and opened the back passenger door for the three to get out as well Blap had to be helped out, as he laid down the whole drive.

"Welcome, G.P. Maximus to Old Eboracum!"

The Planet Mayor was almost as tall as Blap and he held out his arms out to give him a hug.

"I'm not hugging you." Blaphaus said, "And you're not hugging me."

The Planet Mayor lowered his arms. "Of course. It's what we do here on good ole Old Eboracum but I get it... so, want to ride my personal train and we can chat?"

"Wotever."

"We'll do whatever you'd like." Zeb said.

Yerkal said, "You have GNN here... you didn't ask."

"My planet, my rules. You are?"

"Governor Yerkal, and this is Governor Zeb."

"This is my Assistant Bella, she'll take care of you two inside while Maximus and I chat."

"We are staying with him." Yerkal said.

"Nope. You're not. We'll be back. C'mon, Maximus, let's take a ride."

He went to put his hand on Blap's back who said, "Don't touch me."

The Planet Mayor and the Galactic President were the only ones in the section of the train they were in. Blap stood and the Planet Mayor sat besides him, studying him.

"So, you're a Toob, am I right?"

"Tooberosum. But I do get called Toob. You really have not heard of my species? Or planet?"

"Nope. Should I have? Have any of your kind ever been to Old Eboracum?"

"How am I expect to know? I doubt it. I'm here now, so there you go."

"Yeah. But the Cabinet forced you to be here. Would you have come if you didn't have a choice?"

"Nope."

"Exactly. So, why are you here? Why did you have them bring you here?"

"You're not that bright, are you? Why do you think?"

"I don't know."

Blap sighed, "Did you hear or see what happened with Canis?"

"Yeah. The truce with them and Cyrakuse... and now there's a Canis Governor."

"Yep. So, Jaboney, they want this planet to be part of the Cabinet. Anybody you know would be a good candidate to be Governor? And I don't want any feces about I have to go talk the King or anybody. I just want a name, where to find him or her so I can go see them and offer the Governor role. So let's cut the chase... who do you recommend?"

"Man, you're a tough one, Toob. Were you happy to be offered the position you're in?"

"Nope. I hate it. But here I am, on this train, with you... so, do you have a name or not?"

"Of course I do. Kwoh Jaboney!" Jaboney grinned.

Yerkal couldn't wait to get back home and tell Peezle about his "adventure" so far. He wanted to look into the backstory of the G.P. as well. He sat looking across at Zeb, who sat playing with his beard. They were left alone with drinks and food all by themselves. They had no idea how long they would have to wait, and what the unfiltered Toob was saying. They didn't like he was by himself.

"So, Governor Zeb, do you have a family back on Chordatta?"

"Yes. Two boys. Mixed species. My wife is a Leetric."

"So that makes them Leedattian's?" Yerkal laughed.

"I guess so. Mixed species are often looked down on."

"Yeah, as a Solicitor, I had to deal with a lot of those situations. This galaxy could be so tough and mean."

"What do you mean *this* galaxy? There's only one galaxy." Zeb pointed out. "The Creator just made this one."

Yerkal nodded, "Of course."

Some believed there was just this one galaxy, others believed there was more than one. Yerkal believed there were other galaxies out there. Bella then walked back into the lounge followed by Jaboney and Blaphaus. Yerkal and Zeb stood up and Zeb noticed the Mayor was very happy.

"So, I take it you have good news?" Zeb asked.

"Sure do! I'm not Planet Mayor anymore! Bella, I'm now planet Governor of Old Eboracum and member of the Galactic Cabinet! You're getting a raise!"

She smiled so cheerful and hugged her boss. "Thank you and yay!"

"Wait, so this planet no longer has a Planet Mayor?" Yerkal asked.

"Correct!"

"For some absurd reason he jumped at the chance." Blap remarked.

"So, Canis is the only planet with a Planet Mayor and Governor?" Zeb asked.

"Unless the other planets want a Planet Mayor and Governor as well." Yerkal said.

"You lot figure that out. Are we done here?" Blap asked.

Zeb nodded, "So, you'll be able to come to Launderington for the Cabinet meetings?"

Jaboney nodded, "Of course! So, what planet is next on your radar?"

"We have to go back to Launderington and figure that out." Zeb said.

"Then let's go." Jaboney smiled, "I'm all yours!"

"You might want to calm down." Blap told him. "You're making this more of a big deal than it is."

Thaw was flying in first class in the shuttle, looking out the portal window at the stars racing by. In the distance he saw the neon glowing multi-colored lights of the Farvegas space station. Other galaxies, he thought? There was no way. But Professor Phence was never wrong. He was the smartest human he knew, his company was the company that built and designed most robots.

Mal went into the dance school on Ceilingida where Blaphaus' holo-image was still on the roof.

"Hello, Mal! How is Governor Nate?" Fadonna asked.

"He's not Governor anymore, Fad. I don't want him around Blaphaus, he's too young and it's too dangerous."

"Awe. How did Nate take it?"

"Hard. Zalez is with him, hoping they can bond and Nate will forget about it."

"Awe. I hope he'll be okay."

"Me too. By the way, please take down Blaphaus' head off this building. The Belhopsa's no longer support Blaphaus."

"Oh..." Fadonna didn't know what to say.

"Father, where are we going?" Nate asked, sitting in the back seat of his father's car.

"You'll find out. It's a surprise."

"Does mother know?"

"Nope, not yet." he replied.

"Will she be mad?"

"I don't think so."

Nate sat back and smiled. "Good, I like surprises."

"So, word is that Planet Mayor Jaboney is now Governor of Old Eboracum now. I don't know what is going on, but this Tooberosum is the best thing to happen to the galaxy. Which planet is next? Are all twenty-three planets going to be part of the Cabinet? We can only hope so... Buterdau Kooper, GNN." He took off his microphone from his black tie and turned away from his GNN news desk.

"That was great as always." his Chordattian producer told him. "Governor Thaw is waiting to holo-call with you."

Buterdau nodded.

He went to his office, sitting behind his desk. The holo-call of Thaw appeared and he seemed to not be himself.

"Hello, Governor. What can I do for you?"

"I've been drinking, Buterdau. I'm on Farvegas."

"Farvegas? Have you been gambling?"

"Yes. And drinking. I went home today to Siahl."

"That's good." Buterdau nodded, wondering why Thaw would contact him and tell him this.

"I spoke to Professor Phence, Buterdau, and he told me a few things which you can't talk about yet, but something you might want to know."

Buterdau said, "Okay then. But if I can't report it, what's the point?"

"I have to tell someone." Thaw said. "We are not the only galaxy... there's a whole universe out there. That's what Phence called it anyway."

Buterdau couldn't help to chuckle. He would never report that, he'd be laughed off GNN. Thaw was really drunk. No way is there another galaxy or a universe, or whatever it was called.

CHAPTER 13

At the Icefence hotel on Launderington, all the Governors sat around the conference table, that Blaphaus stood at the end of.

"I'm so glad to be part of this Cabinet with you all as Governor. I did great things on Old Eboracum and I'm sure could help with great things for the whole galaxy." Jaboney was saying. He turned to Bodie who sat next to him. "Your Planet Mayor made a big mistake, he could've been Governor."

"Guess he didn't think about it." told Bodie.

"So, G.P. Maximus, you're going a great job. Your ratings are through the roof." Zeb smiled.

"Ratings? What ratings?" Blap asked.

"Every month ratings are done asking the planets what they think of the G.P. and yours are great. Getting two planets to join the Cabinet is a big help."

"So, Thaw, how was trip to Siahl?" Zeb asked.

"It was okay. Family matters." he lied.

Southington said, "So, we think Mesas should be next. We don't really know anything about that planet though. Do you know anything about it?"

"Ummm... Nope. Not a clue." Blaphaus said, "Why should I?"

"Is there anyone here that knows about Mesas?" Dawber asked.

"I heard it's very hot and a Leetric wouldn't be able to survive on it." Thaw said.

"Then good job you're not G.P. then." Blap told him.

Gillian the Jiraffa said, "I think I can handle the heat... depends how hot it is. I volunteer to go with the G.P. for this trip."

"I like the heat as well, so I'll also go. Blaphaus, how do you like the heat?"

"Put it this way, I don't. Why is this planet hotter? There's just one sun..."

"They have to have it hot for their species." the Gink said.

"Well, that doesn't explain why it's hotter than the others." Blap said, "Any of you lot know a scientist?"

"Thaw, you know a scientist, right? A human on Siahl..."

"Professor Phence, yes, but he wouldn't know why."

Blaphaus said, "I know one person who would know."

"Who is that?" Southington asked.

"Zalez Belhopsa, the head of Dook Energy."

Yerkal swallowed, "I don't know..."

"You're a Solicitor, Yerkal, I'm sure you're pretty smart. Wot's your last name anyway?"

"It's just 'Yerkal.'" Southington replied.

"Ummm... I doubt that. Yerkal, you're human, right?"

"Ah, yes. Why?"

"Well, some species have only one name... but humans have a first name and last name..."

"Like you do." Lluhdor pointed out.

"Yes, we normally do on Tooberosum. Most species do."

Bodie said, "On Canis we just have one name... unless our parents get super creative... I know a good chap named Princess Margaret Of Snowdonia. And he's a chap. His parents must've had a real big sense of humor."

"Or your friend is not a 'chap.'" smiled Noam. "Ever think about that?"

"You lot give me a headache." Blap said. "So, Yerkal, wot's your last name? Or is it Yerkal and you have another first name?" Blap asked, "And you know wot will happen to you if you lie to me."

Zucaritas growled, "What is it, Yerkal?"

Yerkal slumped in his chair, "Can we just focus on the situation at hand? Mesas is the next planet..."

"Wot is your whole name?" Blaphaus asked, "I'm not going to ask you again."

"It's... Peezle."

"Peezle?!" Blap asked. "As the Peezle that was Traf's bloody Assistant?"

"Is Peezle a common name amongst humans?" the Gink asked.

"No, I never heard of a Peezle." Jaboney replied.

"I knew a *Peasel* once." Bodie said, "How do you spell your name, Governor?"

"Are you Peezle's husband?" Noam asked.

"Ummm..."

"Where is Peezle?" Lluhdor asked, "We can ask him."

"Okay! Peezle is my husband! But he's not the reason I wanted to be Governor..."

"Then why?" Blaphaus asked.

"It was Zalez's wife's idea... she asked me to come here to try to be Governor, as she didn't want her son to be Governor."

Blap said, "I'm pissed. You're fired..."

"No!" Southington stood, "Stop firing everyone who pisses you off."

"He lied, lady, and..."

"You don't lie?" Thaw asked.

"No." Blap said.

"He didn't lie, just wasn't that honest." Dawber said.

"Well, anybody who is connected to that family I don't want to deal with."

"You just recommended Zalez..." Zucaritas said.

"Damn you all. Okay, Peezle, you're not fired. Yet. You're going with me to Dook Energy before we go to Mesas. Long neck, you're going too."

Gillian nodded with her long neck. "Yes, Galactic President."

"And you." Blap said to Southington.

"That's good. The trip will do me good."
"Then book a flight." Blaphaus said.

Ever since Nate was five-years-old and learned what his father did for a living he loved to go to the space station and see where his father worked. He was so lucky that once again he got to go for a "work" day with his father, and without Romana this time. Some of Zalez's crew were pleased to see Nate again, he was generally loved by everyone. They spent an hour just walking around, meeting so many people who worked there. Nate noticed that so many different species worked there, it was cool. He wondered why he went to an all human school, there were so many species, with interesting backgrounds. One thing he noticed though was there wasn't one Tooberosum on the station at all.

"Father, how many Tooberosum's do you think exist?"

"I don't know. Why do you ask?"

"You don't have any here that work for you."

"They keep to themselves on Tooberosum I think. Except for Blaphaus. Maybe more will start leaving their planet." he shrugged, "I don't know."

"Father, I've been trying to research Tooberosum's, and Blaphaus."

"Yeah? And what did you find out?"

"Just a description of them, and that they weren't seen for a long time. No one even went to their planet. It's weird, right? Why are they so mysterious?"

"Son, I have no idea. I just know that if they're all like Blaphaus then..."

Nate was going to tell his father his theory on Blaphaus but a balding man rushed up to them.

"Hello, Mr. Belhopsa, Nate. You must be so proud your boy is Governor..."

"I'm not Governor anymore." Nate said seriously.

"Oh? I'm sorry. Anyway, there's a shuttle heading this way to the station, and wish to land."

"Nekkod, you know that only Dook shuttles can come here..."

"It's the G.P. with a few Governors, sir. They said it's important. Want me to tell them you're not here?"

"Mr. Blaphaus is coming here?" Nate asked.

"Maybe he wants you to be Governor again." Nekkod smiled.

"No, have them meet me in my office."

"What about me, father? Can I see them as well?"

"Sure. Just don't tell your mother."

Nekkod watched as the yellow private shuttle from Old Eboracum landed in the hangar section of the space station. He stood nervously as he watched the Toob, the attractive blonde female Governor, the skinny handsome male Governor and the tall long necked Jiraffa Governor walk down the ramp.

"Welcome to Dook Energy, Galactic President, Governors. Mr. Belhopsa is waiting for you in his office, his son is there too." Nekkod smiled.

"Terrific. His bitch of a wife isn't, is she?"

Nekkod didn't know what to say. "Ummm... no, she's not here."

"Good." Blap remarked.

Nekkod walked them into the office where Zalez and Nate were.

"Mr. Blaphaus, hello!" Nate smiled. "I'm so sorry mother slammed the door in your face."

"Does she normally do that to important people?" he asked.

"Hello, Nate." smiled Southington.

"No, she's very protective. I think the assassination attempt freaked her out." Zalez explained.

"That was a lousy assassination attempt." Blap said, "You don't yell feces before you pull a weapon. I'm not a Smidge, I'm a big target." Blap motioned to Yerkal. "So, Belhopsa, do you know who this is?"

"I have no idea. Hello, I'm Zalez Belhopsa, head of Dook Energy."

"Yerkal, Ceilingida's Governor. I guess I'm your successor, young man." Yerkal smiled at Nate.

"Nice to meet you." Zalez shook Yerkal's hand.

"Nice to meet you as well." Nate shook Yerkal's other hand.

"So, tell him your last name." Blap said.

"Peezle." Yerkal remarked.

"I don't think you need to do this." Southington said.

"Sure I do. His last name is Peezle, Chordattian. Do you remember that name?"

"Yes, Noj Peezle. He's a friend."

"And you don't know who Yerkal is?"

"We never met." Yerkal said. "Zalez, what the G.P. is trying to say is I'm Noj's husband."

"Ahhh. Nice."

"Tell him how you got to be Governor."

"Maximus, that's not why we're here." Southington remarked.

"It's my main reason I'm here. Tell them, Peezle."

"Mal contacted me. It was her idea." Yerkal said.

"Mal? Why? For what?"

"So I can replace Nate. I guess she wanted Blaphaus to replace him quickly."

"Mother would not do that." Nate said.

"It's true."

Zalez said, "I will talk to Mal about that. Is there another reason you're here, Blaphaus?"

"Yup. Why is the planet Mesas so bloody hot?" Blap asked.

Gillian said, "That's the next planet we are going to... but we heard it's really hot there "

"I guess they like it hot there." Zalez said. "There's quite a few species that live there."

"Do any of the Mesa work here on this station?" Nate asked.

"Good thinking, Nate." Southington remarked.

"There's not a Mesa species." Zalez said.

"The galaxy has one sun, so why is that planet hotter? Is it next to the sun?" Gillian asked.

"It's not nearest to the sun. In fact Ceilingida is closer to the sun."

"That planet gets too hot for me." Blap said, "I don't want to deal with the Mesas heat. Zalez, you're coming with us. You're going to find out why it's so hot."

"I can't leave Nate here by himself."

"You're not, he's coming as well."

"His moth..."

"I don't care about her. As G.P. I'm telling you what's happening."

He turned and walked out the office. Gillian and Southington followed as Yerkal whispered to Zalez and Nate.

"I'm so sorry." apologized Gillian. "He wears me out."

Mal opened the front door of the house and went inside to see all the lights were on, and Romana sitting in the couch listening to music.

"Hey, Romana, are you here by yourself?"

"Hi, mother. Yeah, I got home from Jos' house and father and Nate weren't here."

"Hmmm. I wonder where they went."

Romana shrugged, "I don't know. Probably somewhere fun. Nate does all the fun stuff."

"That's not true."

"He got to leave the planet. I never left the planet!"

Mal sighed, "Well, he won't be leaving the planet again for a few years."

The yellow shuttle approached Mesas, which was a very tan looking planet from space. The shuttle started to shake as it got closer. Blap was buckled against the bulkhead where he stood. The others were seated, and were holding onto their seats armrests.

"Father, I'm scared." Nate said, tears in his eyes.

"We'll be okay." Zalez remarked, feeling scared as well.

"We are experiencing some turbulence so remain seated. Or standing. Or else." the pilot said over the intercom.

"Are we going to die?" Gillian whispered to Southington.

"No, we will be okay."

The pilot said, "We are about to enter the atmosphere of Mesas…"

The shuttle shook violently for five minutes before it came down to land. There was no inside spaceport on Mesas, just an outside landing area. Nate had thrown up all over his shirt, and Gillian rubbed her long neck in pain.

"We are coming in for a landing." the pilot said over the intercom.

The shuttle came down and landed in the desert, amongst the other crafts. It's door opened and the ramp lowered down. The six walked down it and onto the hot sand.

A long faced gray species approached them, wearing a t-shirt and shorts. His legs were black and white striped and his black hair was sticking up like a mohawk.

"Hello. Welcome. I'm Dibo. Do you need a tour guide? I could be a guide. I know this planet."

"Where is the nearest city?" Southington asked.

"City? What's that? A place to go to the bathroom?"

"No." Blap said, "Civilization."

"Civil what?"

Yerkal took off his jacket and tie, he was sweating so much and his hair was getting messy. "Do you know who we are?" he asked.

Dibo shook his head. "Nope. Should I?"

"Do you know what a human is?" Southington asked.

"You-man? What's that?"

"For crying out loud." Blap muttered, "We are not going to find a Governor here."

"Governor? What's that?" Dibo asked.

Gillian asked, "Dibo, do you know who the Planet Mayor is?"

"I don't know what that is."

"And you want to give us a tour?" Blap asked.

"Yes, I know this planet." Dibo nodded.

"Sure." Blap said, "Let's skip this planet. This is bloody ridiculous."

Nate saw a small gray haired and big pointy eared species walk by with a cane.

"Hello, mister!" Nate waved.

The little one was shorter than Nate. He stopped and turned to the boy.

"Are you a child?" Nate asked.

"A child? I'm old enough to be your grandfather if I was human, which I'm not."

"You know I'm human?" Nate asked.

"I just said I'm old. Yes, I know you humans. They don't normally live long on this planet."

"We are not going to be here long." Nate said.

"That's good, because you'll die."

Zalez walked over and put his hand on his sons shoulder.

"Do you know what species I am?"

"Yeah, a Chordattian. There's a few of your kind I know. Not the funnest species. Now if you don't mind..." he then spotted Blaphaus who was arguing with Dibo, and Gillian was trying to stop them. Southington was waving her hand in front of her face, trying to fan herself.

"That's a Jiraffa. We have those here. And isn't that the new G.P.?"

"You know him?" Zalez asked surprised.

"Yes, I pay attention. Is he here to try to get this planet to join his Cabinet?"

"Yes, that's the plan. Also we want to know why this planet is so hot."

"It's the sand. The sand is hot... and there's a big heater in the planet's core. We like it hot here."

"We could tell." told Zalez. "So do you know who the Planet Mayor is?"

"What? Yes I do. His name is Rüppell. He lives miles from here. Miles. Thousands of miles. In a town."

"A town? There is a town here?" Zalez asked.

"Not here. There."

"Why would the spaceport be on this side of the planet?" Yerkal asked.

"I don't know. I didn't design it. You should pick me as the Governor. I'm Bilby. I'd love to be Governor."

Blap walked over. "I'm dying on this dirt pile. That long faced arse is not getting us anywhere."

"G.P., this is Bilby. He can help us. And he explained why the planet is so hot. He also knows who the Planet Mayor is." Yerkal pointed out.

"And he wants to be Governor." Nate smiled.

"Terrific. Let's just take him then."

"We have to talk to the Planet Mayor first." Gillian said walking over. "Southington is very sick from the heat. She's going to stay on the shuttle. Where does the Planet Mayor live and work?"

"On the other side of the planet." Nate said.

"I have a vehicle that will get us there." Bilby told them. "I hope you'll fit on the back of it, G.P."

"Do you know what species he is?" Nate asked.

"A Toob I was told. I never seen one before. Thought you were a thing of legends."

"No, I meant what species is the Planet Mayor?" Nate asked.

"Oh. He's a Lycalopex. You're a Toob. Never seen one before."

"Well, here I am." Blap said, "I'm drowning here in sweat. Let's go."

Nate saw that Blap wasn't even sweating. What did Blaphaus mean he was sweating? He wondered if Tooberosum's did sweat.

Yerkal said, "I'll stay on the shuttle with Southington if that's okay."

"Sure, that would be good." Gillian pointed out.

"Have a good trip." Yerkal nodded.

Mal was getting frustrated, she couldn't reach her husband anywhere. She was really getting worried, and thought of one person who might be able to help. She sat in her bed and Peezle's holo-call appeared above her info-pad on the bedside table.

"Noj, hello."

"Hey there, Mrs. Belhopsa. How are you?"

"I'm okay. Have you heard from Yerkal? How is he doing as Governor? He is Governor, right?"

"Yes, he is. He seems to like it a little."

"That's good. I think my husband and Nate are missing, Peezle. They are not at home and I can't reach them. Do you think you can ask Yerkal to help? Can you help?"

"Um, sure. I'll contact him and get back to you. I can come to Ceilingida if you want. I'm not working so..."

"Yes, please. Thank you."

"Don't mention it. I'll be there this afternoon."

Mal smiled, but she still was worried.

Little did Mal know that her husband and son were on the hottest planet in the galaxy. Nate felt ill with dried vomit on his shirt next to fresh wet vomit. His hair was wet with sweat and his face was beet red. His dad had the top part of his overalls pulled down and his black thick furry body glistening in the sun. Gillian was okay with the heat but wasn't enjoying the flying buggy ride. She sat next to Blap who stood on the back of the flying buggy, facing the opposite way. He felt dizzy and miserable and was hating life... and for the first time wishing he was back home. Bilby did not seem bothered by the heat, but he was bothered by the weight on the back of his buggy.

"How much more?" Nate whined.

"We would've been there already if the back load wasn't so heavy." Bilby retorted. "The weight can't get this vehicle as high off the ground as I want."

"You lot owe me big after this." coughed Blap, hardly moving his mouth. The buggy landed in front of a small hut looking building.

Bilby turned to them all. "This is it."

They all got out and Zalez asked, "This is where we'll find the Planet Mayor?"

Bilby nodded, "Yes. He's the red furred one, probably at the back table playing a game of stabber."

Zalez was the first one to walk inside, seeing it was a bar. He looked down at Nate. "Son, wait outside please."

"Why?"

"This is a bar, you shouldn't be in here."

Nate looked up at the fans in the ceiling. "But it's cooler in here."

"Okay, just take a seat at that table by the front door."

Nate nodded and said, "Okay, father."

A green feathered species with a small black beak approached them.

"Hey, I hate talking to beings, but you have no shirt on, sir." he pointed to the sign above the bar that said: "You Must Wear Shirts At All Time."

Zalez nodded and apologized. "Sorry."

He pulled the top part of his overalls up and put it on.

"We're here to see the Mayor." Gillian told the feathered species.

"Planet Mayor Rüppell is over there playing stabber."

They looked to see the red furred Canis looking being playing cards with a species that looked like Bilby. Behind the bar the bartender looked liked Dibo, the tour guide they met when they first got to the planet.

"What are you?" the feathered one asked Blaphaus.

"The Galactic President." Blap told him.

"The Galactic President? Why would you be here in this bar?"

"Because I'm a glutton for punishment."

At the bar a hard-shelled black and red species turned around, long antennas sticking straight up.

"Hello. I'm Bocks. I hear you're looking for someone to be Governor."

"What? How do you know?" Gillian asked.

"Because my planet talks a lot about it." Bocks replied.

"Your planet?" Zalez asked. "What planet are you from?"

"Cakerlak."

"One of your kind tried to assassinate me." told Blaphaus. "You're not going to be Governor."

"You have to go to Cakerlak sooner or later, am I right?" Bocks asked.

"I don't have to go anywhere."

"What have we here?" Rüppell approached them. "Bocksy, are you bothering these customers?"

"No, Rüppell, just making small talk."

"Well, don't. Hello, welcome to Mesas, I'm Planet Mayor Rüppell. You're the Galactic President, a Tooberosum, right?" He got on his tip-toes and studied Blap. "Never seen one of your species before."

"You look like a Canis." Blap told the Planet Mayor.

"Ha! My grandparents were from Canis. That's a nice planet, but not as hot as this one. Don't you love the heat?"

Blap said, "Nope. Not at all."

Gillian asked, "So, how does this planet stay so hot? It's not the sun..."

"We were told there's a generator underground..." Zalez remarked.

"Hahaha. That's what so many people think. Do you know what's close to this planet?"

"No, we don't." Zalez said.

"A space station... the Faeligion Church. The heat from it somehow comes to the planet... heats up the atmosphere. I didn't know the Church was so hot. Luckily we all love the heat here."

"I don't." Blap said.

"Neither did the last G.P. When this planet first started to get hot I reached out to the G.P. Traf and he asked how hot the planet was and I told him 104 degrees and he said no, he's not coming here. But we know he spent time at Church. So, you being here is a big thing. I would love to be Governor and work with you."

"So you know why we are here?" Gillian asked.

"Yes, you're looking for someone to be Governor... and I'd love to be the one. I'll even go with you to Cakerlak. I get along with them pretty good, and I know who to talk to there, right Bocksy?"

"Yep."

"So, you want to be Governor and will be part of the Cabinet?" Gillian asked.

"Yeah, if Traf would've asked I would've said yes. So, what do you think?"

"Done." Blaphaus said. "That was easy."

Gillian said, "We will let you know when we plan to go to Cakerlak."

"No prob. Just holo-call me and I'll be there." he shook Blaphaus' hand. "Man, that's like shaking a dead Leetric."

Blap pulled his hand back, not replying.

Professor Phence walked up the stairs to the House back on Launderington, and went inside to be greeted by the House robot that scanned the human.

"Hello, Professor Phence, how are you today?"

"You know who I am?"

"Yes, sir, it's your company that built me. Phenceway."

"Ha! Of course. I'm here to see Governor Thaw."

"I'll send him down for you, Professor." told the robot.

The door buzzer buzzed and Mal opened the door to see Noj standing there. She gave him a hug and said, "I'm so glad you're here! Come on in."

She led Peezle in and Ten followed, with his proper legs.

"Hello." Ten said.

"Oh. Hello." Mal said, "You're taller."

"Like I should be. No more stupid little purple legs."

"Ma'am, Ten has something to tell you." Peezle told her.

"Mrs. Belhopsa, I know I apologized for knocking O-U's head off, and you accepted my apology but I don't think you really one hundred percent mean that. I will make it up to you and stay here as your robot, until you get another. Especially with your husband and son missing."

"Thank you." Mal said half smiling. "Peezle, did you get in touch with Yerkal?"

"No, I've been trying."

"What do you think is going on? Do you think it has something to do with the assassination attempt?"

"I have no idea." Peezle said, "I will try to get in touch with him again."

Back on Mesas, Bilby was flying his buggy again. Everyone was in the same position as before, and Nate once again was feeling sick.

"Father, I don't feel so good."

"I know, son, I'm so sorry. We'll be back at the shuttle soon."

"I'm never coming back to this planet as long as I live." complained Blap. "Unless that bloody Church moves."

"I wonder if the citizens of this planet really likes the heat?" Gillian asked.

"They're bloody stupid if they do…" told Blap.

Ahead they saw the shuttle where it sat.

"Yay! We're almost there." moaned Nate.

A few minutes later the buggy stopped next to the shuttle and they all got off it.

Depo walked over to them and said, "Hi there, y'all, welcome. Do you need a tour guide?" he saw Nate's shirt was covered in fresh wet vomit. "Boy, oh boy, you're so smelly."

"Leave them alone!" Bilby waved his cane at the long faced Depo.

Blap and Gillian went up the ramp, and Zalez carried his son who was really sick.

"Is Nate okay?" Yerkal asked.

"No, I don't think so." Zalez sat Nate in a seat. "Tell the pilots to fly to Jubilee Hospital on Ceilingida."

Yerkal nodded and made his way to the pilots cabin. Gillian looked at Southington who did not look good either.

"Jupha, are you okay?"

Southington slowly shook her head.

"She's not well either, Zalez."

"Both humans, but Yerkal is okay."

Yerkal came back in to the main hold and took a seat buckling in.

"Shut up, all, this is your pilot, buckle your asses in, we are about to take off and head to Ceilingida. I hope we don't have turbulence again."

Governor Thaw sat behind his desk as Professor Phence sat across from him. Thaw taped his jaw, sitting back and thinking.
"So, you're saying now that this galaxy has definitely been invaded?"
"It's very possible, Governor. We just don't know by whom yet."
"But the species we have we know which planets they are from... even the planets not part of the Cabinet and we haven't been too."
"There are species that don't have planets, Governor."
"I know, but we still know where they are from."
"Do we? Are you sure about that?"
"Give me a species that you claim is not from this galaxy, Professor."
"Okay. Tooberosum."
"Tooberosum? That planet is right here in this galaxy."
"Is it? Have you been there?"
"No, but... you're saying our Toob G.P. is from another galaxy? Invaded this one?"
"How many Toobs do you know? Or seen?"
Thaw said, "None. But they stay on their own planet."
"But Blaphaus didn't. Think about it."
"I went to Firvegas and got drunk, and gambled a lot of money because what you showed me... there's more galaxies out there and a whole universe, or whatever you called it. I respect you, you're so smart but saying the Toob is not from this galaxy."
"Exactly."
"Well, if that's true then this is the worse invasion ever."
"Or the best one." Phence said seriously.

"Zalez!! Where the hell have you been?!" yelled Mal at the holo-call of her husband in the living room. "Where's Nate?!"
"Darling, it's a long story. I'm on a shuttle, with Nate. Meet us at Jubilee Hospital."
"Jubilee? Hospital? What's going on?"
"I'll explain when you get here. Don't bring Romana. I'll see you later."
The holo-call ended and she turned to Peezle who sat in a chair, with Romana sitting besides him.
"What's happening, mother?" Romana asked.
"I don't know. Mr. Peezle, come with me. Romana, I'm taking you to the dance school. Fadonna will watch you."
"But I want to go with you."
"Not yet."

    The yellow shuttle came down slowly to land on the roof of the hospital, directed by a robot waving a red light stick. When the shuttle landed the ramp descended and Zalez rushed down it, carrying Nate in his arms. Nurses met him with a stretcher and he carefully put Nate down on it. Yerkal and Gillian helped Southington down the ramp, and nurses put her on another stretcher. Blap slowly walked down the ramp and a nurse asked him.
    "Galactic President, do you need a stretcher as well?"
    "No... I'm good."
    "Are you sure?" Yerkal asked. "You're barely speaking... and moving..."
    "I said I was fine." he snapped.
    He followed them to the lift slowly feeling anything but good, but the last thing he wanted was for doctors to examine him, or probe. He just hoped he didn't pass out, because that would not be good. That would ruin everything...

CHAPTER 14

Mal couldn't get to the hospital quick enough with Peezle sitting in the passenger seat of her vehicle. Inside the hospital Blaphaus, Zalez, Yerkal and Gillian sat in the waiting area in the lobby. Same place Peezle met the Toob for the first time. And when he and Mal walked into the lobby this time they saw Blap in the corner as he was stared at by the other beings in the waiting room. Zalez stood up and approached Mal, arms opened wide to hug her. Mal didn't open her arms to hug him at all. Yerkal walked up to Peezle and they hugged and kissed on the lips.

"Where the hell is my son?!" Mal exclaimed.

"Shsss... people are listening..."

"I DON'T CARE!!" she shouted out loud.

"Your wife is getting worse and worse." Blap called over.

A Cyrakuse was staring at him and Blap commented. "Stop staring, that's rude."

"What is *he* doing here?" demanded Mal.

"We were with him. It's a long story. Let's go to the cafeteria and sit and talk."

"Where is Nate?!"

"Where's Romana?" Zalez asked.

She punched him hard in his chest. "WHERE IS NAAATTTTEEEEE!!!!!" she screamed.

"Calm down. He's okay. He was very dehydrated..."

Gillian walked over and said, "I hate to interrupt but we have to contact the Cabinet. Would you want to help?"

"You know Yerkal is now Governor is, don't you, lady?" Blap asked her. "Nice move. It worked." He said sarcastically.

"I'm not talking to you. Dehydrated?" she sat in a waiting room chair. "How?"

Zalez sat besides her and took her hand in his. "I thought it'll be a good idea to cheer Nate up and take him to Dook, but then Blaphaus and the Governor's showed up and I was asked to come with them to Mesas as that planet is so hot, and I might be able to figure out why. It was so hot there it made Nate sick as well as Governor Southington. They were both dehydrated, so I had the shuttle come here and land on the roof of this hospital."

"You took him off planet when you knew the last trip he took made him ill?"

"He wasn't ill, he was tired. And Dook isn't that far away."

"And Mesas?"

"Not too far."

"Turns out the heat of the planet somehow is from the Church space station, but I find it hard to believe." Blap said.

"Why is Noj Peezle with you?" Zalez asked.

"Because I couldn't get in touch with you or Yerkal so I asked for his help."

Yerkal said, "I'm glad you did." He gave his husband a hug.

"It's a bloody family reunion." muttered Blaphaus.

Just then Doctor Mecca walked into the waiting room and saw Blaphaus right away.

"Well, I'll be... a Toob... your kind don't get out often, do you?"

"No. And I don't blame them. The galaxy sucks."

"Can I touch you, G.P.?" Macca asked.

"Nope."

"Well, congrats on becoming Galactic President."

Mal stood, "Can we see our son? Nate Belhopsa."

"Yes, he's doing good. So is the Governor lady."

"Can I see her?" asked Gillian.

"Yeah, follow me. They are in rooms next to each other."

Blaphaus went over to the robot receptionist desk and said, "Can you call an Ultra ride for me?"

"Mother!" Nate cried for joy as she rushed into the room and gave her son a big hug. He laid there hooked up to an IV-robot with his smelly shirt off.

"Nate! Are you feeling okay? Your face is a little red."

"It's not sunburn, mother. Are you mad?"

"Yes, but at your father, not at you."

"Don't be mad at father. The station he works at is amazing! He didn't know Mister Blaphaus would show up. I never want to go to Mesas ever again."

"You won't."

"Is Ms. Southington okay? She's nice."

"I don't know, but I think so."

In the other room Southington laid in the bed, also hooked up to an IV-robot, getting fluids just like Nate.

She smiled up at Gillian's face. "Where's Yerkal?"

"In the lobby with his husband. It was good to see Peezle again. I miss him, and Traf."

Southington smiled, "So do I. Where's Blaphaus?"

"I don't know. He was in the waiting room."

"So, was the trip a success?"

"Yes, Planet Mayor Rüppell is going to be Governor. He seems nice."

"I'm glad. This is going to be successful... considering. Does the Cabinet know anything?"

"No, not yet. I was waiting to see how you were doing first."

"Okay. What planet are we on?"

"Ceilingida. We are at Jubilee Hospital."

"So, we'll just fly back to Launderington with the G.P. and Yerkal then tell the Cabinet what happened."

"Well, as soon as you're discharged and little Nate is discharged we'll leave here."

"How is Nate?"

"I think he's good. His mother is mad. No... more than mad. Furious. She screamed at Zalez."

"Oh, boy. So much drama." Southington said.

Blaphaus stood outside the hospital and watched a Ultra vehicle drive up.

"Tooooobbbbb!" the Chordattian driver yelled as he got out the vehicle and opened the passenger door for Blap.

"Calasteel? Wot are you doing?"

Blap got into the vehicle, Calasteel got behind the wheel and drove off.

"When the call for the ride came in the robot receptionist mentioned a ride for the G.P. I'm so happy for you! How did this happen?"

"Don't ask me. The Cabinet were desperate I guess."

"Well, since I fired you your life got better. I did you a favor. Ha ha."

"Sure. If you say so."

"So, what were you doing at the hospital?"

"I had to go to Mesas, that planet was bloody hot."

"So you got sick?"

"Not me. Not really."

"Well, look..." he held up one hand to show he wasn't wearing a glove.

"No gloves and I'm growing my face hair in as you could see. I'm not going to be pretending I'm a human anymore."

"Good for you." Blap said sarcastically.

"Yeah, girls dig beards I found out. So, where are we going? The spaceport?"

"No. My house. But you're going to just drop me on the corner. I'm not telling you where I live. No one will know where I live."

Calasteel nodded, "I don't blame you. You're the G.P., Maximus, you're a big shot."

Doctor Macca told Zalez and Mal, "Nate is going to be discharged. The IV-robot gave him plenty of fluids but make sure he gets rest and drinks plenty of fluids."

"Thank you, doctor." Zalez shook Macca's slimy hand.

Mal picked up Nate's blue shirt and coughed. "It smells like vomit!"

"I threw up a few times, mother."

Macca went into Southington's room and told her and Gillian, "You're free to be discharged, Governor. I wouldn't travel today to Launderington. Is there a place you can go to rest and drink fluids?"

"I'll see." Southington said.

Gillian replied, "Yerkal lives on this planet. We can ask him and Noj."

Yerkal and Noj sat in the waiting area in the lobby as Doctor Macca walked back in. He looked around for Blaphaus but he wasn't there.

"Where is the Toob G.P.?" Macca asked the Peezle's.

They looked around and saw he was gone.

"He must've left." Yerkal said, "When we were talking."

"He slipped out." Noj said.

"How can something that big just slip out?" Macca asked.

The Belhopsa's and the two Governor's walked into the lobby and Gillian said, "Where did the G.P. go?"

Yerkal stood up, "He left."

"Well, where would he go?" Southington asked.

"His house probably." Zalez said, "Wherever that is."

"Well, I hope he comes back." Gillian said

"Well, if he does I want to check him out. He's unique." Macca said and walked out the lobby down the hallway.

"Yerkal, I'm not supposed to fly anywhere today. Can we stay at your place?" Southington asked.

Yerkal glanced at Noj, they didn't live on Ceilingida, they lived on Launderington, but obviously couldn't say that.

Mal knew their secret and replied, "Our house is bigger. You're welcome to stay at our place for the night, Governor."

"Thank you. Gillian, are you going back to Launderington?"

"No, I'll go with you tomorrow."

"You can stay at our place as well." Mal said.

Peezle went over to the robot receptionist and asked her, "Do you know where the G.P. went?"

"For security purposes I can't tell you." the robot receptionist replied. "He is the Galactic President after all."

"I know." Peezle said sighing.

Zalez said, "Mal, I'll take Nate home if you want to go pick up Romana from the dance school."

"No. You pick up Romana. I'm not letting Nate out of my sight again unless he's in school."

"It'll be nice to know how the trip to Mesas is going." Zucaritas remarked at the House meeting room on Launderington

"I'm sure they are okay." Jaboney said.

Thaw looking worried, but trying so hard to hide it added, "I say we all go home. It's getting late. I'm sure we'll find out tomorrow."

They all nodded and started to stand up.

"Thaw, are you worried about something?" Lluhdor asked.

"Me? Ummm... no. Nothing." Thaw replied, "Everything is fine."

The next day the yellow shuttle flew to Launderington's spaceport straight from the hospital. On the ship was the pilot and Gillian, Southington, Yerkal and Peezle. They had a good night at the Belhopsa's house, where everyone slept good. Romana thought it was so much fun to have everyone there, and was so glad to see Nate was okay, and her father. Nate wanted to go with the Governor's, he wished he was still Governor. Maybe one day.

"So, how are we going to explain that Maximus is missing?" Gillian asked.

"Are they going to be mad?" Yerkal asked.

"I don't know about mad..." Southington said, "Actually Zucaritas might be mad."

"It'll be okay." Gillian said. "I don't think Blaphaus is missing for good."

The Cabinet sat at their places at the long table. The only ones that weren't there was Southington, Gillian and Yerkal.

"Where are the others?" Zucaritas asked.

Dawber replied, "They are on their way. Southington contacted me earlier."

Bodie, the Canis Governor looked around the room with a patch over his missing eye.

"Is this how it always works?" he asked.

"Not usually." Noam remarked from across the table. "But these are different times. We have a different kind of G.P. now."

"I mean the patch."

"Yeah, you look great, Bodie." Jaboney smiled.

Just then Southington, Gillian and Yerkal walked into the room. Gillian and Yerkal took their places and Southington stood at the end of the table.

"Where is Maximus?" Zucaritas asked.

"Ceilingida... I think." she replied.

"You think?" Eastora asked. "Where would he be?"

"It's a long story. I will start by saying the trip to Mesas was a success... we have a Governor from there now. It's Planet Mayor Rüppell. He's all gung-ho. Canis is the only planet right now that has a Governor and a Planet Mayor."

"That's good." Zeb said, "Is Rüppell coming here?"

"I need to contact him and let him know, but yes, he will."

"So, why is the G.P. on Ceilingida?" Jaboney asked. "Shouldn't he be here?" Jaboney wanted to be Galactic President and if the Toob was missing he had a chance.

"I got really sick on Mesas, as did Nate Belhopsa. The heat on that planet is not good... for most humans. Luckily Yerkal here was okay with the heat, enough to stay with me in the shuttle to make sure I was okay."

Yerkal said, "The others went to meet Rüppell."

"Wait. The boy was there?" Zeb asked.

"And his father." explained Gillian.

"That's not good the boy got sick, or you Southington, but the boy is a civilian."

"He's good now, we stayed over night at the Belhopsa's."

"You didn't stay at Governor Yerkal's house?" asked Lluhdor.

"They offered first." Yerkal replied quickly.

"So, we went to Ceilingida to get liquids at the hospital, and then somehow Maximus left."

"Left the hospital?" Zeb asked.

"Yes, but he lives on that planet so probably went to his house."

"We need to know where he lives." Zucaritas remarked. "He's not going to stay there forever."

"Send the GBI." told Jaboney.

"Not yet." Zucaritas said.

"We can try to holo-call him." Thaw said.

"We tried this morning." Gillian said, "But no luck."

"This is not good." Zucaritas said, "We can't let the press know."

"He might gab to the press." Noam said. "I had a feeling this would happen."

"Contact Rüppell at least." Zucaritas said. "Have him come here. We will wait and see what happens with Maximus."

"What planet is next on the list?" Jaboney asked. "I can go there and try to get the planet to join if we can't get in touch with the Toob."

At the Belhopsa house the door buzzer buzzed and Ten opened the door to see Blaphaus standing there.

"Oh. Hello, Galactic President. There's no one here."

"Where are they?"

"I don't know."

"Wot are you doing here? You killed their robot."

"I belong to the Belhopsa family right now."

"And you don't know where they are?"

"No."

"Wotever." Blap turned to go.

"Galactic President."

Blaphaus stopped and turned around.

"Want me to give them a message?"

"Tell then I hope the boy is okay. And I'm sorry. And it's good you are not a shorty anymore…"

Peezle laid in bed wishing Yerkal was next to him. It was weird for him now that Yerkal was a Governor, and working with the Cabinet and Peezle was not welcome to be by them. He thought it was nice to see Southington and Gillian again, even though it was brief. They were the some of the ones that were nice to him. Most of them didn't understand why Traf needed an Assistant. He was glad that he wasn't Blaphaus' Assistant. Just then a holo-call of Yerkal appeared full size in the bedroom.
"Yerkal! How are you?"
"You didn't hear from the G.P., did you?"
"No. He would not reach out to me."
"He's still missing. Who do you know on Ceilingida that can find him?"
"Hmm… Ten might be able to. Or I can ask Zalez. We already went through this before looking for him."
"Well, we need to find him quickly."
"Okay, I'll see what I could do."

Blaphaus drove his vehicle not knowing what he should do, and he hated that feeling. He always knew what to do. He tried to remember how many planets were on the list. Not many, which meant that Tooberosum was coming up. Blaphaus thought he could go somewhere, and hide but knew they might find him, no matter what he did. He had one way to hide but vowed he wouldn't do that, no matter what. He sighed and cursed under his breath. He decided to just drive to the spaceport and fly to Launderington, but he wasn't going to pay for it. Where was Zalez? He was Blaphaus' main acquaintance on that planet, or any planet. He knew one place that he could try and find him or who can contact him… the bloody dance school with the annoying music.

"Helllloooo!" the new Governor Rüppell said to Gillian's holo-call as he sat playing stabber on Mesas. "How are you?"
"Hello, Governor Rüppell…"
"I like the sound of that. Governor…"
"Good. Are you able to come to Launderington and the House?"
"Sure! That should be easy!"
"Good. The Cabinet is looking forward to meeting you."
"Ditto, love. I'll see you soon."
The holo-call ended and he stood up and said out loud, "Drinks are on me!"

****

Blaphaus was half disappointed his holo-image wasn't on the roof of the dance school. But the annoying music was still playing as he walked in. The women stopped dancing and turned to see Blaphaus standing there. None of the women was Mal but the fat one named Fadonna was there.

"Galactic President, sir! How are you?" Fadonna asked. "Ladies, look who is here!"

"I see." one of them said, crossing her arms.

"Where is Belhopsa?" he demanded.

"She doesn't work here today. It's Starday and on Starday she doesn't work, just during the week."

"You know how to contact her?" he asked.

"Yeah, I could."

"Then do it."

"Why is the G.P. asking about Mal?" a woman whispered.

"Maybe she's having an affair with him."

"Nooo. That would never happen. Look at him, he's ugly and has no legs."

"And his body and head just are one big thing."

Fadonna held her hand info-pad and Mal's twelve inch holo-call appeared wearing a pink bikini. Blap stared at her from behind.

"Fadonna, what's up?" Mal asked.

"There's someone here that wants to talk to you."

Fadonna turned the info-pad around so "Mal" can face Blaphaus.

"What on this planet? What are you doing, Blaphaus?"

"Hello. I know you're not my biggest fan all of a sudden, and I really have no idea why. But I want to know how your boy is doing."

"He's fine. No thanks to you."

"It's not my fault he was hanging out with his father. Where is Zalez anyway?"

"We are trying to have a family day. He's here."

"I need to talk to him."

Zalez's holo-call appeared next to Mal's. He was naked, except for a bathing suit. His black hair all over his body was wet somehow.

"Blaphaus, what are you doing? You left the hospital yesterday..."

"Yep. To go home. I hate this, but I should go to Launderington."

"Then go."

"But I need a shuttle. Is there a Dook shuttle I could use?"

"You're asking for help?" Zalez asked, "That's not like you."

"Yeah, well, I have other planets I need to go to, right?"

"Okay, I'll send a shuttle for you. Head to the spaceport."

"Good."

"You're welcome, Blaphaus."

"Hmph. Thank you, Belhopsa."

"Mother, father, you do like G.P. Blaphaus?" Nate asked sitting on the pools steps.

"Of course they do." Romana said before she jumped into the pool.

Mal and Zalez both were lounging on the long poolside chairs. One of the best things about Ceilingida were the resorts, and the one they were at, the The Grand Ceilingida Resort was one of the nicest. A lot better than the Nights Inn down the road, or the Hotel Ate.

"We do, but him coming into our life's changed so much." Zalez said.

"I used to like him." Mal replied. "Now I'm getting to know him..."

"He is nice, and I don't think he has a lot of friends." Romana said from the pool.

"There's a reason for that." Zalez remarked. "But we're his friends."

"I think there's other reasons he doesn't have friends." Nate asked. "But I'm not saying why yet."

"Well, you are wise, Nate." Mal commented.

"I do have a favor to ask." Nate said.

"Sure, Nate." Zalez replied.

"When it's time for Mr. Blaphaus to go back to Tooberosum I want to go."

His parents said at the same time, "Okay."

"We'll see."

Peezle walked through the spaceport, going right near the spot in the concourse where Traf fell which seemed like such a long ago now, but in reality wasn't.

"You could have caught him, you know."

Peezle looked up to see Blaphaus standing there, with the robot-cams hovering not far.

"There has to be a better way to travel than have those annoying things buzzing around." he remarked.

"What are you doing here, Blaphaus?"

"That's G.P. Blaphaus to you. Wot are you doing here? Isn't your husband Governor at work?"

"Yes, I'm here looking for you actually. The Cabinet is worried..."

"Yeah, yeah, they probably thought I went AWOL. I did think about it. I'm heading to Launderington now, the Chordattian arranged for a Dook shuttle to take me. You're welcome to come."

"That would be at Gate A I think... yeah, I'll come with you."

"Terrific. Want to be my Assistant?"

Peezle said, "Ummm... really?"

"Yep. For now. Don't get too excited, Peezle, things are going to change real soon."

CHAPTER 15

Rubyspears stood inside the spaceport on Launderington waiting for his pick-up. He stood up straight when he saw the G.P. and Peezle approach him.

"The Toob... I mean Galactic President. I wasn't expecting you."

"Surprise." Blaphaus said sarcastically.

"I thought I was just going to be picking up you, Mr. Peezle."

"Well, there's a reason I might not tell you I was with the G.P."

"True. Follow me, the limo is out here." Rubyspears led them off. "So, I haven't seen you since the funeral. You're been having an exciting life, right?"

"Exciting? I wouldn't say that." Blap replied.

They went outside and over to the waiting limousine vehicle.

"So, I take it you're going to the House?"

"Yep."

"How do you go into it? There's steps..."

"I haven't seen inside yet." Blaphaus said, "And probably never will."

"They just need to built a lift next to the steps. You go in, it lifts you, you go right inside. Easy." Rubyspears pointed out.

Zucaritas rushed down the steps of the House just as Blaphaus and Peezle got out the vehicle.

"Maximus! Where have you been?"

"I don't have to be here all the time, Cyrakuse."

"You went to Mesas, and then went to a hospital on Ceilingida without getting in touch with us. Then you disappeared."

"I went home."

Zucaritas noticed Peezle standing by the vehicle.

"Why is he with you?"

"He is my Assistant." Blaphaus said, "You can thank him, he's the reason I'm here." he lied.

Peezle wanted to correct him but didn't.

"Well, you can't just disappear and not tell anyone."

"Yes. I. Can."

"Don't make us put security on you 24 hours a day, Maximus, because we can."

"Yeah. Yeah. So, where are the other fools? Inside I'm guessing."

"Yes, and the Mesas Governor is on his way."

"Great."

Peezle went up the steps to the front door of the House.

"Where are you going?" Zucaritas asked.

"To see my husband."

"You're not allowed in there..."

"He's my Assistant, yes he can." Blap said. "Are we meeting at the hotel or wot?"

Zucaritas signed, "I guess so."

A few minutes later he walked into the meeting room followed by Peezle to everyone's amazement, especially Yerkal's.

"Noj!"

"Call me Peezle."

"Everyone knows he's your husband." Zeb remarked.

"I'm Blaphaus' new Assistant." Peezle told them.

"Where is the G.P.?" Southington asked.

"He's outside." Peezle replied, "You can thank me for bringing him to Launderington."

"We really need to figure out a way to get him to come in here." Zeb said.

"So, what's the plan?" Jaboney asked.

"We need to tell him where we are going to next." Dawber told them.

Outside the Ultra vehicle pulled up and Blap and Zucaritas watched Rüppell get out of it.

"Hey, Blaphaus, G.P. Toob! Why are you standing out here?"

"See how I look? See those twenty something bloody steps?"

"Oh, yeah, you're the no legged species. I feel for you. I'll tell the others you are here, unless you told them." he smiled at the Cyrakuse.

"They should know. I'm Goveror Zucaritas from Cyrakuse."

"Rüppell from Mesas. Nice to meet you."

He went up the stairs and went inside to get scanned by the House robot.

"Governor Rüppell, welcome." she said.

"A robot? Nice! We don't have those on Mesas. The heat shuts them down."

"I'll let the others know you're here, Governor Rüppell."

"Great. The G.P. is outside by the way."

Peezle walked down the steps with Yerkal, holding his hand.

"Wot are you two doing?" Blap asked.

"Blaphaus, Uridae is your next planet." Peezle said. "Who do you want to go with you?"

"I know nothing about that planet. It better not be hot."

"It's a little colder as it's far from the sun. The species there are the Uridae. They are very friendly."

"Then they won't like me. Don't you have a white Uridae on the Cabinet?"

"No, he's a Bipolarab from Ankerage. The Bipolar are related to the Uridae though." Zucaritas said.

"Okay. The Bipolarab, Thaw and Southington will go." Blaphaus told them.

"Southington still doesn't feel great from Mesas." Yerkal said.

"What about the Gink? Or the Pilosa. He's quite, and doesn't speak. Best species ever."

"I'll let Governor Waydo know." Peezle said, "And Governor Thaw and Governor Kaktovic."

Blap smirked, "And if you two can stop holding hands, Peezle, you're coming too."

"Which Peezle?" Yerkal asked.

Later on, the yellow shuttle approached the green planet Uridae which seemed to have a lot of lakes. The spaceport was tucked in between a lot of trees and lakes with a big city outside the forest. The G.P. walked through the spaceport followed by Peezle, Thaw, Kaktovic and the slow walking Pilosa. GNN robot-cams hovered nearby watching them. They saw a tall black furred Uridae standing with the letters hovering above him that said, "Welcome Great Galactic President Blaphouse Maxipad."

"They spelt my bloody name wrong." Blaphaus snorted.

"It's okay."

"The Uridae are not the smartest in the bunch." Kaktovic remarked. He went over to the black Uridae.

"Hello, I'm Governor Kaktovic. I'm with the Galactic President."

The Uridae looked at Blap. "That's the oddest species I have ever met... or seen. Hello, I'm Kennedy, I will be your driver to the Planet Mayor. I'm glad you didn't bring all fifteen Governor's here. I don't have room in my vehicle."

"There's actually eighteen now." Thaw said.

"That's a lot. Follow me." Kennedy led them through the spaceport.

"So, Galactic Blaphaus and a few of the Governors went to Uridae to meet with the Planet Mayor there. So far the G.P. has had great success with getting the planets to join the Cabinet. The Uridae should be a synch. Buterdau Kooper, GNN."

The Planet Mayor's headquarters was a large brownstone looking building, with three steps up to it. Blaphaus, standing in the vehicle looked out the window to see the steps of the building.

"Great. Bloody steps." he said under his breath.

Kaktovic chuckled, "You know I can just pick you up for those steps. Look at my muscles." he showed his arm muscles.

They got out the vehicle and before Blap could say anything along the lines of "don't touch me," Kaktovic grabbed him from behind and lifted him off his feet.

"Hmmm. You're not as heavy as you look."

"Don't ever touch me again." Blap snapped at Kaktovic after he was put down.

Kennedy led them inside and a brown Uridae approached them.

"Hello, you must be the Galactic President. It's an honor to have you here, with your family."

"They are not family. Trust me."

"No, two of them are more like our family." the Uridae said, "I'm Theodore. Follow me."

He led Blap and the Governors down the hallway to a room that didn't have a door. The room was round and almost seemed like a cave design. Behind a desk a Uridae slept, the black and ginger face laying on the desk asleep and snoring. This ones fur was almost had a reddish hull.

"He sleeps a lot." whispered Theodore. He crept up next to the sleeping one and whispered into his ear.

"Planet Mayor, you have company."

The sleeping Uridae did not even flinch or move or stir.

"Well, if he can't be bothered to wake we'll be going." Blap said.

"No, he'll wake up." Kaktovic replied. "Right, Theodore?"

Theodore nodded and tried again.

"Planet Mayor, you have company... very important company."

Nothing. The sleeping Uridae still snored.

Thaw asked, "Is the Planet Mayor always like this?"

"Yep," nodded Theodore. "I will try again. Planet Mayor, can you wake up? You're embarrassing us."

Still nothing.

Peezle asked Blap, "What do you want to do?"

"Leave. I can't take the bloody snoring anymore. Uridae, once you lot get your feces together let me know." he turned his leave the room. The Pilosa walked over to the desk and slammed his fist down hard and loud on it. The sleeping Uridae woke up suddenly and looked up.

"What happened?"

The Pilosa said in a quiet and smooth voice, "Hello, Planet Mayor, I'm Governor Waydo from Hittittippi, and I'm here with the Galactic President Blaphaus Maximus. You were expecting him, I believe."

The now awake Uridae stared at Waydo. "You're a Pilosa. Hello, cousin. My best friend is a Pilosa."

"That's great. I'd like you to meet the G.P. though."

The Planet Mayor looked up to see the others in his office, and looked at Kaktovic.

"You're a Bipolarab... hello, cousin."

Kaktovic nodded, "Greetings, Planet Mayor."

"You're a human?" the Uridae asked Peezle.

He nodded, "Yes, sir."

"Which planet do you govern?"

"I don't. I'm the G.P.'s Assistant."

"Hmmm. You assist how?"

"Don't know really."

Blap said, "He was Traf's Assistant... I hope I don't die on his watch."

The Uridae stood up and asked around the desk and shook Blap's hand.

"It's a pleasure to meet you. What brings you to Uridae?"

Theodore said, "Sir, you should introduce yourself."

"Oh, yes, of course. I am Tremar. I'm the Planet Mayor. What species are you?"

"Tooberosum." Blaphaus replied. "You heard of us?"

Tremar shook his head. "Nope. Well, I think your kind was mentioned in a children's nursery rhyme. I think,"

"I don't think so." Blaphaus replied.

"Yeah, I could be wrong, but it'll come to me." Tremar shrugged.

"So, do you know who would make a good Governor?" asked Kaktovic.

"Governor? We are not part of the Cabinet."

"No feces. The deal is they want this planet to be a part of it." Blap said, "That's why we are here."

"For hundred of years we were our own planet, not part of any group of planets."

"That could change." Kaktovic remarked.

"Why? There's no point." Tremar shrugged.

"You know wot, I totally agree." Blap said. "We don't need this planet to be part of the Cabinet anyway." Blap mentioned.

"Wait, would this planet be the only one not part of the Cabinet? I don't want to feel left out."

"This one, Cakerlak and Tooberosum." Blap remarked.

"Why not those other two?"

"One planets species tried to kill me and the other is my planet and there's no chance they'll play along." Blap said.

"What is the perk of being a part of the Cabinet?"

"Beats me." Blaphaus remarked,

Waydo said, "The galaxy would be so much better if all the planets were united."

"In case there's an invasion." Thaw added.

Everyone looked at the Leetric.

"Invasion? That's not going to happen." Kaktovic said.

"Yeah, who would waste their time invading this galaxy?" Blap asked .

Thaw glared at Blap.

"Okay. I'll find a Governor for you." Tremar said.

"Not you?" Kaktovic asked.

"We don't need someone who just sleeps all day." Blap said. "We have a few Governor's that don't do anything already."

"I have someone in mind." thought Tremar. "But you have to take a train to meet him."

"Sure." Kaktovic nodded. "Just tell us where."

"I'll take you to him. Theodore, you will come with us."

Theodore nodded, "Okay. But I'd make a good Governor as well."

Blap realized he didn't like trains. He already rode a train with Jaboney and now he was on another train with the Governors, Peezle and two annoying Uridae. Tremar was again sleeping and snoring. The train pulled into a station and Theodore nudged Tremar.

"Planet Mayor Tremar, we are here."

Again Tremar did not stir or do anything.

Blap said, "Pilosa, wake his arse up." He walked off the train as Peezle and Thaw followed him.

Thaw turned to Kaktovic and took him by the arm. "I have a question." he whispered. "When you lifted Blaphaus up the steps you said he wasn't as heavy as he looks. What did you mean?"

"He just felt lighter. Almost hollow, but not quite. It's hard to explain."

"We need some blood work from him." Thaw commented.

"Thaw, you're paranoid." Kaktovic chuckled.

"We are here." Tremar said walking off the train with Theodore. The town they were in was a very crowded area, with stands selling all kinds of goods, and food. There were decorations as well, lanterns dangling above, hitting Blap in the head as he couldn't bend down. Kaktovic was able to bend down with no problem.

"The one you recommend for Governor is here?" he asked.

"Yes, he lives over there." Tremar pointed.

Blap said to Peezle, "I hate crowds."

"Every Uridae here is black and white, and none of them are paying attention to us." Peezle remarked.

"Good." Blap muttered.

They went into a very fancy and decorated building with a low ceiling that Blaphaus barely fit in. Inside the house smelt of burning incense and Blap tried his hardest not to gag. The black and white Uridae looked up, wearing his silky red robes and straw pointed hat.

"Planet Mayor." he gave Tremar a hug. "How are you?"

"I'm good. Look who I'm with." he motioned to Blaphaus and the Governors.

"Not Uridae that's for sure. What's going on?"

"This is Galactic President..." he frowned, "Maxipad, right?"

"Blaphaus Maximus." told Thaw. "He's a Tooberosum."

"Tooberosum?" the black and white Uridae asked. "Those were told in stories
and nursery rhymes. Species of legend."

"I knew it!" Tremar exclaimed. "I told you! Galactic President, this is Penya, my
oldest friend."

"We are here to ask you something." Kaktovic commented. "The G.P. has a
question for you."

"No I don't." Blaphaus said, "Except for how can you put up with that smell?"

"Ask him." Thaw said.

""How do you stand that smell?"

"No, he wants you to be Governor of this planet." told Thaw.

"Governor? I want to be Emperor." Pinya smiled.

"Call it what you want." Blap said.

"Do you want to Uridae to be part of the Cabinet?" Penya asked. "Is it hard
work being Governor?"

"It's hardly any work." Blap said.

"And I could be Emperor?"

"Sure. Wotever."

"Then yes, we'll make it official." told Penya.

"Fantastic." Tremar smiled.

Blap said, "Good, I'm going outside, I can't stand this smell anymore."

He went outside and Peezle followed.

Thaw's holo-call appeared on the table in the meeting room at the House.

"I'm going to contact Buterdau so he can report this but it's official, we have
another new Governor and Uridae is part of the Cabinet now."

"Terrific!" Zucaritas smiled.

Noam sat on the table and said, "Don't come back here, go to Phytnes right
away. Take the new Governor with you, it might be easier to convince that Planet
Mayor that way." he said.

"What about Blaphaus' policy of one planet a day?"

"He'll live." Zeb said. "We are so close to the end."

Thaw nodded, "I'll tell him."

Thaw said to Penya, "Gov..."

"Emperor. Call me Emperor."

"Okay... Emperor. We are going to Phytnes right away. Can you come with us?"

"Yes, as Emperor I'll be glad to."

They went outside where the others waited.

"We are going straight to the next planet." Thaw told them.

"Not me." Blaphaus said. "One planet a day, remember? And today I hit my quota by going to this planet and Launderington."

"The Cabinet said it's best we go now. We are taking Penya with us."

"That's good." Kaktovic said. "Get it over with. Then only two more to go."

"This is the last one. I'm not going to the other two." Blap said.

"If we go to Phytnes now it'll save a lot of time." Kaktovic explained.

"Fine. We'll go to the next planet now. Then I'm going to Ceilingida. There's something I want to do tomorrow there."

"Deal." smiled Thaw.

"Let's get to the train." Tremar said, "I need a nap."

In the Cabinet meeting room, none of them could believe it. This was a long time coming, and they had Tostone to thank. It was his idea for the Toob to be G.P. and even though Blaphaus wasn't really doing anything, it was the perception that he was.

Eastora leaned forward and said, "We need to thank Tostone for this. His whole plan is working."

"Not yet." Zucaritas replied, "Not until the last three are set."

Jaboney said, "How are you going to handle the Cakerlak situation and get the Toob to his planet?"

"I think we will offer a Cakerlak to come here. I have an idea about Tooberosum,"

"We need to know why the Cakerlak tried to assassinate Blaphaus. I can go to where he's locked up and find out." Yerkal said.

"Good idea." Jaboney said.

"Want anybody to go with you?" Dawber asked.

"No, I'll be good."

"Word from the Cabinet on Launderington is that there's now another new Governor from Uridae. Galactic President Maximus and some Governors are now heading to Phytnes. Then just two more planets to go too. Buterdau Kooper, GNN."

As they made their way through the spaceport hours later on Phytnes Thaw watched Blaphaus' every move. There was still something about him that didn't add up.

Kaktovic said, "Apparently we have to get our own ride to the Planet Mayor's mansion."

"Does he know who I am?"

"Yes, and a member of his staff said that the Planet Mayor doesn't care."

Penya said, "There is sure a mix of species on this planet."

A brown Uridae walked by and waved and Peezle was the only one that waved back.

A Canis walked up, all black and tan and shaggy looking.

"Mr. G.P., sir, can I have your autograph?"

"What is your name, Canis?" Kaktovic asked.

"Griffin. I'ma huge fan, well done getting Bodie to be Governor."

"I don't do autographs."

"How about an holo-image with you then?"

"No." Blap said.

"He's a little touchy today, Griffin. Maybe next time."

"Fine. I get it. He's busy."

They all walked off leaving Griffin standing there shouting, "I love you, Blaphaus Maximus!"

Kaktovic said, "Can you believe that? You have a fan." he chuckled.

They went outside and Blaphaus noticed the weather was warm and pretty humid. He liked that a lot better than Ceilingida's weather. Peezle pointed to a bus vehicle and remarked.

"That's the vehicle we'll be using."

They went over to it and Blap noticed there was a step up to get into it.

"I'm not going."

"I'll pick you up again." Kaktovic said.

"You're not touching me again."

"Why don't you want to be picked up?" Thaw asked, "Or touched?"

"Because I don't like being touched."

The driver of the vehicle had no legs and arms, and was one long skinny body with scales. His body was wrapped tightly around the throttle that drove the vehicle.

"What are you? You have no legsss but ssskinny armsss." the driver hissed.

"He's a Tooberosum." Kaktovic explained.

"Yeessss, I feel bad for you. I'm a Sssquamata. And don't say what'sss the 'sssquamatta' with me. I hear that ssshite all day long. Watch thisss."

The vehicle lowered so Blap could just walk straight in.

"If only the House could go that." Peezle chuckled.

The Planet Mayor's mansion was huge, sitting on the edge of a cliff that over looked a huge ocean. Most of Phytnes was an ocean, with islands here and there. It was one of the most good looking beautiful planet out of the twenty-three. The entourage was met at the door by a tall, fat black haired being with long curved horns. The black hair almost looked like a large fur coat, it was hard to see where his jacket and fur met.

"Hello. My name is Enitittuk. Welcome. You're the Galactic President I take it?"

"You're the P.M.?" Blap asked.

"Me? Heavens no, I'm just the Bovie butler."

"Well, is the Planet Mayor here?" asked Kaktovic.

"Yes, of course. He is by the pool, waiting for me to bring you."

He led them through the huge mansion out to the back where the swimming pool was. Sitting besides it where a large gray Pachyderm sat, eating with his large trunk on his face, flapping his huge flat ears, and licking his long tusks. A female Cyrakuse was laying on his lap. She was orange with black stripes, same as Zucaritas.

"Welcome, Galactic President. You're a Toob, I see." the Pachyderm remarked. "My name is Haathee, I'm the Planet Mayor on this planet. You're doing a grand job as G.P. so GNN says."

"Then if GNN says then it's true." Blap remarked.

"Really? Hmmm. I actually get my news from my good friend Rüppell... Governor Rüppell now."

"You know Rüppell?" Thaw asked.

"Yes, he's been here, I've been to Mesas. I love the heat. How did you like it, Toob?"

"Like wot?"

"The Mesas heat."

"I hated it. It made a friend sick."

"And a Governor." Kaktovic remarked.

"That's too bad. Toob, how do you like water?"

"Wot?"

"Water? Do you like it?"

"Wot do you mean?"

Haathee nodded to the Cyrakuse female on his lap. She quickly got up and leapt at Blap knocking him backwards into the swimming pool. He quickly sunk to the bottom, with no bubbles coming out of his mouth. He hit the bottom of the deep end and just laid there on his back.

CHAPTER 16

"Blaphaus!!" Peezle cried, he wasn't prepared to see the second G.P. die in front of him.

The rest happened so fast, Thaw and Kaktovic both dove into the deep end and swam down to Blap who was drowning. They each grabbed a side of him and struggled to move him... now he was heavier than they thought. Kaktovic swam up and broke the surface of the water.

"We can't move him! We need help!"

Penya took off his silky robes and straw hat and wearing just his pants he jumped into the pool feet first. He struggled to swim down to the bottom but did so. He took Blap's head and helped them drag Blap up to the low end, the pool steps and finally laid Blap down on that concrete. The silver fob fell out of the inside pocket of Blap's jacket and Kaktovic discreetly grabbed it and tucked it into a pants pocket hoping no one saw. Thaw tried to give Blap mouth to mouth but he seemed not to breath. His arms started to shake and his fingers twitched. He then started to cough a lot, but his mouth hardly moved.

"Why would you do that?" Waydo asked.

"To see if he was real, to see if anybody cared about him. Guess three of you do."

"I can't swim." Waydo said. "Hoe would've dropped of it was he and I."

Thaw walked over to Haathee, giving the female Cyrakuse a dirty look.

"We came here in good faith offering you and your planet to be part of the Cabinet. Penya here just became Governor..."

"Emperor..."

"Governor. We have this planet and two planets to go. But with that little stunt Blaphaus is going to say forget it."

"If he lives." smirked Haathee.

"Why the bloody feces am I looking up at the sky? Will someone stand me up?!" cried out Blap.

Kordiak, Thaw and Penya helped Blap to his feet. He went right over to the female Cyrakuse and waved a green skinny finger at her face.

"You did this!"

He turned to Haathee and grabbed him by his truck, squeezing it hard. Haathee struggled, and tried to speak. "I can't breathe... let go off my truck..."

"You had her push me in the pool..."

"Maximus, let go of him." Thaw ordered.

"No. He's the second species that tried to assassinate me since I was made G.P. I'm over it. I didn't have this bad luck since I was back on my own bloody planet. All you planets should just go to war and wipe each other out."

"Let him go." Kaktovic ordered.

Blap signed and let Haathee go and turned to face them.

"Anybody going to call the GBI? Have them arrest him." Haathee said, rubbing his trunk.

"No, we are not going to do that." Thaw said.

"So, as G.P. he's just allowed to harm someone?"

"And they are allowed to just shove someone into a bloody pool before they know they could swim? The bloody GBI should be arresting them, like that Cakerlak was arrested."

Thaw said, "We are not going to call the GBI or the local bizzes or rozzer's."

Bizzies and rozzer's were the two types of police officers that were all over the galaxy.

"So, I'm open target. And it's okay? This job is ridiculous. Find your own Governors." Blap stormed to the mansion.

Peezle followed him, "Where are you going?"

"Bloody crazy. Leave me alone."

Peezle stopped walking and sighed. He knew being Blap's Assistant would be rough. He was done being involved with the Governors and politics.

Thaw asked Haathee, "Would you *want* to recommend a Governor? Be part of the Cabinet?"

"As long as he's G.P., no. Not interested." Haathee said, arms crossed.

"That's too bad." Kaktovic said. "This will be the only planet not part of the Cabinet."

"Well, that's too bad. But I doubt the Cakerlak will be part." Haathee remarked.

"That's to be determined." Thaw said.

Blap walked through the mansion followed by Enitittuk.

"Mr. Blaphaus, where are you going? Why are you treading water through the mansion? The Planet Mayor will be mad."

"I don't care. His girlfriend was the one that pushed me into the bloody pool."

"Where are you going?"

Blaphaus walked outside as a long purple vehicle drove up and a Cyrakuse that looked liked Zucaritas a little, and the one that pushed him into the pool, got out, wearing a purple suit. Either side of him were two Cakerlak. They were different than the one that tried to kill him. They were black with two legs and six arms and wore coats and hats, and blasters.

"Oh, great." Blap muttered.

"Who are you?" the Cyrakuse asked.

"You don't know? Don't you watch GNN?"

"I'm too busy for that... as Planet Mayor..."

"Planet Mayor? Planet Major for wot planet?"

"Cakerlak. And you are irritated I don't know who you are."

"Wait. A Cyrakuse is not Planet Mayor for Cakerlak?"

The other Governors and Peezle walked out the front door behind Blaphaus.

"Would you trust a Cakerlak to be in charge of anything, let alone the Planet Major? Again, what are you doing and dripping wet?"

Thaw stepped forward, "He's Galactic President Maximus, I'm Governor Thaw, this is Governor Kaktovic, Governor Waydo and Governor Penya..."

"Emperor." the Uridae said.

"I'm Governor Lana Joorg, and again why are you here?"

"We are here to meet the Planet Mayor for Phytnes." Kakerlak explained.

"I think your wife is here." Peezle said.

"Why would she be here?" Joorg asked.

"I don't know, but she shoved me into the pool." Blaphaus said.

"I don't think she's..." he noticed three of the others were wet as well. "Did you all go swimming in the pool fully clothed? Enitittuk?!"

Enitittuk stepped out and went over to Joorg. "Yes, sir?"

"What's going on? Where's my wife? Is she here?"

"Umm."

Joorg said, "I'll find out myself."

He stormed off past Blap's entourage and went through the mansion to the outside pool area where Haathee sat by himself.

"Planet Mayor Haathee..."

"Why, hello, Joorg, you're early." Haathee said.

"I'm always early. Have you seen my wife?"

"Your wife? No, Joorg, why would she be here?" Haathee lied.

"That's what I thought. Why are a bunch of wet species here?"

"They offered me Governor and wondered if Phytnes would want to join the Cabinet."

"And you said?"

"I said no. I don't like the G.P."

"Hmmm. Do you think they'll ask me?"

Inside the door way that led outside Thaw said to Blap, "Go out there and convince them to both be in the Cabinet."

"I'm not going anywhere near that pool, or that female Cyrakuse."

Kaktovic said, "She's gone, her husband is here. If you convince them both you want have to go to Cakerlak. You'll just have one planet left."

"Actually, zero left. I'm not going to Tooberosum."

"Then this would be the last of the 'tour.'" Thaw said.

"Hmph." Blap walked back outside, staying away from the pool.

"Hey! You two!"

"I thought you left." Haathee remarked. "Or are you back to attack me again?"

The two Cakerlak pointed their weapons at Blap.

"Calm down, or I'll tell the fancy Cyrakuse here your secret."

"What do you want?" Haathee asked.

"I don't want anything. But the Cabinet wants you to join them. Both of you and your planets. You'll be Governors, not useless Planet Mayors."

"Is Tooberosum going to be part of the Cabinet?" asked Haathee.

"The Cakerlak do not like to be part of anything." Joorg remarked.

"Meanwhile one of them ruined a nice peaceful day on Launderington trying to kill me. And you're not a Cakerlak. It's your call, wot do you say?"

"Are you going to Cakerlak?"

"Never."

"Then I will go back there and announce that I'll be their Governor."

"Terrific. And you, Haathee?"

"If Joorg says he agrees then I agree, and we'll forget what happened here, right?" he winked.

"Yeah. Wotever." Blap turned to the others. "I'm officially done. Now send me home. My job here is done."

The Cakerlak who tried to assassinate Blaphaus sat in the interrogation room on Launderington that had a one way window. Yerkal walked in and sat at the table across from him.

"Hello, I'm Governor Yerkal Peezle, and I'm also a Solicitor on this planet. How are you?"

"What planet are you Governor of?"

"Ceilingida."

"But you're here? Is that legal, Governor?"

"As Solicitor... not Governor. I'm not here to talk about myself, I'm here to talk about you. What's your name?"

"I don't have to tell you my name."

"No, but it'll make life so much easier for you."

"Neop."

'So, Mister Neop, you do know that trying to assassinate the Galactic President could put you in prison for life, right?"

"Really." Neop scoffed.

"Yes, really. You did it in the middle of the day and live on GNN..."

"All I did was shout out at the Toob. I never pulled my weapon, or fired it. So technically I didn't try to assassinate him... or anyone."

"Okay, but why would you even call out to him or even think about murdering him? He hasn't been Galactic President for long. What did he do?"

"Him? He did nothing personally. But the Toobs and the Order of Blattodea have been enemies for years."

"The Tooberosum's?"

"Yes, those no legged freaks..."

"Who are the Order of Blattodea?" Yerkal asked.

"Ooohh... the Order was here a long time ago. Solicitor, I'm *not* the enemy, you can have every frigging planet in the galaxy all together but when times comes that won't mean a thing."

Yerkal sat back in his chair and felt a lump in his throat. He decided right then he did not want to be Governor anymore.

The holo-call of Thaw appeared in the meeting room of the Cabinet.

"Well, I have good news... it's a long story and we'll explain when we get back but Cakerlak is ninety percent done and Phytnes is one hundred percent done. It was touch and go, but it's all good. I'll let you know more when we get back."

"Glad to hear." Southington said. "Can't wait to hear the news. We'll meet again in the morning."

Thaw's holo-call disappeared and the Cabinet looked happy, but now they had to figure out the Tooberosum problem.

"So, all that's left is Tooberosum." Zucaritas remarked. "How do we convince Blaphaus to go there?"

"We don't." Eastora said, "We trick him. I have an idea but we are going to need help."

On the shuttle, Blaphaus said to Thaw, "I'm going to be dropped off on Ceilingida, right?"

Thaw nodded, "Yes. But we need you again tomorrow."

"Tomorrow morning I have plans. Something I need to do. And if you think I'm going to Tooberosum you have another thing coming."

"You have nothing to worry about, Blaphaus." Thaw smiled. "Promise you will go to Launderington tomorrow?"

"Yes. Wotever."

Thaw got up and went and sat next to Kaktovic and whispered, "So, Blaphaus was heavy when we tried to get him out the pool. Do you have an idea why?"

"I'm not a biology expert but maybe the Toobs get heavier when they are wet?"

"I don't know. Is that possible?"

"Anything is possible."

Yerkal went to the flat where he and Noj lived. He took off his jacket and tie, and went to the kitchen for an alcoholic beverage. He definitely was not going back to the House. He just had to convince Noj not to be Blaphaus' Assistant, and send his husband to the House to let them know to look for his successor.

On Cakerlak, the figure with the antenna walked into the dark room which had one light over the huge Cakerlak, who sat on a throne.

"Weta, I want to tell you that this planet now has a Governor and is now part of
the Cabinet, which is run by the Tooberosum. All planets are now art of the Cabinet… but one.'

"Good." the huge Caterlak said, "That should not be a problem. Everything will
go to plan, just stay quiet."

The figure in the dark nodded, "I understand."

Peezle walked into his flat and went into the kitchen to find Yerkal sitting on the
floor drunk.

"Yerkal? Are you all right?"

"Noj, I don't want to be Governor anymore. And I don't want you to be Assistant
to Blaphaus." blabbered Yerkal.

"Okay, but why not?"

"There's things that are way deeper than we want to know."

"So, are you going to tell the G.P. and Cabinet?"

"No. I don't want to talk to them. Can you tell them? Please?"

"Fine, I'll take care if it. I'm Blaphaus' Assistant anyway."

Kaktovic went into his office on Launderington and pulled out the silver fob
that fell out of Blap's jacket pocket. He pushed the button on the side of the device
and a holo-recording of Traf appeared but kept cutting in and out and saying a
word here and there.

"Hello… recording… predecessor… Cabinet chose wisely… Galaxy… will be
invaded… nothing's stopping… galaxy… seven planets… Tooberosum… anywhere… you… Creator… care."

He frowned wondering how Blaphaus got this and if he should tell anyone else
about it. Again there was word of invasion and Tooberosum. He decided this would
be his secret… for now.

The next day Blaphaus drove his vehicle on Ceilingida. After the pool fiasco
he realized that he really did have enough. It took awhile for him to be fully dry,
and he wondered what happened to the fob he had in the inside pocket of his
jacket. He would somehow find it, but he wasn't too worried about it. He had
something that he really wanted to do, and that definitely wasn't going to be anymore traveling after the trip to Launderington… and the other planet.

Meanwhile, at the House on Launderington, the Cabinet was showing up,
even the two latest Governors were, but the only one that wasn't there was Yerkal.

"Well, there's a lot of you." Joorg remarked. "It's like a smorgasbord of
species."

Zucaritas went over to him and the two Cyrakuse shook hands.

"Welcome to the Cabinet, fellow Cyrakuse. I see you are part of the Tigris sub-species like me."

"Yes, and my wife is as well. I'm a lot skinnier than you as well, my friend." he patted Zucaritas on the belly.

"I'm older than you probably. So, how did you get to be the Planet Mayor of Cakerlak?"

"Let's just say I walked into it. I'm glad to be Governor and part of the Cabinet now though."

"Good."

Haathee now was the biggest and tallest Governor and was afraid to sit in the chair. He loomed over Noam and said, "We might need a bigger room and table."

"We might need a bigger chair for you."

"Ha. I like you, little Smidge. I pooped bigger turds than you."

Noam muttered, "I don't know if that was a compliment or an insult."

"Are we all here?" Southington asked.

Governor Ace said, "The Ceilingida Governor is not here."

"Well, we are not going to wait for him." Thaw said, "Are we?"

Lluhdor replied, "I think we should."

"We can get started." Southington said.

"Where's the G.P.?" asked Joorg.

"Back on Ceilingida probably." Zeb replied. "This meeting we don't want him here."

Eastora said, "He couldn't climb the steps anyway."

"Joorg, you can have Yerkal's chair for now. Haathee, are you okay to stand?" Kaktovic asked.

"Sure. For now." he moaned.

"So, let me get this straight, we have to figure out a way to get Blaphaus to Tooberosum as he's not going to go there no matter how hard we ask." Jaboney commented.

"He's dead set on not going to anymore planets." Thaw said, "Thank the Creator that Joorg was on Phytnes."

"Heathee and I have a good trade relationship and are good friends. We like to visit each other's planets."

"Yesterday, Eastora, you said you had an idea but would need help." Southington remarked.

"Yes, who is Blaphaus close with?" Noam asked.

"He doesn't seem to be close to anybody. He's very standoffish." Bodie remarked.

"Even though he got us all together." Thaw said.

"We know he didn't do anything really." Dawber added.

Southington said, "He seems close with Zalez and the young boy Nate."

"Exactly. So, what if we use the boy as bait? And Zalez? What if we all plan a trip to Tooberosum but don't tell him."

"Not take him?" Zeb asked.

Noam added, "We'll take him, but he won't know until he gets there."

"We don't know if Tooberosum has a Planet Mayor, so who do we approach?" Zeb asked.

"They must have someone in charge, and running the planet." Joorg commented. "They can't run around willy-nilly, can they?"

"What about if they don't?" Jaboney asked.

"We'll cross that bridge when we come to it." Thaw said.

"How do we use Zalez or the boy?" Zeb asked.

"We invite them to Tooberosum on 'behalf' of Blaphaus. But don't tell him." explained Eastora.

"That's good, but isn't the point of getting the Toob to his planet?" Jaboney asked.

"Yes. Don't you think he'll come if the family is going?" Dawber asked.

"I don't think so." Thaw said. "Have you seen how stubborn he is?"

Rüppell said, "No one is that stubborn, everybody."

Most of them laughed.

"You didn't see how he grabbed my truck." Haathee remarked.

"He grabbed your trunk?" frowned Joorg.

"That's because he was shoved into the pool." told Waydo.

"What happened on Phytnes?" asked Zeb.

"Nothing. It's all fine." Thaw said. "I don't think using Zalez's family will work. We need another pawn."

"How about Peezle?" Dawber said.

"Which one?" Zeb asked.

"Noj, his Assistant. We can talk to Yerkal about it."

"Where is Yerkal anyway?" Lluhdor asked. "He's very late."

Yerkal sat in the living room in their flat, sat slumped in the couch, looking rough, shirt unbuttoned, hair a mess, bags under his eyes, and drinking from a bottle of wine. He knew what he had to do, and he knew he had to do it while his husband was at work. But first, he had to finish the bottle of wine.

Blaphaus meanwhile drove up to the school on Ceilingida and got out. He went up the ramp to the building and went inside to the main office. The two female receptionists were startled when they saw him.

"Ooohhh!!! You're the Toob G.P.! Welcome!"

"Is the principal here?" he asked.

"Yes, he's in his office."

"Good." Blaphaus said, making his way to the principals office down the hall-way.

"We need to let him know you're here first…" one of them called out to him.

"Too late." he barged into the office.

President Garcey jumped to his feet startled, "Galactic President Maximus! What a big surprise! I've been following your adventures in GNN. I'm so im-pressed…"

"I'm *depressed*. So, where are the Belhopsa ankle biters?"

"Do you have ankles?" Garcey asked seriously.

"Where are the kids?"

"In their classroom. Do their parents know you're here?"

"I doubt it. Did you open up the school for other species yet, or still just have humans?"

"Still just humans, Galactic President. We have to address it to the school board, there's a lot of red tape…"

"Just get it done. Now take me to their classroom."

"Sure, but can I ask why?"

"I need to tell them something before I go to Launderington."

"Sure, my friend. Follow me."

Ms. Beezlee was addressing the class, talking about maths.

"Okay, class, can you think of the integers for x, y, and z so that $x^3+y^3+z^3=8$?"

Nate raised his hand. "I can, Ms. Beezlee."

"I'm sure you can, Nate. Go ahead." she sighed.

"One answer is x equals 1, y equals -1, and z equals 2."

"That's good, Nate. But what about the integers for x, y, and z so that $x^3+y^3+z^3=42$?"

He chuckled, "Yeah but, Ms. Beezlee, x equals -80538738812075974, y equals 80435758145817515, and z equals 12602123297335631."

"You're a show off." Nog laughed behind him.

Ms. Beezlee said, "You're right, Nate. Class, that's the beauty of maths. There's always an answer for everything."

Just then the principal walked into the classroom with the Toob behind him. The kids looked so excited but not as much as Nog who has been biting at the bit to see and meet the Toob.

"Nate! Your friend is here!!"

"I know." Nate stood up. "Mister G.P. Blaphaus, what are you doing here?"

"Hello, boy." Blap said.

"Hi, Mister Blaphaus!" Romana ran over to him.

"Romana, sit down." Ms. Beezlee told her firmly.

The other children started getting up and going up to the Toob who backed up.

"Children, sit back at your desks." Garcey said. They all groaned and did so.

"It's an honor to meet you." Nog said, "I heard a lot about you."

"All good I hope."

"Oh, yes! Nate is so lucky."

"Not really. Have you met his mother?"

"Mr. Blaphaus!" snapped Nate, "That's not nice!"

"Wotever."

Ms. Beezlee said, "Let's see how good the Galactic President is at maths. So, do you know the integers for x, y, and z so that $x^3+y^3+z^3=8$, Galactic President?"

"Yeah, a bunch of bloody numbers. That feces is not going to help anybody in the future." he replied.

The class all giggled and laughed. Blap went over and stood in front of Nate's desk.

"So, boy, I want to thank you for everything wot you have done. I hope you're feeling better."

"I am, yes."

"So... you know I'm supposed to go back home, to my planet..."

"Forever?"

"No. Hell no..."

"Watch your language." Ms. Beezlee told him.

Blaphaus sighed, "Boy, I don't want to go to that planet, but I know I don't have a choice. Everything will change after that... and after that I doubt I'll be G.P., so I want you to be my successor."

Everyone in the classroom gasped, even Garcey and Beezlee.

"Nate, you're so lucky." Nog commented.

"I asked mother and father if I'll be able to go to Tooberosum and they said they'll think about it. I want to go with you."

Nog said, "I want to go as well."

"No." Blaphaus told him, "Kid, you might not like what you see. It's not wot you think."

"Mr. Blaphaus, I've been trying to do so much research on your planet and species and came up with nothing. Please let me go."

"Look... I said no. But when I go to Launderington I want you to come as well."

"Ummm, Galactic President, I don't think Nate's parents are going to approve..."

"We'll see." Blap interrupted Garcey.

"I would love to be Galactic President, sir, I'm just a child. I don't think I'll be a good Galactic President, I have school."

"Fine. You're right." he went to the door.

"Bye, Mr. Toob!" waved Nog.

"That's just not cool." Nate told Nog. "Show some respect. Where are you going, Mr. Blaphaus?"

"Launderington. Have a good life, kid, and your sister too." he walked out the classroom.

Nog said, "Did you see he did not even blink?"

"Okay, children, back to maths." Ms. Beezlee said.

"Have a good day, class." Garcey left the classroom and followed Blaphaus. "You're really going to resign?" he asked him.

"Probably. I don't know. I'm exhausted. I'm losing my mind." Blaphaus said.

On Launderington, Peezle made his way down the hallway to the Cabinet room which was now guarded by Joorg's bodyguard from Cakerlak. They recognized him and let him into the room.

"Peezle!" Southington exclaimed, "Where's your husband?"

"Hello, all, I'm here to tell you that Yerkal is resigning..."

"Resigning? Why?" Jaboney asked.

"This is insane. We are never going to be ahead." Zucaritas grumbled.

"I'm sorry about my husband. Something is worrying him but he won't say. I don't know what to say. Everything was so simple when Traf was G.P."

"I don't know why I agreed on being Governor." Jaboney said, "You beings can't get your feces together."

Thaw said, "We all know that Blaphaus does not want to be G.P., and wants to resign. Let's call his bluff. Let's invite him here and tell him as long as he picks the next G.P. he can resign. But... we will all be on the shuttle and that shuttle will go to Tooberosum."

Zucaritas nodded, "That's a great idea. Raise your hands if you all agree."

They all did so.

Peezle's holo-call appeared on Zalez's desk in his office on the Dook Energy space station.

"Noj, what's up?"

"The Cabinet is going to trick Blaphaus and take him to Tooberosum."

"Why?"

"Because they are not giving up. They want to see Tooberosum, and take Blaphaus with them. I don't know what to do."

"Let them know I want to go as well." Zalez said. "I'll head to Launderington."

Mal once again was back in Principal Garcey's office because of Blaphaus.

"Hello, Ms. Belhopsa, I'm sorry to have you back here so soon." they shook hands.

"What happened now? All these years I've never been called to come here until this last week or so."

"G.P. Maximus was here and wanted to speak to the children... mostly Nate.
You're not going to believe this but he offered Nate the Galactic President
position."

"He did what?!"

"Yeah, he, I'm afraid, Ms. Belhopsa, is losing his mind. I don't understand, but I
want you to know."

"I really appreciate it. I'm so fed up with this G.P. Why did Traf have to die?"

"I'm sorry. I did try to holo-call your husband but he apparently is on his way to
Launderington."

"What? Why?"

"I don't know. For work I'm sure."

Mal frowned, something was up. Something didn't make sense. Maybe Yerkal
could fill her in.

Blaphaus made his way through the spaceport, with the GNN robot-cams
once again hovering around him. He made his way to the Gate where the yellow
shuttle from Old Eboracum was waiting for him. He didn't know what was going to
happen but it wasn't what everyone thought. The Cabinet and he were going to be
in for a big surprise.

A little bit later he got out the Ultra vehicle in front of the House and looked up
at the steps.

"Hey! I'm out here!!" he yelled.

The House robot heard him and went through the glass doors and looked
down at him. She turned and went back in. Bloody robots, he thought. A few minutes later Peezle and Thaw walked out and went down the stairs.

"Blaphaus! You're here!" Thaw smiled.

"Where are we meeting?" Blap demanded.

"Where would you want to meet?" Thaw asked.

"I don't care. You all want to go to Tooberosum? Let's go. I want to get this over
with."

"What? You are wanting to go?"

"I never said that. I said let's go, this is what you lot want. Bring everybody. It'll
be a party."

Thaw glanced at Peezle, not believing it. Once again things were working out.

"I'll let them all know right away." Thaw said going up the steps.

"Zalez is on his way here. He's going to want to come." Peezle told him.

"Good. More the merrier."

"I have something else to tell you, Blaphaus… Yerkal is not doing good. He won't say why, but he resigned. Ceilingida needs another Governor again."

"Then guess wot, Peezle? You're Governor."

"But I don't live on Ceilingida."

"Neither did Yerkal and no one cares. Congrats."

Thaw walked into the meeting room and smiled, "You're never going to guess what Blaphaus said."

"I'm just surprised he's here." Zucaritas remarked. "But what did he say?"

"He said we are all going to Tooberosum… with him!" Thaw announced.

Not one Governor could believe it.

The tiny two being craft approached the green planet, the robot pilot flew it as Professor Phence sat next to him. Phence frowned, wondering why he couldn't see any other color, different shades of green, and craters, and rocks and dust.

"Is the whole planet like this?" Phence asked.

The robot-pilot checked the scanner and nodded. "Yes, Professor, the whole planet. But I am not sure you would call it a planet."

"No life forms? Nothing?"

"Nada. It's barren. I think it's called a moon."

"I want you to land anyway." Phence told him.

"Okay, but the moon has no atmosphere."

"I have a spacesuit."

The craft came down to land and a few minutes later Phence stepped out onto the moon's surface, wearing a red spacesuit and helmet, tethered to the craft so he couldn't float away. The weather was pretty cold, and the green sand under his feet seemed normal. He kicked it and just a small dust cloud came up and up and up. Phence didn't know what to think… except it could only mean one thing. There were only twenty-two planets in the galaxy… and a sun and a moon.

CHAPTER 17

All twenty-two Governors, Peezle, Zalez and Blaphaus were on the yellow shuttle, now dubbed "Space False One" by Governor Jaboney. The holo-call of Planet Losergram was in front of Bodie, coming from his info-pad.

"You're going where, Governor Bodie?" Losergram asked.

"To Tooberosum! Can you believe it?"

"Nope. I hope you have a good time. I'm proud of you, Bodie. Do the Canis proud!"

"You know I will."

"Nice eyepatch by the way."

"Thanks." Bodie grinned.

Lluhdor sat next to Kaktovic and said, "What do you think we are going to find out on Tooberosum?"

"I have no idea. And it's weird, Blaphaus has not said a word since we left the House."

Do you think he's nervous?"

Kaktovic replied, "If so we'll find why soon enough."

Thaw sat looking out the portal window as the stars. He wished he could get in touch with Professor Phence before hand and invite him on this historical trip, but he had no idea where Phence was. Zalez unbuckled from his seat and went over to Blaphaus who stood against the bulkhead in the back behind the seats. Blap did not blink, and didn't seem that he was breathing.

"Blaphaus, are you okay? Are you alive?"

"Unfortunately."

"You know Nate would be so jealous of me right now. He really wanted to go to Tooberosum."

"I know. But this trip is not for him. I visited your kids at their school. I offered Nate G.P."

"You offered him what?"

"To be my successor. The xenophobic principal kind of talked me out of it. That kid is going to be very successful. Keep an eye on him. He has more wits than any of this lot."

"Thank you, Blaphaus. You're really not as bad as you might want people to think."

"Yeah? You'll see."

Peezle used his pocket holo-pad to try and get in touch with Yerkal but no luck. Dawber and Southington sat next to other, just like at the House.

"How are you feeling about this?" Dawber asked Southington.

"I don't know. How are you feeling?"

"Like we are flying into a frigging trap." Dawber replied.

"I hope not." Southington said, "I don't think Blaphaus would lead us into a trap or something that can hurt us."

"I hope you're right, Jupha. But honestly, how well do we know him? He can wipe the whole Cabinet out on this trip. We could all be going into a huge death trap."

Southington laughed nervously, "Stop it, Cris. You're scaring me... making me nervous."

"I'm just saying."

"I know. I know."

Zeb sat next to Zucaritas, also like in the Cabinet and asked, "Zucaritas, what are you thinking?"

"That again there's two Cyrakuse in the Cabinet." he glanced over at Joorg.

"I mean about going to Tooberosum."

"Oh. Hmmm, that I don't trust Maximus as far as I can throw him and I am weary."

"Me too. We have to have faith this is worth it, right?"

"Sure, Zeb, keep telling yourself that."

Noam glanced his shoulder at Blaphaus just standing there. He shook his head, thinking how much he hated the Galactic President. Zalez held his small holo-pad and Mal's holo-call appeared.

"Zalez, where are you? I could tell you're sitting down."

"On a shuttle going to... Tooberosum with the Cabinet and Blaphaus. Don't tell Nate please."

"With Blaphaus? We are supposed to stay away from him."

"I know, but as head of Dook Energy I had to go."

"Well, I hope he's trustworthy."

"Me. Too. Something is not right with him, though. He doesn't seem himself."

"Well, he went to the school this morning and offered Nate in front of his whole classroom the G.P. position. Luckily Garcey nipped that in the bud."

"I know. He told me."

"Governors, sit down, put your seatbelts on, we are entering the Tooberosum atmosphere. Creator knows what's going to happen now." the pilot said over the intercom.

"Mal, I have to go. I'll let you know what happens."

"Am I going to see it on GNN?"

"No, they weren't invited. Yet."

Tooberosum from space looked like most of the other planets... rivers, lakes, an ocean and a lot of green. There was a spaceport on one side of the planet, the near side to the other planets. Going through the atmosphere wasn't bad, but as soon as the shuttle came out of the clouds it was surrounded by five golden wide winged flying crafts, with some sort of logo on the side. Two of the crafts were on each side of Space False One and one was directly behind it.

"This is the CRSF... state your business." a male voice said through the comm in the pilots cabin.

"CRSF? This is the Cabinet shuttle, from Launderington, care of Old Eboracum, with the whole Creator-damn Cabinet members and the Galactic President."

"Please turn around and head back. The Prime Ruler does not answer to or welcome the rest of the galaxy. Turn around or your ship will be destroyed with everyone in it."

The pilot was glad that only he could hear the threat, not the others.

"Look, I don't know who you are, but you do know the G.P. is one of you, right?"

"I hardly believe that to be true, outsider."

"Oh, really? The G.P. is a Toob..."

"A Toob?"

"Yes! As in Tooberosum."

"That's impossible."

"Yeah, well, let us land and you'll see."

"Hang on."

There was silence for a few minutes. The pilot expected one of the Governors to walk into his cabin and ask why they weren't landing.

"The Prime Ruler says you are free to land. You will be met at the spaceport. Any tricky business we will still destroy your craft."

"Trust me, there's going to be no tricky business." the pilot crossed his fingers.

The shuttle came down to land inside the spaceport followed by one of the crafts. The pilot noticed through the windshield that the few crafts that were there were read with a white stripe along them. They looked like they weren't made for long trips.

The Governors got up from their seats and Blaphaus unbuckled himself from the bulkhead and looked out the nearest portal.

"Welcome home." Zeb said to him smiling.

Blap replied with just a grunt. The ramp descended and Thaw, who was nearest to the door held out his arm.

"Let the G.P. go first."

"I don't think so." Blap said.

Jaboney stepped forward, "I'll go first." He walked down the ramp into the bay. Most spaceports had a bridge that would attach itself to the craft which led the passengers right into the spaceport, but not this one. The others slowly started to go down the ramp, Blaphaus hanging back on purpose.

"Are you scared?" Peezle asked him.

"Not yet."

Just then they were all surrounded by humanoid forms wearing green soldier type uniforms, faces covered by helmets, and heavy weapons pointing at them.

"*Now* I'm scared." Blap muttered to Peezle.

"Hello! I'm Kwoh Jaboney, Governor of Old Eboracum! We are here with Galactic President Blaphaus Maximus." he smiled, arms held out wide.

"They all have legs." whispered Noam to Eastora.

"And they look almost human." Eastora whispered back.

"They have weapons and a military." said the Illiger. "Only my planet has that. This is not good."

Just then a figure in a dark green uniform with medals all over it stepped forward. His face wasn't covered to reveal reddish fur, small beady eyes, small round ears and two buck teeth. He definitely wasn't a Toob.

"I am Brigadier Egap, from the Castor Royal Space Force. Where is the Toob?"

The Governor's parted to reveal Blaphaus standing there.

"Toob, you're under arrest."

The next thing they all knew Blaphaus was grabbed by four of the soldiers and his wrists were cuffed behind his back.

"You know what I am?" Blaphaus asked.

"Yes!" Egap said.

"You can't arrest him. He's the G.P." Thaw pointed out.

"The Prime Ruler will meet you all, except the Toob, at the Lodge. I'll escort you there. Who is in charge now?"

Thaw stepped forward, "I'll be in charge."

Jaboney looked down sadly, he wanted to be in charge.

"I feel sorry for you then, Leetric." Egap remarked, chuckling.

Blaphaus knew this would be bad, but not this bad. His handcuffs were yanked off and he was shoved into the dungeon like cell, with water dripping from the ceiling.

"Careful, you'll snap my arms off."

The iron cell doors slammed shut in his face. Blap looked around the cell, there was nothing in it and it smelt damp. He tried to step aside from dripping water.

The Prime Ruler sat on the far side of the large wooden table that was a giant ring. In fact everything in the room was made out of wood. The Prime Ruler looked like Egap, same species but had dark brown hair and wore a black suit and tie. He stood up and approached the mix of species that Egap led in.

"Mr. Prime Ruler, let me introduce you to this group of species." told Egap.

"Bon joor, hello, everybody. Take a seat. This is something new for Castor. Having all you different species. Some of you are so odd looking. Please take a seat, there should be enough for everyone."

They all sat around the large ring shaped table. Haathee hoped the chair wouldn't break under his weight, but the wood seemed strong enough.

"I'm Castor's Prime Ruler, Denostrebor. We never had visitors on this planet before. I hope my Royal Space Force wasn't too rough."

"I thought my planet was the only planet with a military." Sudgen commented.

"Once upon a time all the planets had a military." told Denostrebor.

Southington asked, "Castor? So, this planet is not Tooberosum?"

"Tooberosum? No, Tooberosum doesn't exist. This is Castor."

"But we were with a Tooberosum. Your soldiers arrested him." Thaw pointed out.

"I know. That's very surprising. Tooberosum's are an ancient race that were the scourge of this galaxy. I thought they were extinct. It's been a hundred years or more since one was seen. And now... there's one that's a Galactic President. How did that happen?"

"Don't you watch GNN?" Noam asked from way across the table.

"No, we don't get that here. We get CBC."

"So, if Tooberosum doesn't exist where did they come from?"

"Another galaxy? Who knows what their planet was named?" shrugged Denostrebor.

"Wait. Let me get this straight... you are saying that the Toob is not from this galaxy?" asked Guoz, the Gink Governor.

"That's exactly what I'm saying. And he's your G.P. That's one of the reasons I'm glad Castor is not part of your Cabinet. So, I have two questions... one is how did he get to be Galactic President and two... why are you all here?"

Thaw said, "It was another Governor that originally had the idea of having Blaphaus as G.P..."

"What happened to the other G.P.?"

"He had a heart attack." Kaktovic replied.

"The Toob was in our lives somehow, the other Governor chose him as everyone was drawn to him for some reason." Thaw explained. "He was the only Toob we've ever seen."

"So, why are you here?" Denostrebor asked.

"We were on a mission to get all the planets in the galaxy to be part of the Cabinet. We saved this planet for last because we thought it was Tooberosum."

"It not being Tooberosum explains why Maximus did not want to come here." Zucaritas remarked.

Zalez asked, "Who powers this planet? Not Dook Energy..."

"Castor Natural Energy. We don't need any help from anybody... we are very self sufficient. So, why are you all here?"

"We thought we could talk to a Tooberosum to be a Governor." Southington replied.

Denostrebor laughed, "That's funny and sad at the same time. Sorry to waste your time, but this planet will never be part of your Cabinet union, even though we share the same galaxy."

"That's understandable." Kaktovic replied.

"So, I have to ask, was it the Toob's idea to come here?"

"No, it was ours." Zeb said, "He said he wasn't coming here until the last moment."

"Well, I'd head back and pick another G.P. if I were you. Maybe from a species you know more about."

"What about Maximus? Where is he?" Jaboney asked.

"He's locked up. I'm afraid he's going to be executed. If he's in this galaxy then a whole swarm of them could come anytime and attack... and even though I have a huge army I'm not ready for that. Are you?"

Pretty much all of them shook their heads.

"I don't think Blaphaus is like that. You said it's been a hundred years. Maybe he's different." Southington commented.

"Do you really want to take that chance?" Denostrebor asked. "I'm not going to put this planet at risk. You have a lot more to put at risk, with hundreds of species."

"Can we see him before the execution?" Zalez asked.

"See him? You can watch his execution if you like. The Castor on this planet will never know he was here. And you can't tell your planets you and he were here. Understood?"

Most of them nodded.

"Good. Because I really wanted my space force to blow your craft out of the sky. But that would get my species talking. I'm just glad your craft was yellow like the space force so no one noticed." he stood up and went to a door in the back of the room. "I'll let you folks chat. The execution will be in one hour. Oh vois for now."

After he left the room everybody started talking at once.

"Quiet!" yelled Eastora. "We can't all chat at once!"

"What do we do? How can we go back to Launderington without him? What do we say?" Kaktovic asked.

"We say that he decided to go back home." the Gink said, "Then we decide who is going to be the next G.P."

"I'll be G.P. if you like." Jaboney told them.

"I say we just see what Blaphaus has to say. We'll ask him at the execution. I just hope the Castor is wrong." Dawber told them.

"Well, this is definitely not Tooberosum so I believe him." Zucaritas commented.

"Makes sense to me." Rüppell replied.

Joorg said, "And everyone thinks the Cakerlak are bad. Maybe this is the reason a Cakerlak wanted to kill him. He knew somehow."

Peezle said, "I really can't believe that Blap could be part of an invasion from another galaxy."

Thaw sat there thinking Phence was correct all along. And they put the Toob in charge.

"Wait until we tell Tostone." Zucaritas commented.

Blap stood in the dark cell hating life. Egap approached and started to unlock the iron door.

"I'm free to go?"

"What? Nooo. You're going to be executed, Toob scum."

Blap didn't say a word except sighed. Everybody was going to be so surprised with what he had to do now. He was led down the tunnel into the execution room. Soldiers were everywhere, and Zalez and the Governors stood to one side, staring at him. A Castor in a black suit approached Blap, glaring at him.

"I never thought I'd say I hated a being, but I hate... no, I loathe you, Toob terrorist."

"Really? That's harsh, we never met." Blaphaus said calmly.

"No one has seen your kind for hundreds of years, I will not let you start an invasion of this galaxy again."

"Wotever, it's hardly an invasion when it's just me."

Thaw stepped forward, "Can we question our G.P. before he's executed?"

"Sure. As long as it doesn't take long. The longer he's alive the more chance we could be in danger."

"You're not amusing." Blap muttered.

"Blaphaus, you were chosen to be Galactic President because you were a Tooberosum, and everyone was fascinated by you. We thought a Toobersoum would be the one to get all the planets together. Because of you twenty-two of the twenty-three planets are now part of the Cabinet."

"Wot? Toothy here didn't want to join the club?" Blap asked.

"No, he didn't. And this planet is not Tooberosum. It's Castor..."

"I never said it was Tooberosum. You lot just assumed. I had no idea wot the name of this planet was."

"Then where are you from?" Southington asked, "Are you from another galaxy?"

Blap sighed, "Yes."

They all looked surprised.

"Told you." Denostrebor said, "No more questions. Time to end this once and for all."

The stone floor between the P.R. and G.P. opened up to reveal a burning pit.

Blaphaus sighed, "Really? You're going to burn me alive? That's a worse death than I could ever imagine. Beats a concussion, broken shoulder and a heart attack I guess. Makes for a good story."

Everyone watched as a tall Castor solider pushed Blaphaus slowly towards the pit. He didn't even struggle.

"You should've let me drown." Blap told the Governors.

Some of the Governors watched, some turned away.

"Isn't anyone going to stop this?" asked Peezle.

Blaphaus said, "Yes. Me. Hold on. I have something to show you all. You're not going to like it. Feces-balls, *I'm* not going to like it."

"You're not going to show us anything, Toob." Denostrebor hissed, getting annoyed.

Blaphaus then reached up to his right yellow eye and grabbed it, pulling it out of its socket and tossed it to the side. He then did the same with his left eye, tossing that to the side. Everyone watched in shock as he took off his purple jacket and threw it down. He reached behind him and touched something, that only the soldier behind him could see. Then slowly he pulled apart his lumpy green body to reveal a human male with short gray hair and stubble, wearing a skin tight black outfit, with a data-pad attached to his chest. His human hands were typing on the keyboard to control the arms and hands and fingers. The Tooberosum "shell" fell behind him as he stood there in front of them all. They all looked at him in shock.

"Who are you?" Thaw asked choking.

"Blaphaus Maximus. Duh." the human male smirked.

CHAPTER 18

"You had legs the whole time!" yelled Noam.

Blap stepped out the "Toob suit," still wearing the three toed shoes that was the Toobs feet. The Castor soldiers all took a step back as well as Denostrebor..

"What trickery is this?" he asked.

"No trickery, just a guy in a sweaty suit." Blaphaus replied. He still had the same voice as before, but a lot less muffled.

"What is going on?" Southington asked.

"I'm so confused." Zeb said, rubbing his head.

"I want you all to leave." Denostrebor said, waving his little finger at Blaphaus' face. "Of all the species to try and be..."

"Yeah, yeah." he started to pick up the pieces of his costume. "Can any of you losers help pick up this stuff?"

Peezle carried the bundled up jacket and Kaktovic carried the "skin" with Haathee's help as they were the strongest of the group. They walked towards the shuttle at the spaceport and up the ramp. Blaphaus carried the yellow eyes in his hands, juggling them as he whistled. All of a sudden he was in a good mood. His secret was out. On the walk back to the shuttle no one said a word. But each had their own thoughts, and most of them were negative. Inside the shuttle Thaw made his way to the pilots cabin to tell him that they are free to go. They all took seats, even Blap did now, still with the data-pad strapped to his body. He unstrapped it from him and dropped it to his bare feet. The costume was dropped in the back row, in a pile of green mess. Peezle put the jacket nicely folded in a seat. Blap stretched his legs and stretched his arms, smiling.

"Feels very good to sit finally." he mused.

Thaw sat next to him and glared, "You know you have a lot of explaining to do... human."

Zalez sat across the aisle from Blaphaus. "No wonder no one could find any information on the Toobs, they are an ancient race. My children adored you. You lied to everyone."

Blap gave him a look, "Pfft. You all lie."

"I don't." Zalez said.

"Sure you don't." Blap scoffed, "Every one lied."

The pilot said over the intercom, "Okay, we are leaving Tooberosum. I hope this was successful."

"So, Blaphaus, explain." ordered Southington, standing over him.

"You made the whole Cabinet look like fools." Zeb said also standing between the rows seats.

"Oh, please. You all made fools of yourselves. You picked me for this, remember? None of you did any research."

"So, you have no remorse?" Kaktovic asked.

"Remorse? Remorse for wot? This wasn't the way I wanted to end things. I told you I didn't want to go to Tooberosum..."

"We didn't. We went to Cantor." Thaw snapped. "Tooberosum is not even in this galaxy."

"It's not in *any* galaxy..."

"What do you mean?" Eastora asked.

"It's made up. You heard of Toobs, but you never heard of Tooberosum. It's an urban legend. No one really knows where the Toobs come from. They might not have their own planet. I just know I'm not from there."

"So, who are you really and why disguise as a Toob?" Jaboney asked.

"I'm not telling you my real name. It's definitely not Blaphaus Maximus though. That name I made up... it sounded pretty good, right?"

"Where are you from?" Bodie asked.

"Are you Emperor somewhere?" Penya asked.

"Not from this galaxy. On my planet and in my galaxy I am kind of wanted man, so I took off before they could catch me. My ship kept on going and I went to the first civilized planet I could find... Ceilingida. Turns out this galaxy is pretty much the same as my galaxy, with a few differences. So, I stayed there."

"What's the name of your planet?" Bodie asked.

"Phulfortha."

"How many planets in your galaxy?" Thaw asked.

"Hmmm... never counted... let me think." he counted on his fingers. "I don't know, it's a small galaxy... eight or nine."

"So, you didn't go back?"

"Nope. I stayed."

"So, why the Tooberosum suit?" asked Gillian.

"I had a suit made of this species called Tooberosums I heard about at a drinking establishment and saw black and white scans of what they looked like. It was a really good design, and comfortable, and didn't look anything humanoid. It hid my height, and everything. This data-pad here made it possible for my arms and legs to work, my mouth and my eyes." he motioned to the data-pad on the floor by his feet. "It's a simple design made by Phence."

Thaw couldn't believe it, if only Phence knew. Maybe he did... he had to ask him.

"Did Phence know what he was designing the data-pad for?"

"I don't know, I never met him." Blap shrugged.

"When you were shoved into the pool did it affect anything?" Kaktovic asked.

"Yeah, almost everything. My eyes wouldn't blink. Luckily my suit didn't fill up with water too bad but I could have drowned. It's during that time when I had a deep feeling I couldn't keep it up, playing a Toob. That water almost screwed up my data-pad."

"What about being a driver?" Zalez asked.

"Wot about it? It was a fun way of making dosh, and learning my way around. I sold my craft and purchased the vehicle which was actually designed for other species with no arms or legs. It worked out well."

"So, you were the Toob all the time?" Lluhdor asked.

"One hundred percent, except when I was at home. That was my time to strip off the suit... and be me."

"So, what changed everything?" Dawber asked.

"Wot changed? Having the Cyrakuse Governor as a passenger! He asked me to be his bodyguard, and the next thing I knew I was bloody G.P."

"With this Toob race, you had no idea about them? I find that hard to believe." Zeb said. "You didn't know their history?"

"Nope. It true. I didn't know they weren't around anymore and such mean bastards. Who would've thought that Castor knew anything about that race. But you guys all thought that planet was Tooberosum, even before I came along. I had no idea wot to expect on the planet... but I knew you weren't going to meet Toobs, and if you did see them would they see through me."

"We knew it was something, then met you and figured it was Tooberosum." Zeb explained. "We all heard of the Toobs, but none of us had seen them."

"Traf heard of them. He left a message on a recording device. Speaking of, one of you have it." he glared at the "Emperor."

"I don't have it." Penya said, "I don't even know what that is."

"Well, one of you stole it from me."

Kaktovic said, "I have it. It fell out your pocket."

"What is it," Thaw said, "What does it say?"

"It's not working." Kaktovic said. "I have it here." He pulled out the fob from his pants pocket.

"Play it." Zucaritas demanded.

"Okay, it it won't work," Kaktovic pushed the side button and Traf's holo-recording appeared and played the whole thing.

"Hello, if you can see this recording I take it you are my predecessor. I hope the Cabinet chose wisely and didn't pick you because you are good looking and a good family man like I was. I am planning on giving up on being G.P. In a few years time I think this galaxy will be invaded... There's other galaxies out there and nothing's stopping them from coming to our galaxy. We need the other seven planets to be reunited with the sixteen. Even Tooberosum... which I can't find anything about anywhere. But I know Toobs are out there. So, whoever you are, I wish you luck. Thank the Creator you'll be able to do a better job than I could ever. Take care."

"See?" Blap asked, "Traf knew more about the Toobs than you lot. Pity he had to drop dead."

"Why didn't you come clean before we made you G.P.?" Southington asked.

"Ego, Blondie. It was an ego thing, I wasn't ready to not be a Toob. I didn't trust anybody. I hated it though. So glad it's bloody over."

"What's over?" Thaw asked.

"The jig is up, Leetric. I'm no longer G.P., you'll have to find some other sucker."

Jaboney held up his hand, "I say me."

"No." Zucaritas said. "We can't go back to Launderington and tell anyone about this, or any planet. No one would trust the Cabinet or us Governors ever again. All this would be for nothing. We finally have all the planets but one working together."

"Good for you, but you know Blaphaus doesn't really exist. I'm human. Explain that to the punters." Blap smirked.

"We are not explaining anything, Maximus. When we land you are going to put back on your costume and continue playing the part." Zucaritas told him.

Blaphaus laughed, "That's the funniest feces I ever heard. I'm gonna burn that feces and maybe move to Old Eboracum. Jaboney, you'll find me a place, I'll fit in nicely there."

"You can live on whatever planet you want, Blaphaus, but Zucaritas is right, no one must know that Blaphaus was fake. We have to keep up with the appearance."

Dawber said to Zalez, "That means you can't tell your family the truth. Can you keep a secret?"

He swallowed, "I don't have a choice."

"Wot makes you think *I'm* going to keep the secret?" Blap asked, "You know how I talk."

"If you say anything and don't do what we ask we will have you arrested." Zeb said, "We have the suit, we can fake pictures that the Toob was assassinated by you."

"That's blackmail." snarled Blap.

"That's the game we have to play." Thaw said. "You don't have a choice."

Southington said, "I'll contact GNN. We'll have a press meeting at the House to announce the Cabinet being full. You'll be a hero, 'Blaphaus,' we'll make you look good as long as long as you play the part."

"Friend, you better start getting back into that suit." Jaboney said.

Blaphaus did not look happy at all.

Hours later, Zalez drove his vehicle to his house where he knew Mal and his children would be. He parked, got out and walked up to his front door. He went inside to be greeted by Ten.

"Welcome home, Mr. Belhopsa."

"Thank you, Ten. What are you doing here?"

"I'm your robot now. It's better for me."

The children were doing their homework on their personal info-pads at the dining room table and they greeted Zalez with smiles and hugs.

"Father, guess who visited us at school today?" Nate asked.

"I heard. Mr. Blaphaus told me. He likes you children a lot. Where's your mother?"

"In the kitchen making dinner." Romana told him.

Zalez went into the kitchen and embraced his wife.

"What's going on, darling? How was your trip to Tooberosum?"

"Fine." he lied, feeling horrible about it, "The Cabinet decided it's best that they keep to themselves. They are nothing like Blaphaus, trust me."

"They're ruder?" she asked.

"No, just different. So, tomorrow is the big celebration on Launderington for the G.P. to officially announce the new full Cabinet. They are going to call it New Galaxy Day or something banal like that. Our whole family was invited to go. What do you think?"

"Please!"

"Can we go?!"

The children cried out for joy running into the kitchen. As always they were eavesdropping on their parents.

Mal sighed, "Okay, just this one trip. It is a school day after all but it's a historical day. Do you think I can invite Fadonna?"

"And Nog?" Nate asked.

Zalez chuckled, "Why not? If Nog's parents say its okay."

"I'll holo-call him now!" Nate ran out the kitchen.

"Invite Principal Garcey as well." Zalez told Mal.

Zucaritas' holo-call appeared before Tostone and Celley, his wife.

"How are you two doing?"

"Fine. We love working for the King." Tostone said, "I don't miss being Governor at all. How is the Cabinet and Blaphaus?"

"Well..." Zucaritas wanted to tell Tostone the truth but didn't. "Greeeeaatttt. So, tomorrow morning on Launderington is the New Galaxy Day celebration. Every planet but Tooberosum is now part of the Cabinet, thanks to Blaphaus and you for having the idea to have him be G.P."

"That's great!"

"Yeah, so you two are invited as well as the King and Lady Gerda. Will you be there?"

"Yes, definitely!" Tostone grinned, "I'm so happy!"

Peezle went into the flat and called out to Yerkal, but Yerkal was no where to be found. He went into the kitchen to see a recording fob on the table, similar to the one that Kaktovic played on the shuttle. He pressed the side and a holo-recording of Yerkal appeared.

"Dear Noj, I love you. I love us. But I have to go away. I found out some news that really scares me... I can't go into it now, but it's something that I need time to research. I will be in touch soon. I love you, take care, watch out for the Tooberosum." Yerkal's holo-recording blew a kiss then ended. Peezle sat at the table and started to cry. He definitely was a cryer. He wondered if Yerkal found out the truth about Blaphaus, and what scared him about it. He then played the holo-recording again, and again and again.

Thaw sat in his office at the House as the holo-call of Professor Phence was in front of him.

"Professor, tomorrow is the New Galaxy Day celebration here on Launderington. All the planets, apart from Tooberosum are part of the Cabinet. You're invited to the celebration, if you want."

"Why exactly is Tooberosum not part of the Cabinet?" Phence asked, seeing what Thaw would say.

"Ummm..." Thaw wondered what he could say, what lie would he come up with. "There was nothing there. It was weird. Maybe in the future we can research it."

"Yes, that will be fine. I will be there for this historical day." Phence smiled, wondering why there was "nothing here." Something didn't add up and he was going to get to the bottom of it.

Some of the other Governors did their own invite, reaching out to others. Joorg holo-called Lila, his wife, Zeb contacted his kids, Jaboney contacted his Assistant Bella, Bodie contacted Planet Mayor Losergram. Southington contacted GNN who would be broadcasting the event live. It was a big day for everyone in the galaxy, except for the Castor.

The next day, the streets of Launderington was full of different species. In front of the House balloons and decorations were hung up with a large banner saying "Happy New Galaxy Day." A crowd formed on the street and around the long reflective pool, and the big white ball that was the Launderington Memorial. This was the same spot where the truce between the Canis and Cyrakuse happened. Just for safety precaution, in case someone wanted to ruin this day, GBI agents were everywhere. GNN robot-cameras also hovered everywhere and Buterdau Kooper and Crisp Jaboney stood to the side. A VIP area was set up in a roped off area at the top of the House steps. where the Belhopsa family, including

Ten, Fadonna, Nog and his overweight parents and Principal Garcey stood. Planet Mayor Losergram also was there, and Professor Phence, as well as all the other guests like the Tostone's and the King and Lady Gerda.

Nate looked up at his father and whispered, "Father, can I tell you something after this?"

Zalez just nodded.

In the House, the "Toob" stood, finally inside. He stayed the night in there and changed into his Tooberosum outfit. The House robot scanned him and said, "You are not real. You are made out of rubber."

"Oh, I'm real all right." Blap scoffed.

The Governors stood around him, making him feel uneasy.

"You know what to do." Zucaritas told him.

"Yeah, yeah, lie to the people. Wot you lot do best. Let's get this feces over with."

"It won't be over with for a long time." Zeb replied.

Music played over the speakers outside, the same annoying music that made Blaphaus cringe at the dance school. He led them outside and the crowd went crazy, cheering. Confetti cannons fired confetti up into the air. A microphone was set up for Blaphaus to talk into and he stood before it, as the Governors stood behind him. He turned to the VIP's and winked he was glad he got the data-pad working again. He waved to the crowd, and so wanted to key in "flip the crowd off."

"Hello, beings on the galaxy." Blaphaus read from teleprompter. "Most of you know me as Blaphaus Maximus, Galactic President... and a Tooberosum..."

The Governors looked nervous, hoping he'd keep to the script.

"But what you don't know is my species are a quiet lot, who keep to themselves. Not me. I am honored to be your Galactic President, representing twenty-two of the planets in the galaxy. For the first time ever the Cabinet is full."

The cried cheered, everyone looked so relieved. In the crowd was the Leetric Erick, Sargan and Ieme.

"I knew we should've gotten to know that Toobie better." Erick said.

"There's going to be a few changes..." Blap continued.

"He's off script." Dawber whispered to Southington.

"I don't know wot those changes are yet, but they will make this galaxy the best galaxy there is. Yes, there's more than this galaxy out there, trust me. I've been there. I have traveled."

There were some cheers and some boos from the believers and disbelievers. Pastor Rellim from the Faeligion Church stood in the crowd as well, watching Blap closely.

"We will welcome any new species from a different galaxy with open arms, like you have welcomed me." Blap continued.

"What is he talking about, Doctor Sahii?" a woman asked in the crowd, spectacles on her face and short blonde hair asked. "And how did he get to the top of the steps? He has no legs."

The shortish white haired, gray skinned older man in the gray suit replied, "Something I have been saying for years. We'll talk later."

Thaw whispered to Blap, "Do you want to keep talking or end this?"

"Everybody, tomorrow is a new day! Celebrate today! Happy New Galaxy Day, everyone! Now let's party!" he smiled, waving his arms. Inside the suit Blap was hating life, but no one saw that, and no one would. The crowd cheered and applauded and the Governors all gave a sigh of relief. Beings on all twenty-one planets celebrated, this was start of a whole new beginning.

"*New* Galaxy Day? It seems like the same bloody galaxy to me..." Blap muttered.

"So, Nate, what do you want to say?" Zalez asked.

Nate motioned for Zalek to bend down and when Zalez did he whispered into his ear.

"I think Mr. Blaphaus is not real."

"Well, Crisp, there you have it. The Tooberosum has done it. Every planet but his own is part of the Cabinet now. What do you think will happen?"

"Your guess is as good as mine, Buterdau, but if I had to go by what my brother, the Old Eboracum new Governor says, things are going to get better and better. Praise the Toob."

"Praise the Toob indeed." smiled Buterdau.

Guoz the Gink's holo-call appeared in front of the big Cakerlak Weta in his chamber on Cakerlak.

"The plan is in effect, Great Weta, the invasion will begin soon. No one will see it coming,"

"Perfect. No one has an idea you're not from this galaxy?"

"Nope. And no one has been to the moon that they think is Gink. No one will see this coming at all."

"Splendid. And the Toob? He's still alive..."

"The Toob is not someone we need to worry about."

He didn't want to tell Weta the truth about the Toob... not yet anyway.

Across the galaxy, on Castor, way on the far side of the planet arrived a dozen green ships, that could be ready to attack. Down on the planets surface, a lumpy green, yellow eyed being with long skinny arms and no legs looked up to see the lights of the ships fly over. He turned and went into the homestead to tell his Toob family that they weren't the only species in the galaxy after all...

TO BE CONTINUED...

THE GOVERNORS AND THEIR PLANETS THEY REPRESENT

1. Jupha Southington - Mencken
2. Cris Dawber - Canola
3. Tone Zucaritas - Cyrakuse
4. Erlas Zeb - Chordatt
5. Lluhdor - Struthionia
6. Noj Peezle - Ceilingida
7. Gillian - Savannahian
8. Noam- Homunculus
9. Thaw - Siahl
10. Guoz - Gink
11. Joer Ace - Lesavia
12. Bradypus Waydo - Hitittippi
13. Kaktovic - Ankerage
14. Heckmondwike Sugden - Xenartha
15. Bert Eastora - Burdernchurdettu
16. Bodie - Canis
17. Kwoh Jaboney - Old Eboracum
18. Pinya - Uridae
19. Haathee - Phytnes
20. Lana Joorg - Cakerlak
21. Rüppell - Mesas

Jason Peverett was born in Balham, London, England in 1968. Jason grew up in Port Jefferson, Long Island, moved back to England in 1984, where he finished school in Burford, a village in the Cotswolds, which is in England and then graduated in 1987. He moved to Orlando, Florida in 1987 and currently still lived there. His father was the lead singer (Lonesome Dave) in Foghat, and he writes a weekly pop culture based blog called Peverett Phile. He loves movies, music and staying indoors as much as possible. He is also a fan of the New York Giants, the band Barenaked Ladies, the gas station Wawa and is a big *Star Wars* fan.

Apart from this book, Jason has released two albums, which are available on CD. "How Do You Know My Name?" by the band Strawberry Blondes Forever which he released with Dan Nowicki and "You'll Be All Right" by Null and Void with Chris Nelson.